The Terminus Protocol

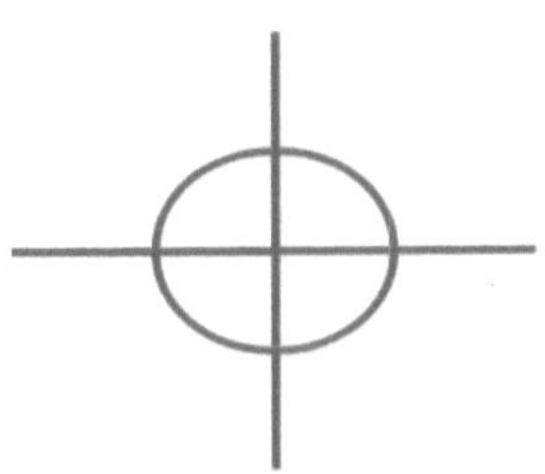

The McGowan Collection Series, Book 11

**Col. Lee Martin
and Terry S. Byrnes CPPB**

Check out all our novels on:

https://colonelleemartinbooks.com

Table of Content

CHAPTER 1

It hadn't taken long after we moved into our Georgetown condo for my wife, Adriana, to begin missing our lovely home, Wolf Laurel, back in the West Virginia countryside. For fifteen of our twenty years of marriage, Wolf Laurel was a bed- and-breakfast inn which was consistently on the list of the 20 most inviting country inns in America. Adriana had owned it for five years before our marriage and another ten before that with her first husband, God rest his soul. But now, no longer a quaint and cozy haven for vacationers, it has only for the past two years simply been Adriana and Bruce McGowan's personal residence.

After giving the better part of my adult life to my country as a military officer, FBI Special Agent and Department of State counterterrorist operative, I had settled back with the lovely Adriana in retirement at our

B&B to take in all the luxuries and rewards that I was due. Occasionally, even though I had officially retired, I had accepted some contract counterterrorist work for the government where it involved using my well-honed investigative and take-down skills for which I was remembered.

Then, just when I thought my life as a government servant was finally in my rear-view mirror, a rather important figure came to see me. It was three months ago that Vice President Bart Collins, the former CIA director and brief national security advisor, drove all the way down to West Virginia from Washington, D.C., to have a chat with me. He was actually asking me to put my retirement on hold for at least a year and start up a counterterrorist team that was being modeled after the highly secret Zulu element honchoed by my old friend and boss, Lionel Byrd. Sadly, Lionel and all but one member of our team had been murdered by one of our own on Team Zulu at the direction of a former congressman who was vying for the Oval Office. I say *former* because it was I who ended up planting a bullet in the congressman's head, making him former *everything*.

But back to the VP, when he arrived at Wolf Laurel and was greeted at the door by the lovely Adriana, he immediately struck up a conversation with her about how a former action guy like me was too valuable to be a sedentary domestic such as I had become and managed to somehow convince her that my taking the position was a great career move. Great career move at my age? What was he thinking? And what was she, of all people, thinking as well?

Anyway, how all this worked was that I would ramrod a highly covert team that not even the president and Secretary of State knew about. While the eight thousand people in the Counterterrorist and Countering Violent Extremism (CT) department at the State Department building on C Street were collaborating with the alphabet agencies such as the FBI, CIA, military law enforcement and Homeland Security to combat foreign and domestic terrorism, my team would exist offsite in a house on MacArthur St. as a shadow element doing much the same thing. Only covertly and with reckless abandon. The team would be made up of serious special ops guys…highly-proficient people who chewed nails and spit bullets. And people they went after would disappear. They'd find 'em, fight 'em, fix 'em and forget 'em. I left out the other f word. Only three people plus the team would know about it. The top boss was the Vice President, as long as he was in office. And he had three years left. Team name…Terminus.

Again, the current president would know nothing about us and our mission. And it was intended that he never would. According to the VP, who made no bones about it with me, the president wouldn't have the guts or the gonads to be associated with or condone Terminus protocol. If he knew that the team was comprised of hand-picked liquidators going off the grid to take out terrorist suspects before the State Department's CT and Bureau's JTTF had a chance to act, the unit would immediately be scratched and its members not only de-programmed but given memory-killing drugs.

I had done my homework on the charismatic Vice President Collins. Even though on the surface he was a low-keyed and relatively-uninvolved personality in the executive office, as most VPs generally are, from the back seat he might have actually been running the country. For the previous three years. Neither the house nor senate was the wiser. Moreover, neither were the Departments of Defense, Justice, and State. Where it came to America's offense against terrorism, he was the shadow president. The world may have seen him as a Bruce Wayne, but in reality, he was Batman. Except he didn't wear a cape and a mask with pointy ears. And it was his intention that Terminus would be the unit who'd answer the bat signal.

As the current president, Charles L. Bertram, was tired and frustrated, and because of his weak foreign and domestic policies, his poll numbers had tanked. He had decided not to run for a second term. And although Vice President Collins had never been in the political limelight and given little executive responsibility, he was still popular and charismatic enough to be chosen as his party's candidate for the November election. However, he would have a tough-uphill battle beating his competition from the opposing party.

Meetings with VP Collins were going to be as clandestine as our missions. They would generally take place in confidence in his office or in mine as needed on the QT, or perhaps even the backseat of his limo at night on a dark street. The National Security Advisor, my friend Ben Marshall, the only other player in our rogue game, would also be present.

My old organization, CTT, was defunct. No teams were left in any of the major cities. The whole concept was dead. Lionel Byrd's replacement, a director named Jenkins, who had taken over the command of our four counterterrorist units had taken the team nowhere. He had neither the leader skills nor stones to plan and carry out the necessary brutal missions with the courage and tenacity of his predecessor. And that had been recognized by the former National Security Advisor, my friend, Preston Johns who by the way had had oversight of CTT. Thereafter, any global and domestic terrorists found and taken out were mainly left to the Bureau's JTTF, and in latter days, Homeland Security.

Even though I was anxious to quarterback this team, what I would miss like the devil was taking part in the action. As I would send my team into the world of danger to execute a mission, all the while I'd be gnashing my teeth that I had not hit the ground with them. While the State Department's CT organization was overt and legal, my clandestine guys wouldn't be. At least that's how I pictured it. As to the team's organization, I'd propose to the VP that my team be comprised of four operatives…two smart, tough guys from the former CTT teams Xray and Yankee who were based in Chicago and Dallas, respectively, a third member, a retired CIA case worker who had joined Team Zulu, my former unit, and the fourth, a guy which I would have trouble placing…a former hit man. I already had in my head the names of the people who would make up the team. Not comprised of blood-thirsty rogues, anxious to pump bullets into bad guys, but at the same time, they'd be scurrilous and relentless when they had to be. I had stayed in touch with three of them, but it had been a decade since I had communicated with the fourth. However, it was nigh time that I did. The thing was, I didn't think he'd go for it. Maybe Collins wouldn't either. Even though who I had in mind was probably still living that life of comfort and luxury with his lovely wife on the island of Antigua, I knew there was something in him that, like me, craved stimulation if not exhilaration. I had seen it in him…seen it in his eyes and in his clenched fists. Seen it in his zeal when he went into action. He was the best shot in the world. Even *I* couldn't compete with him. But would he bite? I'd at least make the offer. I had been on the job a month. At first, there were no meetings with the VP and just one with NSA Marshall. The State Department's CT operatives were the official game players. As they would be receiving and gathering the Intel on terrorists and other subversives, through our own resources we would as well. If the mission required Terminus attention, even before the JTTF was out of the gate, our Bat Team would already have ignited the firestorm and be in process of sweeping up the ashes. Swift and punishing. No trophies, no accolades. No limitations.

Since we were not legally sanctioned, my team and I would be paid out of a secret government account. The National Security Advisor (NSA) had set that up. Ben was a friend of mine going way back. More recently, he was the guy who had dispatched me to get the goods on a good-old-boy militia organization in upstate West Virginia which I found out had planned to explode an EMP bomb over Washington to cripple the D.C. area grid. The terrorist was another friend of mine who had been booted from our CTT organization and held a grudge. His plan came to an end, however, when I introduced him to yet another friend, Mr. Glock. Mr. Glock planted a couple of slugs in his chest at center mass.

And so, it was set up where I would build this super-clandestine CT element operating under the direction and oversight of Vice President Collins and NSA Ben Marshall. I would become Lionel Byrd, but only leading *one* intrepid counterterrorist team rather than four. Although no one else knew about us, we had at our fingertips every Intel and technical resource that every other counterterrorist elements within the government had.

Back to Adriana. I thought she was adjusting well that first month to our new condo and life in the nation's capital; but lately I had become worried about her. Returning home from work one evening I saw that she had been crying. I placed my arms around her and she melted into me like warm butter, soaking my shirt collar with her tears.

"What's wrong, sweetheart? I've never seen you like this."

"I'll be okay," she snuffed. "Just not a good day, that's all."

"Tell me about it. Did something happen?" "No. That's just it. Nothing happened." "I'm not understanding," I said.

She stepped away from me and dabbed at her wet cheeks. "I'm…stronger than this, and am embarrassed to have you see me cry like this. It's just that…I'm stuck here in this condo all day. I don't know anyone. All my friends are back home. This area is just too congested for me. I don't have my car and wouldn't get out into the Washington traffic if I did." She then paused and allowed a slight smile to grace her lips. "In telling you this, I feel like a wuss. I think that's what people call it. A wuss."

I brought her back into me. "My dear, it grieves me to see you like this. If you want to go back home, I'll quit today. We'll get in the car and leave. The government can just send me my pay and…"

"No, Skip. Absolutely not. We made this decision together. It's something that will fill *your* void and just because I'm a bit lonely and have no desire to get out in this Washington rat race, you're going to continue working with the government. You promised Vice President Collins one to two years and we're going to stick with it. The operative word is *we*."

I then thought I'd throw a little humor her way to make her smile again. "You mentioned the rat race. Yeah, it's fast-paced out there alright. But the problem is, even if you win, you're still a rat." Must have been very *little* humor. It didn't faze her.

"Tell you what, sweetheart, I want you to start going back home on the weekends. I've know I was selfish in taking this job and in the process have wounded your spirit. I didn't need to go back to work and you were self*less* in giving up the life and house you love, even if it is for two years. Here's what I want to do. Every Friday afternoon, I'm going to rent you a car to go home then return on Sunday night."

She grinned and shook her head. "Not on your life, Bruce McGowan. Me drive out I-66 in Friday afternoon traffic? Then get into that Sunday evening parking lot with people returning back here from the weekend? I don't even want to get behind the wheel when the Washington traffic is thin. No, I'm staying here with you. No more tears and no more feeling sorry for myself. I'm just going to put on my big-girl panties and suck it up."

"Nothing big-girl about your panties, my dear." I gave her my best Groucho Marx eyebrow treatment. "Speaking of that, maybe you'll allow me to…"

She finished my sentence. "…get into them. Hmmm. I think that will make me feel a heck of a lot better. *Before* dinner or after?"

"Both."

And so, after having my dessert first, at the pleasure of Mrs. McGowan, we took a walk along M Street down about three blocks to a restaurant I frequented B.A. (before Adriana) when I was an operative on Team Zulu. I love Mediterranean food and Novalie's served the best. It was a new experience for Adriana who of course had never been there but also because this West Virginia girl had never tasted Mediterranean cuisine. I'm not demeaning her by saying that, but having spent years managing her bed-and-breakfast without a vacation outside of the U.S. there were many things she hadn't experienced. However, after she hooked up with me, we did however travel to places like Paris, the Caribbean and Ireland, sampling their traditional foods. No falafel or moussaka, though.

It was a beautiful spring evening, sixty-two degrees, light breeze, and a sunset of orange and violet hues peeking around Georgetown's three and four story buildings. As we walked hand-in-hand, the further we trekked, the more relaxed she seemed. Of course I thought I had taken care of that an hour before. But she was smiling and playfully bumping into my derriere with hers. I knew then she was going to be a great dinner date forgetting all about feeling sad and alone that day. We would need to have more time together evenings like we were enjoying, and on weekends.

There was much to see in D.C. and I expected we'd be taking a lot of spring walks along the Washington mall beneath the cherry blossoms amidst the stately marble and granite government buildings and monuments. If you got beyond the crowds and the lines of people pushing and shoving at the Metro, I always thought Washington was a wonderful, impressive experience.

Following our dinner of shawarma, couscous, a greek salad, and a bottle of crisp Riesling, we hoofed it back along M Street to our condo. It was dark when we reached our steps. For perhaps twenty minutes we sat on the steps talking and watching people passing by…a few teenagers acting out, an elderly gentleman in a tweed coat and Scottish tam o'shanter cap, navigating with his cane, and a couple in love, stealing kisses, walking so close to one another I thought at first glance they were one person. And the vehicles. Being Georgetown, many of the passing cars we saw were Mercedes and BMWs. And then there was that Bentley.

Adriana turned her face toward me and asked, "So how is it the government is paying for us to live in this ritzy neighborhood considering you're just a low-ranking government employee? What kind of job is it, anyway?"

"Remember, it was the vice president of the United States who sought me out. He and the national security advisor wanted someone with my experience to build a counterterrorist team to their specifications. The unit I supervise will be one of the most important organizations in the department. The VP has designs on how it will be staffed and what missions we will perform."

"Uh, Mr. McGowan, *you* won't be performing missions, especially the type of missions as before." She paused.

"I *am* correct, aren't I?"

"I will dispatch people to do what I used to do. And you are correct; I'll be sitting behind a desk pushing people's buttons. I don't have a team as yet, but have a pretty good idea who will be on it. We are at this point still in the organizing stage."

"Just remember, husband dear, we have an agreement. I'm proud that you are an important man to people high up in the government, but you promised you wouldn't…"

"And I will abide by that promise. You can take it to the bank."

She smiled and leaned into me. "How 'bout you taking me upstairs instead for dessert, part two."

CHAPTER 2

Monday morning, the 4th of May, while sitting at my desk at the house on MacArthur going over a series of Intel reports and inter-departmental messages, my cellphone rang. "Bruce, Bart Collins here."

"Good morning, Mr. Vice President." "Naval

Observatory, 1400 hours. Be there." "Will do so, sir."

The house on the Observatory grounds was, of course, the vice president's home. It was the late 70s when the VPs ceased living in private homes and took up residence at One Observatory Circle, likely for security reasons, being only a heartbeat from the Oval Office. As the VP's official office was in the Eisenhower Executive building next to the west wing of the White House, I figured Collins did not want any curiosity hounds wondering who the strange face was that had become a regular visitor.

It was a short walk…all of three blocks. I stopped in a

Starbucks along the way for a strong black coffee. No fru-fru crap for me. I bought the VP a cup as well. I remembered he liked sugar and cream in his. It would be the first time after moving into my office digs that I would personally meet up with Collins. The NSA, Ben Marshall, had stopped by my building for a chat the week before. It was just the two of us meeting as no team was in place yet. Actually, all I was doing that entire month was sitting alone reading myself in on department memos, emails and Intel. As I would be privy to any and all Intel coming down the chute, I had just two days before finally gotten my security clearance reinstated, the highest in the government, Top Secret-sensitive Compartmented Information (TS/SCI). I was provided with an assistant, an attractive no-nonsense forty year old blonde named Debbie Freeman. She was a twenty-year State Department analyst from the Harry Truman building who Ben said was guaranteed to be trusted to keep our team and activities confidential.

Considering I was meeting with the VP at his VP residence in the large, white house on the Naval Observatory grounds, I had left my Glock and boot .380 at the Terminus house. Since I had no badge and had yet to receive my official ID, getting through security and the metal detector could have gotten messy. VP Collins had, however, already arranged for my passing through by posting a secret service agent at the end of the conveyer to transport me to his quarters. When I was then directed to Bart Collins' office, he stood waiting ready to greet me at his open door like I was some kind of dignitary. He held out his hand and I shook it.

"Well, Director McGowan, we meet again. I had intended for us to have a face-to-face meeting like this before now, but I wanted you to get settled in and well-versed about what's happening on the terrorist front. I hope you have been fully on the receiving end of all the Intel reports and both in and out messaging on the Justice and State Department tracks."

"I'm sure somebody is wondering who the new guy is that was added to the list of recipients."

He smiled and nodded. "Let them keep wondering. Come in and have a seat. Something to drink?"

"Thank you, no. I stopped for a coffee. And here's one for you."

"Merci," he replied.

The vice president was a stately-looking man, tall, silver-haired, and wearing a gray suit with a turquoise tie. Not only was he the former CIA director but a Missouri congressman for two terms, four years. Even though he was considered a milquetoast politician by the public and the press, I had compared him to a sleeper car I once owned…looked like every other Oldsmobile Cutlass on the road, but under the hood was a beast with the same 455 horsepower engine as the 4-4-2.

Collins took his place behind his desk as I took the soft, easy chair opposite him. We had some small talk about our settling in at the condo in Georgetown with him asking if it had been to our liking and especially how Mrs. McGowan was doing. I told him the condo was totally satisfactory but that Adriana, being away from her country comfort zone was having some adjustment issues. He nodded and said he understood how she must feel. But then, satisfied all was well in the McGowan family, he quickly got down to brass tacks. "I trust you have by now envisioned how you intend to structure your team and would soon be ready to bring them in. Before we talk missions and responsibilities, I want you to tell me who you have in mind to bring in with you, that is unless you want to rely on some of my recommendations from my Agency tenure."

"I am asking you to consider four of my own recommendations, sir. I know you would have them vetted via background checks, reviewing service history and performance, also determining whether they are professionals or merely killers and thugs. Rest assured, I would not suggest anyone from the latter category."

He settled back in his chair. "I know you wouldn't. I'm sure you have given the composition of the team your utmost thought. So, talk to me."

"Like I previously conveyed, I have narrowed down my choices to four individuals with another as an alternate or even a solid fifth."

"If you think you need a fifth operative for depth purposes, we will consider it."

"First, I would like to bring back a guy who I operated with from the old CTT element, Mike (Mickey) Johnson, from the Dallas team, a very bright and resourceful Black gentleman who Byrd himself groomed. The second candidate is a retired CIA operative I came across a few years back named Pierce Stryker. We collaborated a couple of times on missions in Libya and Pakistan. He's tenacious and a force to be reckoned with when tasked."

"I know Stryker," Collins added. "He should be maybe fifty-five now but was a young thirty-something when I was director. I have to agree he would be Terminus material; however, I do remember him being a bit of a hot head."

"I can control that. But I think he has mastered his temper as he's gotten older. He was traveling through West Virginia a couple of years ago and gave me a call. We had a drink at a local pub and I saw that he had mellowed out considerably. We talked about the old days and he said if he ever had another opportunity in the field we are discussing, he would like to do some contract work. As to the three of them I mentioned, all could hit the ground running if I gave them a call."

"Your third?"

"This guy would probably tell me to take a long walk off a short pier when I approached him. One of the missions the former National Security Advisor pulled me in on was to find him to join me on a mission. He was a Marine sniper and considered the best long-distance shooter in the world. He's the guy who took out the infamous Viper and helped me take down the Jamaal ul-Fuqra bunch."

"And how I remember that. I was with the Company at the time but I didn't know it was you and the guy you are talking about who killed that outfit. All I heard was that some former Marine took the head off the maggot at over a thousand yards."

"It was a highly classified mission that only the president and NSA knew about. So I guess Eagle One *did* keep it all under his hat."

"Tell me more about this sniper fellow and why you think he could serve on this team. He'd certainly need more credentials than just being a great shot."

"Well, he was a CIA case worker after the Marines."

"When was that?"

"Back in the '90s. He left in '98, I believe."

"I wasn't director until 2000, so I wouldn't have known him. What's the bottom line on him?"

"Well, sir, you may not want to hear this, but up until I met him in 2008, he was working as a hit man."

Collins quickly leaned forward. *"A hit man?"*

"It's not like it sounds. He had been coerced by a couple of high-up justice department people to kill people who had literally gotten away with murder.

They had either escaped prosecution because they weren't given their Miranda rights or released by liberal judges on some technicality."

"Like that old movie The Star Chamber."

"Exactly. The U.S. Attorney General's office held past indiscretions over his head, telling him he would go to jail for a lengthy time if he didn't kill for them. But, they paid him handsomely. And by the way, the NSA paid him a million bucks for killing the Viper."

"I reckon he'd be disappointed with what we would pay him…if we in fact decide he *can* join Terminus. Are you really good with him?"

"I am, sir. But I don't believe he will want to give up his island lifestyle to go back to pulling triggers. His wife would also have a say in that."

"Well, you can see about it. What's his name?" "Atticus

Steed."

"Steed. I would want to interview the guy and ask my battery of questions… I can think of two or three right away. You mentioned a fourth person. Who would he be?"

"Actually, a she. One of the first special ops women in the military, and then she served six years as an FBI special agent. She is one tough gal, having taken part in both military and Bureau missions in the Sudan, Iraq, Afghanistan and Kuwait a couple of which were the Desert Falcon missile defense operation and Neptune Spear where Bin Laden was taken down."

"So she was a SEAL."

"Yes, as of 2016, when women were first allowed to be a part of combat missions."

"Impressive. What's her name?" "Angela Lovato."

"Hispanic."

"Cuban-American, sir." "Does she speak Spanish?"

"Third generation but she's fluent."

"Good. You would need someone bilingual."

"Actually, two other of my proposed operatives are multi-lingual…Stryker who speaks Italian and Greek, and Mr. Steed who is fluent in Arabic and Hebrew." "He's Jewish?"

"No, sir, but he spent two years in Israel after

schooling. Supposedly, it was a Mossad agent that taught him to shoot before he joined the Marines."

"So he has some experience with the IDF." "Yes."

"Sounds like a well-rounded team. Obviously, you've given a great deal of thought to staffing."

"I have."

"From what you tell me, I suppose I'd be good with your selections, maybe even Steed. But I'd like the NSA and I to sit down with these people, if they agree to come in. That doesn't mean I don't trust your judgment, but as we know, this will be no ordinary counterterrorist unit. We don't want any renegades out there."

"Of course, sir. I will contact them all to see how many will agree to sign on. Maybe none of them will as I don't know if they're working in any post- government careers."

"You do that, Bruce. Do you have any questions for me?"

"Just one, sir. What's a good lunch place around here?"

CHAPTER 3

I had all their numbers locked in on my cellphone. Would they be available? Would they even answer my call? I was sure each of them would recognize my number rather than allow it to go to spam or voice mail. I had talked with all of them at some point in the last couple of years. Whether retired or taking on another business, a lot of us special ops and law enforcement people stay in touch, even if we just say, "Hi…how ya doing." And as people like us are always hungry for a little excitement in our lives, I was counting on at least three of them to come aboard with me. Steed was especially going to be a long shot. No pun intended.

Mike Johnson answered on the first ring. He was working security there in the D.C. area for a large packing company. When I told him what I had in mind, he didn't miss a beat. "Yes, I'd be interested. Could be like the old days."

"Meet me on the Washington mall opposite the Museum of American History, 1400 tomorrow."

"You got it, Bruce."

I wasn't readily able to get hold of Stryker. He's one I wasn't sure about. CIA types were strange dudes…and unpredictable. I called and left him a message. I was just getting ready to head for home when he called back.

"Bruce McGowan. How the hell are you?"

"Well, some days I'm the pigeon…other days, the statue."

He laughed. "Same old Bruce. Always wise-cracking. You know I was just thinking about you the other day and our joint investigation into the U.S.S. Cole attack. Man, that was over twenty years ago."

"Twenty-three to be exact."

"Harrowing times, Bruce. Then it wasn't long until 9-11 happened. What the hell has happened to our world?"

"Yeah, I ask the same question every morning when I get up and turn on the news. But, the reason for my call is to ask what you're into now and if you'd like to get back into the fray."

"How so?"

"I'm setting up a super-covert counterterrorist team that will have no connection to the Bureau, State Department or Homeland Security. I'm in Washington working for someone high up in the chain."

"Who would that be?"

"Can't tell you, Strike. I'm hiring four or five to make up the team. I'd like you to be one of them. The job is here in D.C. What are you doing now?"

"Just retired and living off my pension. Tell me how your deal works."

"We receive the Intel and then go after people of the terrorist persuasion. The only difference in us and all the other counterterrorist teams is that no one will know who we are or where we are at any time. We make sure the Intel is valid then take out the threat. We will be swift and deadly. Anybody taken prisoner will be subject to every illegal interrogation method ever devised. Once we have the information, the dude is never heard from again."

"Sounds intriguing if not salivating." "Interested?"

"You could say that."

"Where are you now?"

"Kentucky, Bruce. Got a house in a town called Blue Grass."

"Sounds like you're in horse country."

"Yeah, near Lexington."

"Are you married?"

"My wife died a couple of years ago."

"Sorry, Strike. What would hold you back from taking the position?"

"Nothing, really. I'd have to sell my house. Don't know if I could live in the high income town of Washington."

"We'd make it worth your while." "How much?"

"We will get into that another time. So you'll think about it?"

"Give me a little time."

"All right." He was quiet for about ten seconds.

"Okay, I thought about it. I'm in. Just give me all the logistics and tell me when you want me there."

"I'll recontact you by Friday. I can't officially offer you the job until you're vetted. Like I said, someone high up in the administration will chat with you."

"Great. Have your people call my people."

I chuckled. "Will talk Friday. Have a good day, Joe."

I found Adriana in a better mood that day. She had gone out to a fresh produce market and brought home a lot of rabbit food to make for supper. "What kind of meat tonight, sweetheart?"

"I thought we would just have a nice big salad. You've been eating too much red meat lately."

As I was in the mood for a thick, juicy steak, I was sure to be famished by nine o'clock. But I just replied, "Hmmm. I didn't work myself all the way up on the food chain to become a vegetarian."

"Which means you're not going to enjoy the salad."

"I will enjoy it, my dear. Maybe tomorrow a ribeye?"
"Okay, I'll concede that. But I'm serious. You need to watch out for your arteries. We don't need any coronaries happening to that aging body of yours. And I haven't seen you go on a run in two weeks."

She was right. I had been neglecting my running game. Tomorrow I would change that. There was a football field a few blocks away with a running track. And I did enjoy jogging the Washington mall when we first came to town…the capitol building down to the Lincoln Memorial, around the tidal basins and back. *But* I was not ready to give up my beef.

I had two more calls to make; but first, I needed to meet with Mickey Johnson on the park bench near the Smithsonian as planned that next day to fill him in on all the details. He was chomping at the bit on the phone. I supposed that with the history of being an action guy like me on the old CTT, a security guard gig would be a complete disenchantment in the work sphere. As I remembered, Mickey should be between fifty and fifty-five but as I also remember him having a lifelong fitness passion, age was not going to be a problem.

Being the prompt, regimented guy that I am, I arrived at the rendezvous site precisely at 1000 hours. He was already there reading a copy of the Post.

Although it had been maybe fifteen years since I had seen him, his Allied uniform gave him away. When I stepped up to the bench, he never looked at me, choosing instead to keep his nose in the paper. I stood there a while without as much as a 'hello' to see how long it would take to notice me. Finally, he said, "Are you just going to stand there and say nothing, Scorpion, (my code name back then) or sit down and offer me a job?"

"I didn't think you saw me," I replied, taking a seat beside him.

He then laid the paper aside and looked at me over his glasses. "I spotted you a block away, my friend. As a matter of fact, I have embossed in my brain every face that has passed by here for the last ten minutes."

"I remember that about you. How's life been treating you?"

"This uniform should give you the answer to your question. My life has been racked the last couple of years by terminal boredom. Off to work in a warehouse at 2100 hours and punching out at 0600 the next day. Waste the majority of the next day sleeping, then start all over again after a run, a shower and something to eat."

"Exciting. Do you have a significant other? I don't think you were married when I last saw you."

"Been through one long marriage since then. I'm not sure if I gave up on her or she gave up on me. I think I just didn't have room in my life for someone who hadn't given me a kind word in years."

"And now?"

"I live alone with my pit bull Jake. We have a great relationship. How about you? As I remember, you were going with and maybe married a beautiful gal back in West Virginia after the CTT years."

"We celebrated twenty years not long ago. Best thing that ever happened to me."

"So, did you totally retire?"

"After CTT, I kept getting pulled in by government muckety-mucks for contract jobs, mostly terrorist-related. Made some decent money but paid for it a few times by collecting lead. My wife was getting tired of me coming home with holes in my body, so to salvage our marriage, I became a house husband."

"Now that *is* boring."

"Well, we didn't come here to talk about what used to be. Let me fill you in on this operation we're developing…"

"Who's we?"

"I can't tell you that; but the idea man is near the top in the political arena." I then gave him the particulars of our planned team and his eyes lit up like a Christmas tree. I thought maybe my tentative offer was *like* Christmas to him. A chance to step out of a threadbare, humdrum life.

"When do I begin?"

"You will have to first be interviewed and vetted. I will set it up for you."

"Who is it that will interview me?"

"I again can't tell you that or how it will be done."

That caused me to think. The vice president wanted to personally chat with all my candidates, but as only the NSA and I would know he was the force behind Terminus, how could that be accomplished? No one else on the team was to know he was involved. It would be on my list of questions the next time we had a dialogue.

"Then it seems you will have some secrets *within* your secret organization."

"A lot of times that's the case, Mickey."

"Of all the other former team members we had in CTT, why me?"

"Mr. Byrd talked you up quite a bit. And I remember you as not only a shrewd and sharp-witted operative but one that could be depended upon when things went down…such as in Operation Fremont."

"Yeah, that went well as I remember. But thanks for thinking about me as you put this all together. Gives me some hope about my dull-ass life. I'll be ready to go at any time."

"Good." I stood and shook his hand. "You still look fit, Hondo" (his former code name).

"Try to be. See you around, Bruce."

CHAPTER 4

I returned to our future team house and sat pondering about my call to Atticus Steed. He hadn't actually been in law enforcement or on any kind of clandestine team. We had become friends and partners from not only the Viper mission but after the Viper's brother had located him to avenge his 'murder.' Both Atticus and his wife Maria had taken the sniper's bullet fired from a boat off shore in Antigua. As Maria convalesced, Atticus and I went after the assassin. What began with me hunting Steed the hit man to accomplish the Viper mission, ended in a fairly close-knit relationship between us and our wives. I had only seen him in action with a rifle but as he had no counter-ops training nor was ever part of a team like we were putting together, I couldn't vouch for his capability to embark on government-driven operations. But my instincts are generally right-on about people and I knew if he was set to task, he would be dynamic in the role of a clandestine counterterrorist operative.

I had spoken with him on the phone the previous Christmas. It was nothing but a friendly call without any business attached or with any discussion of the past. What was then was just history. I dialed his number. It was Maria who answered.

"Hi, Bruce," she greeted, without me even saying a word. "I recognized your 304 area code when it appeared. How have you been?"

"Just dandy…and you two?"

"We are wonderful. Atticus just stepped out of the shower. I'm sure it's he who you were calling. I'll get him."

"Tell him to put some clothes on before talking to me. I don't want that image in my brain."

She laughed. "You're funny." "Yes I am."

"Bye, Bruce. Here's Atticus. There was a pause and then his voice came on the line. "Hello. U.S. Marines. Providing America's Enemies an Opportunity to Die for their Country Since 1775. How Can I Help You?"

"Now *that's* what I wanted to hear," I replied. "How the hell are you?"

"Better than I deserve."

"To what do we owe this phone call."

"Just a question. Are you still liking living on a tropical island like a king?" "It's been a magical experience."

"Been? That sounds past tense. Are you planning on ditching your dream to come back to civilization?"

"Well, we've been here for fourteen years now. I think Maria would like to return to the USA to spend some time with her mother since her father passed away. She also misses all the dress shops, fine restaurants and well, America in general. Maybe I do a little myself."

What he said opened the door for me. Something I hadn't expected. "If you do that, would you keep your cottage there in paradise?"

"I think so. It probably wouldn't take me long to get a belly-full of American politics, out of control crime in the cities, and the impossible traffic. I'd be coming back here less than a month later."

"Do you have a U.S. state in mind?" I asked him.

"We haven't really talked seriously about it. Maria's mom is in southern Pennsylvania. Maybe there…maybe a little further south."

"Like the D.C. area."

"Did I mention the traffic?"

"You did. But it depends where you are and what time of day it is."

"Okay, McGowan, what gives? We're continuing this conversation longer than I envisioned. What's on your mind."

"Just as I remember, you read people very well. And even over the phone."

"If you'll further remember, I went back to college at the University of Health Sciences Antigua and got a masters in Psychology."

I had forgotten that. If he came in with us, we'd then have a psychologist on board as part of the team. Icing on the cake.

"I want you to mull something over, Atticus. If you're thinking about going back to stateside, you'll need something to do."

"Uh huh, and you just have something *for* me to do, which is why you're calling."

"You had always said you were intrigued with what I did for the Department of State and wished you had had an opportunity after the Marines to do something like that. Well, I'm giving you that opportunity now."

He laughed. "Me work for the government after all I went through with them? Have you been into Adriana's cooking sherry again?"

"It's not what you think. I will be in charge of a shadow operation separate from the counterterrorist elements of the State Department, Homeland Security and the alphabet agencies. What we will be doing is super-clandestine and unknown to not only all other government agencies but the American people as well. Not even the president will know."

"You're either talking about what you did a few years ago or you have gone rogue out on your own."

"Very similar to what I did before. Nothing rogue or mercenary to this opportunity."

"Well, Bruce, thanks for thinking about me, but if we

did come back to the mainland, I would have an 8 to 5 job that would not give Maria cause to worry about me. You know what I'm talking about; you have gone through that with Adriana. But wait a minute, you're in backwoods West Virginia and…"

"Adriana and I are living in Washington now…at least we will for two years. But we still have our house there in Greenbrier County."

"And so, you've already taken over such a team you're talking about."

"Putting it together as we speak."

"Bruce, I have to tell you…as much as this sounds intriguing, I don't think I'd be cut out for this. Anyway, it's definitely something Maria wouldn't go for."

"Well, I'm going to leave the offer open for you to consider. Of course it would require you to relocate to the D.C. area…maybe Maryland, Northern Virginia, et cetera."

"And exactly when were you going to bring your team together for a first meet- up."

"I have in mind the 5th of July at 0900 if I can corral the rest of them. At that meeting, you and others would be interviewed, then a background check completed.”

“And you would expect me to pass that?” He then laughed.

“I’m sure all has been forgiven and anything on paper totally expunged.” “Stuff like I did is not easily erased from people’s brains.”
“Anyone who had known about your government-ordered hits will be out of the system, in jail or dead. Anyway, the person heading up this team will be keeping it secret from anyone else in the justice, law enforcement or political arenas.”

“And that person is?” “Can’t tell you that, Atticus.”

“Secret dude heading up a secret organization with secret missions.”

“About the size of it.”

“Pull together all your candidates but leave me off the list, Bruce.”

“Is that your final answer?” “I believe it is.”

“Well, if you change your mind, you have my number.

I’ll send you the address.”

"Thanks for your call, Bruce. Give Adriana my love and best."

"Same to Maria. Don't be a stranger."

And that didn't go like I had hoped it would, especially after hearing that Steed and his wife were contemplating going stateside. Still I had the fifth candidate to contact on my list…Angela Lovato.

It had been years and I can't remember how long since I had seen Angela. I was a contractor dispatched by the NSA back then with the old CTT team and had been partnered with the FBI on a mission in the Beirut area in 2018. I remember the special agents kept asking who we were…mercenaries, CIA, thugs…but we kept a silent tongue. The agent team had assumed the lead but our CTT went off tangent, located and then erased the terrorist menace. When the agents found the house where the terrorists were camped, they found four bearded dudes dead. We were brutal in the take-down but compassionate and merciful to their families who were found huddled in a corner scared shitless…literally. It had all been pretty damn messy with all the blood and shit.

So Angel, her nickname, and I had communed briefly at a drinking establishment outside the town's limits after the ordeal was over for a fruity Sharbat. Iraqis frown on consuming alcoholic beverages in their country, so we settled for the traditional fruity drink. We didn't mind killing their people over there but didn't want to insult them by violating their customs. Angel kept trying to pump me for information, also wondering what the hell we were doing there as part of the task force; yet we didn't take part in it. "Or did you?" She asked. "Was that you ahead of us?" I danced around her questions. But even though she gave me her number, I didn't stay in touch with her since I was married. But even if I wasn't, I made it a point to never go out with a woman who could kick my ass. Not a bad-looking thirty-something gal with short hair, still looking Special Ops-like in appearance and tough as cowhide.

I made the call, thinking as it was ringing, she likely had a different number after nearly seven years, so why was I wasting my time?

"Hello." It was a woman's voice, but was it hers? "Is

this Angela?"

"Who wants to know? If you're a telemarketing prick or a scammer, just tell me right now and I'll…"

"You'll hunt me down and torture me."

"I know your voice from somewhere. Now who the hell are you?"

"Does 2018 in the Iraqi town of Salah ad Din ring a bell?"

"Yes, that's it. McCowan or somethin' like that." "McGowan We shared a conversation and some sharbat."

"Yeah, I remember now. You're one of the spooks that went with us on Operation Delta."

"Wasn't CIA. I'm sure I told you that." "Then who were you guys?"

"Just operators in the State Department chain. I think I can tell you that now."

"Well, it's good to hear from you. Tell me you ditched that wife you kept talkin' about and decided to look me up."

"No, I'm still married, but I did decide to look you up."

"Well, McGowan, I don't go for that stuff. Gets too messy. A doting wife back home and a paramour on the side."

"Not why I'm calling, Angel. I wondered if you were still with the Bureau or doing something else."

"I left the FBI last year and got my private detective license."

"Where are you?"

"Back where I grew up in Oklahoma City." "How's that going for you?"

"Slow as a herd of turtles stampeding through peanut butter."

I laughed. "I think I remember how quippy you were in our conversations."

"Why the call, McGowan?"

"Call me Bruce, Angel. I was just wondering if you were still with the Bureau and if not, what you were doing. I am putting together a hugely covert counterterrorist team headed up by a guy high up in the government. Your name and face popped into my brain. Interested?”

“Maybe. I'd have to know a hell of a lot more about it.”

“Would you be available to fly into D.C. and interview with us on 5 July?” “Let me check my calendar. I've been hired by some guy's wife to follow her husband who says he's goin' on a July 4th golf trip with some guys. She doesn't believe it. He's a business dude and is away from home a lot. She found semen in his drawers and lipstick on his pants after his last *business* trip. I had stalked him on an overnight deal here in the city, but as he was intentionally being evasive, I wasn't able to get any good shots of him.”

“Is that what you want in a career…working for suspicious wives to get the goods on their cheating husbands? Not much gun-play in that.”

“Is what you're wantin' me to do involve shootin' people?”

“Counterterrorist activities have many dimensions. Gun-play comes in a good bit.”

“Then I'm interested. I just looked at my calendar while you were talkin' and other than a couple of gigs, I've got nothin' goin' the next couple of months."

"The address is 412 MacArthur not far from the White House."

"Unless I get a hundred grand job between now and then, I'll be there, McGowan."

CHAPTER 5

And so, the offers were out there. I had had in mind perhaps a dozen former agents and operatives with whom I had fought terrorism through the years but the people who would get first refusal, if it came to that, had the traits, skills, and personalities that I thought would make a great Bat Team. When VP Collins sent the Bat signal went up, I was sure these four could hit the ground running, three of which had no spouses who could get in the way of them answering the call. I'm sure I would find myself envious that they would be out there knocking heads and planting slugs while I was sitting at my desk waiting for them to return. Would it be possible to slip in with them occasionally just to fire up my engine and get my heart racing? Adriana told me I needed to make sure my arteries weren't clogging. What better way to do that than send through the arteries a firestorm of adrenaline.

Before the day ended, I called the VP on his private number. As he recognized my number, he answered on the third ring. "Afternoon, Bruce. Talk to me."

"Well, Mr. Vice President, all four of my proposed candidates have been contacted. Two appear to be firm, one is a maybe but should accept and the fourth declined."

"Which one declined?"

"Atticus Steed. He and his wife are living the life of luxury in Antigua."

"No wonder he declined."

"However, Steed and his wife are talking about moving back to the states so that she can be close to her ailing mother. If they move close to D.C., I think I can reign him in."

"Okay, but don't bet the house on this guy. And I'm still not sure about him."

"I think you *will* be once you interview him. And by the way, I was wondering how you would carry out the interviews. You made it clear we will be in every respect clandestine. No one would know you are the creator of Terminus and have primary oversight of the team."

"We will set up two rooms at your office house with a

two-way mirror in between. They won't see me but I'll see them. I will ask them questions and all they'll hear is my voice which will be audibly altered."

Sounds like something out of the show Law and Order…and rather avant- guard."

"Maybe the set-up is a little unconventional, but necessary. I will slip in and out at your side door. Will make sure no one sees me."

"Also very cloak-and-dagger, sir."

He chuckled. "When will you bring them in?" "I gave them a tentative date of 5 July." "Why then?"

"It was mainly arbitrary, but as I have been doing methodic, day-by-day planning as to team development, responsibilities and individual expertise when it comes to missions, I figured I'd be done around the first and can then sit back and assess what I have. It also may take me a couple of months to get potential team members to commit. I'll be on the phone with them to assure they will show on the 5th for their interviews."

"And the woman?"

"Lovato? I'm sure she's in. After I told her she was a candidate for the team and its missions which I carefully parlayed, I could hear her heart thumping like a drum over the phone."

"Good. Between now and then, Bruce, I want to have a few meetings with you to go over in detail what I envision for this team. You of course are experienced in mission planning and conduct. I won't stand in your way or question your tactics. I will be sure that you receive the Intel on Terminus-necessary scenarios before it goes to the agencies. It will be like giving you a running start. Terminus will be engaged when drastic measures need to be taken where I and the National Security Advisor believe that conventional counterterrorist methods should not be employed. JTTFs are not always the way to go when a small team of infiltrators and saboteurs can quickly and efficiently get the job done."

"Agreed, sir. And I am confident that the people I chose to serve on Terminus will do it in a swift and punishing manner. When the smoke clears, the media, politicians and justice departments within the system will all be scratching their heads wondering *what the hell happened?* Our motto at CTT was the three Bs…Be swift, Be brutal and Be gone. The same will apply to Terminus."

"The very zeal I want from you, Bruce. Put it together. Let me know if 5 July is on."

"Roger, sir."

After our conversation, I spent an hour or so rehashing in my brain policies and information as to how terrorist information comes down the pike, who gets it first and who makes the decision to send which Counterterrorist operatives. The responsibility to acquire and disseminate terrorist Intel belongs to the NCTC or National Counterterrorism Center. When knowledge of a terrorist threat is realized and analyzed, the information is then placed into the Terrorist Identities Datamart Environment (TIDE) network. Terminus would be on the receipt list but as a blind cc. The VP and NSA would assure I get the info first and then would have dialogue with me about the immediate deployment of our team. By the time the other CTs planned, prepped, secured visas to enter the country, determined CT unity, integrated all CT agencies for control purposes, and then deployed, our element would already be making people die.

As to mission conduct, I knew each of the operatives I had selected was intelligent, decisive, quick-thinking and could place rounds mass center without blinking an eye. They were pretty much like me, but had a long way to go to *be* me. I know that sounds arrogant, but a fact. By the time I was through with them, however, they would be close. Until we were up and running officially, even though we *weren't* official, there would be long days of off site training, conducting situational reaction scenarios and polishing up on their shooting skills. They would have the latest and best of firearms, tactical gear and gee whiz devices…everything that the JTTF had, except the armored vehicles, and the other CT elements. Weapons, ammo, explosives and gear would be inside a well-secured small warehouse only a block from the team house. Otherwise, during the conduct of regular business, everyone would be dressed in casual business attire that was commiserate with the sign on the door of our house, *Brightstar Inc.* Brightstar was nothing but a front, a fictitious, fallacious business that no one need have the interest or curiosity in entering the building. If they did, my personal assistant, Debbie, would greet the person and inform that the office was a private business that didn't warrant on-site customers. To make the business in any way credible, however, I needed to come up with an idea of who we were on paper and what we did.

Most days I drove the Suburban to work which left Adriana stranded, vehicle wise, during the weekdays. She had chosen not to bring her van from West Virginia to D.C. as she had no desire to go anywhere to which she couldn't walk. She vowed never to get out in the Washington traffic with all the government people out in the mornings and afternoons and tourists during the middle of the day and definitely not venture onto the Capital Beltway which was a 64 mile interstate part raceway and part-parking lot. She had everything she wanted to do within walking distance in our Georgetown community. However, a couple of days I decided to walk the two and a half miles to and from our condo to my office house. As I had worried about her being out on the street during the day, I never thought I myself would ever come upon any danger, morning or evening, along the way. One would think.

It was the 17th of June and the temperature was supposed to be cooler thanks to the previous day of rain that brought with it a nice northwest breeze and lower humidity. I didn't get away from my desk until seven-thirty, so after calling Adriana to tell her I wouldn't be home until about eight-thirty, I closed up and hit the pavement.

On my trek along Pennsylvania Avenue, I glanced at but paid little attention to the White House. Seen it, done it. After I had entered the Foggy Bottom area, I skirted the Potomac and then came upon the Exorcist Steps where Father Karras took a fatal tumble. Of course Karras was a fictional character in the book and movie, The Exorcist, but I had never visited the steps nor had taken the detour to do so. I stood at the bottom, looked up to the top, wondering if the padre was thinking "Heaven, here I come" as he bounced down to the bottom. I then smiled and continued onto M Street. After passing a few nifty clothing stores and a sports shop, suddenly a hooded figure began running from an ABC store, crashing directly into me. Both of us ended up sprawled onto the sidewalk. The bottle of booze he was carrying broke and splattered, drenching me, him and a wad of money that came flying out of his hand. His pistol scooted along the sidewalk out of reach.

I looked over at the man and said, "*Well,* prick, appears you just robbed the liquor store."

He then got to his feet, whipped out a knife and attempted to slash me. However, I pulled my Glock from its holster and slammed the butt against his head. He hit the concrete again and began shouting obscenities.

"I introduced you to one end of my Glock; would you like to see what comes out of the other?"

"Shit, man. Take it easy with that."

"Now get your ass up," I barked, placing the muzzle into his neck beneath his chin.

Seconds later, a D.C. patrol car came speeding up to the curb, its siren dying down. Two officers quickly exited with guns drawn. One of them aimed his pistol at me and yelled, "Police! Drop it, sir! Let me see your hands!"

I laid the Glock down on the sidewalk and raised my hands. That's when the perp began running. The second officer shouted "Stop! Police!"

He didn't and continued on down the street.

"Shoot the bastard!" I yelled. But the cop didn't. He instead gave chase. That was going to go nowhere. The suspect was young and athletic and the cop, fifties and carrying more than two hundred fifty pounds. He then stopped, touched the radio on his shoulder and began talking.

The cop who had a bead on me then told me to get down on my knees, hands on my head.

"Officer, I'm sure you can see what happened here. The man robbed the liquor store and literally ran into me.

You see the money here and his gun over there. I had him in custody."

"You a police officer?" "No."

"Then why do you have a gun?" "For protection from things like this." "Do you have a permit?"

"Yes, West Virginia."

"Your license is no good in D.C. unless you have a permit issued here. As to your state, we do not have preemption laws. You have to apply for a D.C. carry permit and complete two hours training. You're illegal, sir, and I have to take you into custody."

"If I give you a number, would you please call it? That person will square this away."

He smirked. "Another guy who knows somebody important and trying to avoid arrest. Who is it, the president?"

"No. But he's high-up on the political food chain."

"It's you, sir, who needs to make the phone call after I take you into the station."

"You give up on an armed robber and bust my gonads even after I subdued the man?"

"Hands behind your back, sir. I need to hook you up."

I did as instructed and as he pushed me against the brick wall, began frisking me.

"Look, officer…"

"Don't want to hear it. Don't give me cause to charge you with resisting arrest."

Well, this was a fine bucket of monkey poop. How quickly a guy's day can change from anticipating a pleasant evening with his beautiful wife and a plate of shrimp and scallops waiting for me at home to what was probably a musty jail cell shared with a drunk who had just thrown up on my urine-soaked mattress.
I'd make that phone call to Ben Marshall as soon as I had the opportunity. If I was only allowed one phone call, Adriana was going to be worried.

I was not booked right away but was allowed to call Marshall who immediately jumped into me. "Is this your idea of keeping a low profile? The VP is not going to be happy. People are going to wonder who you are and…"

"Come on, give me a break, Ben. This wasn't my fault. An armed bandit literally ran into me as he was running out of a store."

"Spare me the details. Let's get you out of there ASAP. I will send a car and a guy with a badge and release order. Should be there in twenty minutes. And for God's sake, get yourself a D.C. carry permit."

"Thanks for your understanding, Ben. Means a lot to me."

"Don't be snide, Bruce. I'm doing my best to take care of you. But you need to stay off the radar."

"Okay, okay, I understand that. Thanks, Ben."

"My car will be there shortly."

A lawyer by the name of Abraham Goldman dressed in a black suit and striped tie appeared at the precinct desk with a federal release form signed by one Judge Amos Nelson. The cop who had brought me in came to the interrogation room and motioned me out the door.

"I guess it's who you know in this town.

Happens all the time. We bring them in and somebody high up on the food chain gets them released."

"I shouldn't have been arrested in the first place, officer. And the charge against me will be expunged."

"Just get the hell out of here, McGowan."

"Gladly. I guess you people didn't catch the perp, huh."

He didn't reply but turned his back. Obviously, they didn't.

I checked my phone when it was returned to me and saw that Adriana had called, wondering where I was since it was now ten fifteen. Since my phone had been taken away upon arrest, I wasn't able to call her back. She had called a second time just before ten and was now understandably worried.

Goldman dropped me at my condo. As I was getting out, he said, "Stay out of trouble, McGowan."

"I try but seems like trouble has a mind of its own. Thanks, Goldman; I appreciate the ride."

When I entered the front door, Adriana had the look

on her face that I had dreaded. "Why didn't you call me back, Skip? I was worried sick."

"Not a good day, sweetheart."

That's when I began telling her how it had ended. "You could have been killed by the guy."

"And I could have killed *him*"

"That's not the response I was looking for."

"I know. I'm sorry. I'm just pissed as hell and didn't mean to be disparaging."

She then turned and stood at a window, staring out into the dark. "I don't like this place, Skip. It's too dangerous and too unfriendly."

"Unfriendly?"

"When I go out, I find the people to be haughty and cold. We've now been here almost two months and I don't know anyone. I don't *want* to know anyone. I want to go back home."

"We talked about this, Adriana. We knew it would be foreign to you and I have hoped you could adjust to it. I don't want you to go. I know we can be happy here together. Can we just give it a little more time?"

After a brief pause, she turned back around. "Alright, I'll try. I know I'm stronger than this. I guess I just need to get a new attitude."

I put my arms around her waist. "And I'll help you. I'll be here for you especially on the weekends. But if you find this time next month you are still wanting to go back home, I will step away from this opportunity and go with you. Our marriage and your happiness are the most important things in my life."

"I don't want you to quit. I don't want to be the reason you would do so. I'll be fine. But…you stay off the streets. You either drive or take the Metro."

I nodded. However, there was no way I was going to cower, avoiding the streets and people who looked like they wanted to have me for lunch. I have faced death numerous occasions and by the grace of God come through all the ordeals with only a half dozen wounds…none of which were close to putting me in the grave. But I replied, "I hear you, sweetheart. I will not give you cause to worry."

CHAPTER 6

That next morning the vice president called me at my desk. "Good morning, Director."

"Morning, sir."

"I hear you got into a little scrape last night."

"I did. I bumped head-on into a robbery."

"So I heard. And Mr. Marshall took care of it."

"Yes. A case where the police overreacted."

"From what I learned, I believe you are correct about that."

"Did you call to rake me over the carpet, sir."

"Not at all, Bruce. You responded exactly as you should have. It's the kind of grit you're made of. Don't worry about it."

"Thank you, sir.'

"Are you in process of setting up those interviews?"

"The background checks came in a couple of days ago and there is nothing prohibitive in their history. I have since lined up Johnson, Sabbitini and Stryker for interview next month on the 5th. Each will be here."

"And both the hit man and the special-ops gal?"

"Still waiting to hear from her but I think we can count Mr. Steed out."

"Continue to press Lovato, Bruce. We need a hard-nosed gal on the team, especially one fluent in Spanish."

"I will, sir. We'll make that happen."

"That's not to say any of them are shoe-ins. I want to be in on the scrutiny."

"Understood. I've made no promises to anyone. However, I'm very confident about the lot of them."

"I'm pleased that you are. I'm relying on your best judgment. From what I know about you, you have tremendous insights about people."

"Is there anything else we need to discuss today, Mr. Vice President?"

"I think not, Director. Just stay out of the limelight. No one needs to know you're anything but the CEO for Brightstar. By the way, I have had that bogus company placed on the exchange and given it both a background and history."

"Have we decided what kind of business it is?" "An HR

company. Personnel management."

"Well," I replied, "I see both the humor and irony in that especially where it comes to our help with assuring there is a secure and safe environment, addressing problematic behavior, and of course, termination."

"I thought you might." "Very clever, sir."

"Thank you. My cleverness is why I was voted into this position." He then chuckled. "I have to go, Bruce. Give me the time and particulars for the 5 July gathering. I'm anxious to observe the folks you selected."

Roger, sir. Good day."

I still needed to nail down exactly when the Terminus candidates were to arrive and that none of them had backed out. As interested as Lovato was in ditching her boring private eye job and moving on in her life, I had not gotten a firm answer from her about coming to our little party on the 5th. I called and left a message on her cell. I imagined that she was somewhere watching through a peephole at a husband cheating on his wife.

After the call, I went to the front desk to spend some time with Debbie discussing what Brightstar actually was…except in reality it wasn't. "Well, that's a coincidence," she said. "I spent most of my years with the State Department in H.R."

"And as far as this team goes, you will be attending to our personnel needs just as you would be in a real business. Of course you are being held to the utmost standards of confidentiality. As we have acquired for you a secret clearance, you will be exposed to a good deal of classified information, which we discussed."

"Who do you answer to? You haven't told me who your boss is."

"My immediate boss is the National Security Advisor, Ben Marshall."

"I did see him in here last week and wondered if that

was so," she said. And then I thought, the vice president would be slipping in on the 5th and she would be setting up for his observation next to the interview room which would include sound and camera. She would see him come in and leave. She would wonder why the Vice President of the United States would be directly connected to our team. She knew we were a clandestine counterterrorist operation, but the VP was way high on the government ladder and his presence in our team house wouldn't make much sense. I had to tell her.

But that's when I again called Bart Collins. Would he be okay with her knowing?

"Sweet little Debbie? Absolutely. Her father was my Directorate of Operations at the Company. I've known Debbie since she was just a kitten. It was I who placed her there at Terminus, you know. By all means inform her. She has the clearance and can be trusted beyond even that of your primary team members, I'm sure. By the way, she also has a black belt in taekwondo."

"I will try not to pick a fight with her."

He chuckled. "But when you tell her I'm actually the one to whom you directly report, and that Ben Marshall is only the guy you'll tell your team members is your supervisor, she will never let on any different."

And that told me something I didn't realize. Ben was a supervisor decoy. That was why the VP and I had been talking rather than me with Ben. I wondered why I was allowed to go two steps up the latter in my phone conversations. Of course it was the VP who came to me and who had summoned me to his office a couple of times. Any mission orders would come directly from Collins.

Marshall would be in on it as an advisor and mission organizer, but not the one to whom I would report. I couldn't believe it had taken me two months to realize that. Stuff was slowly sinking in.

I then went out to the lobby where Debbie was sitting. The room appeared to at one time have been a parlor. Debbie was blonde, petite and had pretty, captivating eyes. Of course I knew I couldn't allow myself to be captivated by her looks. Anyway, not only were we both married, I was her boss.

"Debbie, can we have a moment?" "Absolutely, Mr.

McGowan."

I took a seat in a sofa chair next to her desk. "You're looking bright and eager today. I thought we should have a chat. I've been meaning to do so but apologize I have had little for you to do so far."

"But I do keep myself busy. What's on your mind, sir?"

"First, I wish you'd call me Bruce."

"Hmm, I'm not used to calling my bosses by their first names."

"Make an exception with me. I think it will make us both comfortable with one another. In conferences that involve our operatives, you would call me Director."

"Understood, Bruce."

"I know you were read in as to your responsibilities when you first came aboard. You know as well I'm in the process of staffing the team."

"Yes. Mr. Marshall sat down with me when I first arrived and told me what I'd be doing. I would provide the H.R and IT support and be both the administrative and logistical assistant to you."

"Were you advised what our team would be doing?"

"Yes. You are called Terminus and when we receive Intel on terrorist factions out there either planning or in the process of performing terroristic acts, you will dispatch either some or all of the team to terminate both them and their mission."

"Pretty well encapsulated. I guess I don't need to give you a long, boring briefing on the team and its responsibilities. The vice president says he knows you through your father who worked under him when he was CIA Director."

"Yes. His teenage daughter used to babysit me."

"I see. Well, I'm going to share something with you that requires the utmost confidence. Even the operatives we hire will not know this. My immediate boss, the creator and architect of the Terminus project is Vice President Collins."

She smiled. "And you didn't think I knew that?" "You

did?"

"He's the one who called me, brought me into his office and reassigned me to here from the State Department."

"Well, why didn't I know that?" I said. "I thought National Security Advisor Marshall placed you here."

"Well, Mr. Marshall probably had a hand in it, but I know he will have little to do with what goes on here."

I smiled. "Well, obviously anytime I need to know something, I'll come ask you."

"And I'd be pleased to provide you the answers." She

was going to work out fine. She'd be my Radar O'Reilly for sure. Except without the glasses and teddy bear.

"Well, as we have merely been ships passing in the water most of the time having only casual conversation, I know now that I can trust you as a confidant to bounce things off you when needed. You will have every piece of information and Intel I receive from either the VP or NCTC that I receive."

Again she smiled. "But I already do, sir."

I laughed. "Well, now that I know how things work around here and that everything is safely in your hands, I'll just go back to my office and work a crossword puzzle."

"I'm glad we talked, Bruce. We are going to make a great team."

"You bet we will."

CHAPTER 7

I finally got a call back from Angela Lovato. "Bruce McGowan."

"That's me. Hello, Angela."

"Alright, what time do I meet you on the 5th?"

"That's what I wanted to hear. We'll all gather at the team house at 0900."

"So, how will this work…you interview me and the rest of the team all at once or individually? I don't want to be sitting' around waiting' on my turn while you're talkin' to other people."

"I'll be in on the interview, but my boss will be asking the questions and getting to know you."

"Which didn't answer my question." "When and what time are you flying in?"

"The evening of the 4th and will be at your location at 0900 on the 5th, just like you told me. Now do I sit around all day or is it all of us together?"

"Individually, Angela. I'll have you interviewed first. Should only take a hour. What you do with the remainder of the day is up to you."

"And who's doin' the interview besides you?" "My

supervisor."

"And you're not gonna tell me who it is."

"Nope."
"I don't know if I like this but guess I'll be there."

"Don't guess, Angela. Be here or not."

"I will. See you on the 5th, McGowan."

Just like I remembered her…abrupt, tart and demanding. But it was her spirit I liked, not to mention her skills.

And so we had three…at least for interview. I actually didn't see any reason VP Collins would not like and choose any one of them. But something could be said or found out about someone that would x-out him…or her. If that was the case, I had two or three alternates.

At noon that day I took a walk along the historic Washington Mall then near the capitol building, stopped at a roach coach trailer and bought a cili cheese dog and an ice-cold bottled Coke. After consuming them on a park bench, I popped in an antacid tablet, knowing that I would have terminal heartburn by mid-afternoon if I didn't. A beautiful day but approaching 90 degrees. I had shed by jacket and tie back at the team house, so to get myself even more comfortable, rolled up the sleeves on my white shirt. The scenery was great, one of them a brunette in short shorts and a blouse rolled up above the waist, and the other a tall vixen with long, blonde hair and short skirt as thin as a newspaper that exposed her thighs nearly all the way up to…well, let's just say her sports section. I wasn't lusting per se, but I must confess *was* greatly appreciating God's handiwork.

A pasty-face mime came up to me and put himself through a bunch of mechanical antics like he was climbing an invisible wall. He was obviously looking for a handout. I just ignored him but he continued going through his motions. Then a cop walked by and told him to "move along." I then had a funny thought. If the cop had arrested him, would he have to tell him he had the right to remain silent? It was time to get back to work.

When Debbie and I departed work at 5:30 that day, I walked her to her car. She lived in Springfield. Since I had not driven the Suburban, I took the Metro. It wasn't that I didn't want to push the envelope and get into another scuffle, I had already had my walk and the temp was still 89. Anyway, I might run into the same cops in Georgetown who would ask me if I was carrying, which I was, and if I had gotten my D.C. carry permit, which I hadn't. It reminded me to take a day and go apply for one. If it was like going to the tag office, I *would* have to take a day because I'd be standing in line with a thousand other people.

My beautiful wife greeted me with a kiss and asked me how my day went. Escorted directly to the dinner table, I found two glistening pork chops on my plate. I didn't deserve her, especially since I had ogled two other beautiful women while sitting on the park bench. Shame on me.

After dinner, I helped clear the table and dried her special dishes that didn't go into the dishwasher after she washed them. We then sat in our living room in front of the TV for a couple of hours whereupon she returned to the kitchen to bring out the Creme Brûlée, the recipe she had brought back from our vacation in Paris. It was a vacation for her but a nightmare for me, considering I ran into an old nemesis of mine who wanted to kill me. But I in turn killed him by pushing his wheelchair off a cliff. It was not as cruel as it sounds. I am not a heartless being. You'd just have to know the story.

As it had been a few days since Adriana and I had been intimate, we later attacked one another with unbridled passion. No, a bridle and saddle were not involved, but maybe something resembling a pommel was. Anyway, for some reason that night, I slept like a baby. Oh wait a minute, I actually *do* know the reason.

Three weeks later, July 4th, Washington was bursting at the seems with tourists. As it was a Sunday and a holiday, the government was shut down; however, residents venturing out would still have to brave the vehicle and pedestrian traffic. And then there was the Independence Day parade through the streets of Washington and that magnificent fireworks display near the capitol building. I stayed home with Adriana and watched it all on TV. I didn't get much sleep that night since the students at Georgetown University set off their own fireworks on campus until after 3 AM. As I was bleary-eyed later in the morning at seven when I walked out the door, I knew I wouldn't be operating on all cylinders at our very important meeting. Who the hell was it who set up the meetings for the 5th and what was he thinking? I then saw his face in my rearview mirror.

Traffic was worse than ever that morning and it took me nearly twenty minutes to go three-and-a-half miles. As I was parking the Suburban in our small parking lot in the rear of our team house, I saw Debbie getting out of her Honda.

"Did you have a good Independence Day, Bruce?"

"I hid all day and buried my head under the covers all night."

"Afraid of fireworks?"

"Something like that." Then I told her about the university bozos.

"Well, I had a marvelous time watching all the festivities, the parade along Pennsylvania Avenue and then on the lawn of the capitol. The music was great and the fireworks spectacular. The president was there mingling in the crowd and I got to shake his hand."

"Whoop-tee-do," I said.

"You don't like the president?"

"I shook hands with him once when he was a congressman and his grip was that of a dead fish."

She grinned. "Yeah, I shook hands with him once and it

did kinda feel like that."

"Well, let's go get this on." We then walked in through the rear door.

"Do you think all of the invitees will be here?" she asked.

"I believe so. The vice president will be arriving a little after nine after we get set up and will let me know by cellphone when he's on site. We need to prep the room he'll be in and test the mic and speaker. I brought some donuts and danish with me and a box of coffee from Dunkin Donuts. We'll split them up between the two rooms. The important thing this morning is that we need to arrange for none of the people coming to not see the VP. Bring him in through either the side or back door but make sure it's not when any of the visitors are getting out of their vehicles. That's why he's coming after nine."

"Yes, sir. I'll take care of all that."

I then said "I will put a sign on both doors for them to enter through the front door. I made that up last week."

"Good move," she replied.

"Okay then, let's get set up. If you will go into the VP's room and turn on the mic and speaker, I'll go to the conference room on the reverse side of the mirror and wait to hear your voice. Then I'll respond to see if you can hear me."

I then grabbed a pastry and cup of the Joe and sat in our small conference room, waiting on her voice. The speaker in the room projected Debbie's voice weakly. I said "How do you hear me?" and got no response. I then went to the next room and told her to turn the volume up on the transmitter. She did and I returned to the conference room. Her voice then came in loud and clear. "Do you hear me clearly?"

"Yes," she replied. Her voice however was intentionally cloaked. The VP's voice would be as well so as not to be recognized.

"Great, then we're good."

I set up two chairs near my audio set, one for the interviewee and one for me. We were ready. It was now just after eight and I returned to my office. I didn't know the questions the VP would ask, but I had two or three to add.

As I expected, and as she requested, Angela Lovato came in early at eight forty- five. She was intent on being interviewed first. Debbie brought her to my office. I stood and held out my hand to greet her. Now sporting a ponytail, I saw that she was petite and warmly tanned.

"You don't look much different from the last time I saw you, Angel."

She smiled. "Wish I could say the same about you." Then she laughed and said, "I'm just messin' with you, McGowan."

"You can call me Bruce."

"Okay then, *Bruce*. Still handsome as ever."

I think she was fishing for the same compliment, but somehow I didn't have it in me. Her face looked the same and had weathered well but more hard-boiled than I had remembered. However, she still had a tight, firm body which belonged on a 30 year old. Her personnel file said she was 47. I was impressed.

"I'll be sure you're first on the list."

"Thanks. I have a plane to catch back to Oklahoma City at noon."

"You couldn't get a later flight? The interviewer may want you to stick around."

"I actually have a big case I'm working on and am required to be in deposition at four, central time."

"Okay, we'll work this out."

There was then a rap on my door and Debbie appeared. "Director, we have someone else in the lobby, a Mr. Johnson."

"I'll be out in a moment." Then I went back to Angel. "I'm going to set you up in the conference room down the hall. Ladies bathroom is on the right and conference room across from it. Pastries and coffee are on a table in the meeting room."

"Thanks, but I don't eat sugar. I'll take the coffee, though."

"And I will be in there shortly."

I then went to the lobby to greet Mickey. We shook hands and I asked him to follow me to my office.

"Okay, when you hear my boss's voice on the intercom, stay focused and let that personality shine."

"Got it, Bruce."

"Also, be assertive but respectful in your interview. The person with whom you'll be talking is high up in the system, so don't be obtuse. The operative positions for which you're being interviewed are similar to what we did in CTT, but even more critical to the security and defense of our country. Be bright and be brief in your responses."

He nodded.

"We have a former SEAL who later became an FBI special agent and who will be interviewed first. She is already in the conference room."

"She?"

"*She*. And I'm pretty sure *she* can kick your ass. So when you meet her, don't be condescending."

"Yes, sir."

While we sat there, Debbie rapped on the door once more. "Director, we have another gentleman in the lobby."

"Who?"

"A Mr. Stryker."

My heart sank a little; I was hoping it was Steed. But certainly glad that Stryker had materialized. "Bring him in, please."

Debbie departed the room but returned a few seconds

later with Stryker behind her. She then left and closed the door behind her. I stood to greet him. "Hello, Pierce. Meet Mike Johnson."

They shook hands and each found a chair. "Mickey then asked, "Pierce? Is that your given name?"

"Yeah, but most just call me Strike."

Stryker was five-nine and a skinhead. When I last saw him, his hair was cropped short and thinning, which had revealed more scalp than fur. His bald head now gleamed under my lights like a flesh-colored bowling ball. "Strike, I was just getting ready to explain to Mike that each of you will take the chair in the conference room down the hall on the left adjacent to a piece of audio equipment containing a mic and a speaker. On the other side of a large mirror in the next room will be my boss, whose name I am not at liberty to divulge. He will ask you a series of questions and you will provide your answers thoughtfully and respectfully. He will be assessing your personalities while probing you about your skills and experiences. Be candid but be truthful. He already has your shields and personnel files from your previous work experience, all of which involve counterterrorism. I have recommended each of you above others I have served with. Don't disappoint me." I checked my watch. "I'm not sure how long this process will take but while the female candidate is being interviewed in no less than five minutes from now, you will remain in the lobby. Understood?"

"Understood," they said in unison.

"My assistant who you met will bring you some coffee and pastries." I then rose and led them out the door and to the lobby.

"Ms. Nelson, would you please make these gentlemen comfortable while I check on Ms. Lovato."

She then whispered. "Yes, sir. Eagle Two has arrived and is set up."
I nodded and retreated to the conference room.

CHAPTER 8

After switching the knob to *on*, I tested the audio. "Sir, this is McGowan. Are you there?"

"I'm here."

"How do you hear me?"

"Lima Charlie (Loud and clear)."

"Here with me is Angela Lovato who will be the first candidate for Terminus."

"Good morning, Ms. Lovato."

"Yeah, good mornin,'…sir," she replied.

"Thanks for coming in. Are you okay with this kind of interview?"

"I'm just wonderin' why it's not in person. Not used to talkin' with somebody I can't see."

"I know it's a little unorthodox, but there's a purpose behind it."

"Which is?"

I began cringing. Don't go there, I said under my breath.

Bart Collins continued. "You've had two stellar but short careers I see…Navy SEALS, four years, Silver Star from your combat service in Special Ops…I believe that was in Iraq after the war…"

"That's where I met McGowan."

"Director McGowan," he corrected.

"Yes, sir…Director McGowan."

"Then you served six years as a special agent in the FBI. You were also decorated there. Something about saving the life of a fellow agent on a raid of an arms dealer warehouse. Lots of accolades in both careers."

"They don't mean squat, sir. The medals are somewhere tucked away in a drawer. It's all about makin' bad dudes go away and makin' America safe from foreign and domestic threats."

"Why a life of action versus working somewhere in the business world?"

"It's what I was born for, sir. I would die sittin' behind a desk lookin' at a computer all day long."

"There may be those out there who might say a woman doesn't have the body and emotional strength to do what a man should be doing. What do you say to that?"

"I have proven myself in combat and on streets of crime which proves them wrong…and sexist. I hope you don't have those ideas."

I heard Collins laugh. "I am not one of them, I assure you. But what questions do you have for me?"

"Will I ever see you or know who you are or will you continue to be a ghost in the wall?"

I let out a disparaging sigh. Come on, Angel, I said to myself. Play nice.

"Probably not. There is a reason you don't need to know."

"Okay."

To get her the hell out of the interview, I then said, "Well, sir. We will be discussing this candidate. I have three more waiting in the lobby."

"That's all I have for Ms. Lovato, Director. I wanted these interviews to be short and sweet. Just wanted to get to know you. Thank you for coming in, ma'am, and thanks for flying all the way here from Oklahoma."

"I guess I expected a bit more grillin' but thanks anyway fro the interview…whoever you are."

I stood and made no hesitation in escorting her out of the room. "Wait for me in my office, Ms. Lovato. The voice from the other room and I will need to talk about you and then you can get on to the airport."

"Yes, sir. Thanks."

When Lovato left the room, I began apologizing for her abruptness. "I knew she was a pistol, but I felt some of her answers were a little abrasive."

"Well, I like her, Bruce. She has spunk and can obviously be feisty. I didn't think at any point she was disrespectful. She just knows who she is in this world. She will be a good operative for your team. She's in."

I shook my head. "I agree, sir, but I imagine she could be like a bucking bronco and I won't have time to rein her in."

"I know you and know you will have no trouble with her. We don't want to tame that spirit."

"Yes, sir. I will have a few words with her in my office and give her the news."

Upon my return to the office, Angel was immediately apologetic. "I know; I blew the interview with my smart-ass answers. Anyway, thanks for setting it up.
Guess I'll just go back home and keep peekin' in windows."

I slid in behind my desk and didn't say anything in response for a moment. Then I said, "You'll go back home but you'll be closing your business, packing and finding a place to live here in the D.C. area."

"The hell you say. I'm in?" "You're in, Angel."

I thought I saw a little mist on her cheeks but it could have been sweat.

"Thank you. Thank you, Bruce. And thank whoever the hell your boss is."

"Now get your ass out of here and come back when I call to give you a starting date."

She then came around to my side of the desk, wrapped her arms around my neck and kissed me. I had to move my face a few inches so that it wouldn't be on the mouth. "I been wantin' to do that ever since I saw you back more'n five years ago."

"Don't be doing that again, angel. Now get the hell out of here."

When she had departed I went to the lobby to bring Stryker in. "Come on, Strike. Down the hall to the first door on the left, You two guys make yourselves comfortable. Have another donut and a cup of coffee. Again, the men's room is down the hall on the right." I then looked at Debbie. "Have these fellas been behaving themselves?"

She smiled. "Perfect gentlemen."

Stryker then took the chair in the conference room by the transmitter. Again, the vice president knew Stryker. Buck was an operations officer in Libya when I met him in 1999 doing PSYOPs work. Another CTT operative and I on our Zulu team had taken down a terrorist in the small Libyan city of Misrata based on Intel transmitted by Stryker. We met with Pierce in advance to learn where and how many terrorist assets there were on the premises, and whether the three of us could route them without any collateral damage or deaths. Unbeknownst to us, Gaddafi was visiting the city at the time and was parading down the main street in an open staff car. Nearly every door on the street opened up and families and thugs alike stood cheering and firing weapons in the air to celebrate his visit.

As we had taken positions of observation on a second story rooftop across the street from the terrorists' house, we were then clearly able to see the three suspects as they stood in the doorway firing in celebration. Each of us set up with the M40 sniper rifles we had taken from our rucks and quickly assembled. Although any one of us could have easily picked off Gaddafi, he wasn't our target. Stryker had told us in doing so would not only result in every gun in Misrata being turned on us, but if we did survive a thousand rounds coming in our direction, our asses would be in a

Libyan prison or a U.S.federal prison for a breach of government protocol. Of course I knew that.

However, as guns were blazing wildly in the air, no one would pay any attention to three men in defilade firing three suppressed rounds into three terrorist pricks, dropping each of them in the doorway.

I was impressed with Stryker, but what I was concerned about there in the conference room was his responses to the VP's questions. The vice president, like me, knew he had a history of being difficult, but as he and I had crossed paths in the past few years, I saw during our meet-ups that age and losing his wife to cancer had done much to turn him into a human being. Still, he looked good. His file placed his age at fifty-six, but he looked forty.

VP Collins had been a little concerned that even though his voice had been modified by an audio program, Stryker may recognize it. When the interview began, Collins never let on in his questioning that he knew anything about him. The voice changer worked well and transmitted a lower, more guttural voice that sounded nothing like the VP.

The vice president asked Stryker where in Kentucky he lived and then talked off tangent a bit about horse racing. Stryker mentioned losing his wife but assured the VP his days of grieving were well behind him. He was now looking to start a new life which involved action. He had missed it and he was still young enough and in good enough physical shape to take on the kind of missions we would carry out.

The veep, playing ignorant of Stryker's missions as a CIA case worker, asked him to talk about some of them.

"I'm afraid I can't do that, sir. Many of them were classified and even if they weren't I would be remiss in telling you about them. They would be confidential between me and my higher at the time."

"It's the answer I hoped you would give me, Mr. Stryker. I know we can trust you as an operative in our business to keep a silent tongue. Thank you for being here. I am good with you, sir." He then addressed me. "Director McGowan, you can bring in your next candidate, but please give me five to get rid of my two cups of coffee."

I then took Stryker to my office for a moment and shook his hand. "Looks like you're in, Strike. I will let you know when we will start up. Of course,

you would have to relocate."

"And I'm ready, Bruce. I have some sad memories back

there in Kentucky. I sold my house three months ago and moved to an apartment. I can get out of the lease, however."

"Good. That's all then. Have a safe trip back home."

I then walked toward the conference room but almost literally bumped into the VP returning from the rest room.

"So, Lovato and Stryker you like, sir."

"Yes. And if your man Johnson is of equal grade, we'll have a team."

"It's now 10:15 so maybe we can wrap before noon."

He looked at his watch. "Yeah, that will be good."

"Your Secret Service agent out there in the car must be getting warm in this heat. I can bring him in to my office, sir."

"*She* will be fine out there. She's from South Florida and is used to it."

That was me making the mistake of assuming the agent was a he.

I then took a brief moment to go check on Johnson in the lobby.

"Mickey, if you would bear with me, I'll be back to get you in a moment. Thanks for waiting."

"No problem, Bruce."

I took a pee break myself, then pulled Johnson out of the lobby. He looked great in his dark suit and speckled blue tie. A different picture of how he looked in the Allied uniform. "Sorry you had to sit so long. Do your best in there."

I opened the conference room door and seated him by the speaker. Bart Collins' camouflaged voice then broke the room's silence. "Good morning, Mr. Johnson. Thanks for being here."

"Thank you, sir. I've been looking forward to meeting you…except I thought it would be personally."

"Don't let this arrangement both you; it's necessary for a reason I can't divulge."

"Yes, sir."

The VP continued. "I understand you're a security guard now, where you were at one time were a counterterrorist operator along with Director McGowan."

"I was, sir."

"And why would you take a job as a security guard rather than maybe continuing into law enforcement, for example?"

"When Director Byrd was killed and our counterterrorist teams were abandoned, I went back to school and got my bachelors in Criminal Justice. I then went through the Virginia State Police Academy and became a trooper for about twelve years then applied for a job in Virginia's Division of Law Enforcement as an inspector. I have to tell you as I missed what I was doing for the State Department so much that I just became disillusioned at the inspector job. I left the state and then my marriage failed. I thought about going back into law enforcement and even applied to the State Department's counterterrorist division which is called CT. But they turned me down. As our CTT unit was highly clandestine, I had no records to prove I trained and served the government as a counterterrorist operative."

"Yes," Collins replied. "That was the problem with covert work. If even the government didn't have your name listed on its list within the State or Justice

Departments, you have no record. And we're sorry about that. With this team of which you're applying, you may not be listed or paid within the State Department's system, but there will be a record kept of your service as you'd be paid out of a special and clandestine account." He then paused. "But then you took a low-pay security job, Mr. Johnson. To my previous question, wasn't that a complete come-down career-wise?"

"It was, sir. With not being able to find meaningful work in law enforcement above being a sheriff's deputy or a town cop, I just took the job to pay the bills. I've been looking around for the past few months. If I am not selected for a position on Director McGowan's team, I will likely go on to law school and become an attorney."

"Good for you. That tells me more about both your tenacity and ambition, even in this stage of your life. You look like you've stayed in good shape and can still chase down bad guys."

"I work out everyday and run the Washington Mall three times a week."

"Well, Mr. Johnson, I will turn you back over to the director. He and I will talk more about you."

"Thank you, sir…" He then grinned. "…whoever you are."

I thought his interview went well. I thanked him also and walked him back to the lobby. "Take care, Mickey. Will call you when the decision is made."

He nodded and we shook hands. As I was letting him out the door. The figure of a tall, dark-haired man in a gray suit and western boots sent a shockwave through my body. Atticus Steed.

CHAPTER 9

While I stood in the lobby with my mouth agape, Debbie addressed Atticus. "Good morning, sir. May I help you?"

"I hope I'm in the right place," he replied.

"This is Brightstar. Is this where you intended to be?"

He then looked back at me. "The very place. Maybe this guy can help me."

"Well, sir, this is not…"

"It's alright, Debbie. I can help him." I held out my hand and we shook.

"Sorry I'm late, old boy. My plane was delayed."

"Good to see you here, Atticus. Debbie, this is an old friend of mine who I hoped we'd see today. Can you go back and tell our interviewer we have a fifth candidate? I hope you can catch him. He's probably out the door by now."

"Yes, sir." She jumped to her feet and walked quickly toward the interviewer room.

I then turned to Atticus. "Come on back to my office."

He looked over the place as we ventured down the hallway. "Nice digs. Old house remodeled. Very cozy looking for a counterterrorist hideout."

When we entered the office and sat down, I asked, "What changed your mind?"

"Maria. I didn't realize how much she wanted to get back to the real world. The fantasy world was great, but I think we were both ready to go. She also wanted to be close to her mother. And I had to have something to do to afford living back here in the east. So, why not?"

"Well then, great. You came at an opportune time. We've had four interviews so far. I hope Debbie was able…" That's when she popped in the door.

"Director, we're set up again."

"Thank you, Debbie. Let's go across the hall, Atticus."

As we walked, he looked at me with a grin. "Director?"

"I have to be called something and that's the title I was given by the boss."

"The National Security Advisor?" "One of my bosses."

We both sat down in the conference room chairs and I heard the VP next door clearing his throat. "Who do you have there, Director? I thought we were done."

"Another candidate, sir, someone from my past with whom I shared a couple of joint contract missions, Atticus Steed."

"So, this is the infamous Mr. Steed. Welcome."

"Thank you, sir. You called me infamous…do you know something about me?"

"You could say that. Director McGowan filled me in on you. A former professional hit man for the government, I understand."

Steed looked at me with piercing eyes.

"Mr. Steed," I said, "if you want this job, we have to come clean about everything. Anything you don't tell him would be found out, anyway."

He nodded. "Sir, I was coerced into terminating people who had literally gotten away with murder."

"I know the story, Mr. Steed. I'm not here to judge you on your past. I do know our government and Director McGowan hired you to assassinate the heir to bin Laden's legacy, The Viper. And you aided Mr. McGowan in taking down the entire Jihad training camp called Jamaat ul-Fuqra."

"Obviously you know more about me than I do you, sir."

"Atticus," I whispered in his face. "Easy."

But the vice president laughed. "Touché, Mr. Steed. I do know that you were the top sniper in the Marine Corps and touted as the best shot in the world. You worked for the CIA a short time as well. I also know from your hit man stint that you have very good investigative and people locator skills. What I don't know about you is if you have ever hunted anyone down legally as a police officer or detective."

"No sir. I've worked *for* law enforcement but not *in* law enforcement."

"Okay. But let me tell you…we're looking for operatives that possess the traits of things like integrity, emotional intelligence and problem-solving. Do these define you?"

"I'd like to think so. I guess my past tells you I've solved a lot of problems."

"That you have, Mr. Steed. Other people's problems. But you've also taken a lot of lives."

"Let me assure you, sir, I had no glee in taking those lives."

"If you had to do it all over again, coercion aside, would you?"

Steed was quiet for a moment, obviously searching for the appropriate answer. Then he said, "No. I have a lot of regrets. Every life I took, I still see their faces when I close my eyes. However, I would have no regrets in taking the lives of people who would hurt Americans by exploding bombs and planting IEDs. My conscience would not bother me in the least."

"Thank you for your candor, Mr. Steed. That's all the questions I have for you. Director, please release Mr. Steed to your office and stay a bit longer to discuss all the candidates."

I motioned for Atticus to leave the room. After he did, I closed the door and sat back down to listen to what he had to say.

"Well, Bruce, that was a truly eclectic group of people. Let me give you my ratings of the lot. From number Four down to number One. Number Four was Stryker. I know him and like him. He's on the team. My number Three is your CTT associate Johnson. He interviewed well and provided the answers to my questions to my satisfaction. And he looks good in a suit. Lovato is my Number Two. I like her spirit and she definitely has the skills for the job. She will also be a good asset considering she's fluent in Spanish. That leaves Steed. Regardless of his past, I like him. Your insights about him are the same as mine. He's polished and his steely eyes match his personality. Good work in putting this team together."

"Thank you, Mr. Vice President. Do we make these offers in writing and under what stationery?"

"Nothing in writing. Call and make the offers. We will not chance anything being intercepted in the mail.

Anybody not good with an offer over the phone is out."

"When do you want them here?"

"I'll let you set the date of hire. They will have to get their own residences and we'll make sure they are bug-free. They are to keep a low profile and talk to no one about even working for the government. I'll have Debbie set up the personnel files and payroll. All official paperwork will be locked in your safe.
When they are all ready to move here and come aboard, set a start date. After the two weeks of training you have set up at Quantico, we will then hit the ground running and start hitting the terrorist threats as they surface. Remember, the Intel hits your computer first. You will immediately respond as quick as the fire department shinnies down their poles. Keep your people accessible 24/7.
Send me your operation plan by 1 August." "Roger, sir."

"Again, good work, Bruce. I'm out of here."

When he was gone, I returned to my office to find Steed in the cushy sofa chair that sat in front of my desk, his cowboy boots propped up on my desk.

"Comfy?" I asked.

He then immediately removed the boots from my walnut desk and straightened up in the chair. "Sorry, Bruce. Been a long trip up from Paradise."

"Did you leave Maria there?"

"She's there. As I knew this would be a quick matter, I didn't want to drag her this distance."

"Okay then, talk to me about what you two decided. Are you firm about moving back?"

"We are. However, we haven't decided whether it will be to Pennsylvania or as far south as here. I don't think her mother is long for the world and I can't imagine making the move there where she is for less than a year."

"Is Maria good with Maryland or Virginia?"

"Actually, if this thing here works out, we'd probably live in Fairfax or Falls Church."

"Would make Adriana happy. She loved Maria and as she has yet to cultivate friendships here, I am sure both would be close."

"How did the man behind the wall think my interview went?"

"He was always concerned about your past, but from your interview and my recommendation, you are at the top of his list."

He nodded without expression. "And I will never learn who this guy is."

"Likely not. But mine is the face you will only need to see."

"How many other members of the team will there be?"

"Four at this point." I then gave him a capsule of each.

"A female operative?"

"You have a problem with that?"

"Not at all. Some of the toughest human beings I've encountered have been women. So when do we begin?"

"We haven't agreed on a date but I'm thinking after Labor Day."

"That works for me. We should be able to find a place

in proximity by then. You haven't talked salary though. Can we live on what you folks will be paying?"

"It won't be a million like you received for the Viper deal but Maria will live comfortably."

"But we don't want to be upside down financially." "Trust me…you two will be fine."

"I'm sure. You haven't disappointed me so far during the time I've known you." "How long will you be around today?"

"I have a flight back tomorrow."

"Adriana and I would like you to stay at our place tonight unless you've booked a motel."

"That would be nice. And it'll be nice to see her again. You don't deserve her, you know."

"I know. Let's grab some lunch. There's a good deli over near the Old Post Office Pavilion."

"Good idea. I'm famished."

CHAPTER 10

Adriana was overjoyed that evening to see an old face from our history as mine was the only friendly face she had seen for over two months. It told me it was time to go home for a long weekend so that she could get back together with her friends. And feel comfortable again in her old bed at Wolf Laurel. The three of us went out on the town, had a scrumptious dinner and a couple of post- dinner liqueurs. We talked a good bit about Maria and how great it would be for she and Adriana to be close by one another. My sweetheart needed a friend and confidant if she was going to spend two years worth of days in a city she couldn't feel warm about.

The next day, a Tuesday, I drove Steed to Reagan before heading in to work.

"I will keep you informed about the start date," I told him. "If you need some help with your condo hunting, let me know."

"Thanks for the lift and especially for your recommendation of me to the guy in the wall."

I nodded. "Give my best to Maria and we look forward to seeing you soon." He then gave me his usual Mr. Spock Vulcan salute. Still a Trekie.

I had another meeting with the VP two days later at his office in the Observatory house. Other than our accidental meeting in the hallway the day of our interviews, it was the first time we had been face-to-face for weeks.

"I'm very pleased at your selection of operatives, Bruce. Let's see if they all play well together. Sometimes people with the personalities and skills like those approved for the team have egos and attitudes that are not congruent with one another."

"I probably understand that more than you think, sir, given my experiences with the military, FBI and CT section. I'm thinking somewhere around 6 September, after Labor Day is when I'll bring them in for their first day and that's when I'll have a day-long Sunday-go-to-meeting session about conduct, behavior and operations standards. For two weeks thereafter, we will have intensive training at the FBI's Hogan's Alley that will involve mock village exercises, situational reaction scenarios and both rifle and pistol qualification. There they will be given role play exercises that involve locating human targets, employing investigative techniques, carrying out offensive and defensive tactics, the securing of evidence, and both lectures and sand table exercises about conducting searches in urban, desert, mountain and jungle environments. Weapons familiarization on the latest arms will go off as well along with using the latest firing techniques such as the Weaver position. It will be rigorous and require continuous decision-making. Each of our operative selectees are in good enough shape to go through this training even though some are in their fifties. I will assess each of their KSAs or knowledge, skills and abilities. Those who years ago went through similar special ops training will find what they experienced to pale in comparison to the training I will put them through. These people will be ready to hit the ground running well before the end of the year. If I had the Army's jump school at my availability, I would also make paratroopers out of them. I know there would be operations which would go quicker and with more stealth if they were dropped in."

Collins nodded. "Perhaps we can arrange for that. I will have Ben Marshall see if we can get them in a jump class at Ft. Moore or Ft. Liberty. As I remember, Marines and special ops people like the UDT have been provided that opportunity for years. This all sounds ambitious but have you arranged entry to Hogan's Alley?"

"Yes, sir. I have a long-serving friend in the Bureau now working as a civilian in logistics who is setting us up. I gave him a tentative date of 10 September."

"Well, you have certainly done your homework, Bruce. Ben told me you're a stellar institutor and strategist. I can't wait to see your finished product with this team and ultimately the results of their missions. Remember, we will deploy them within minutes of receiving the Intel. They must be trained-up to be immediately responsive and lightening quick. The element of surprise will not just apply to terrorists but everyone else in the counterterrorist business who will find the job done by the time they hit the ground."

"You can depend on that, Mr. Vice President."

I felt exceptionally good about our meeting. Everything was falling into place and I had the VP's confidence. I would personally call each of the selectees and officially offer him, or her, the position. I had not intentionally mentioned the word Terminus and all they knew at this point was they would be part of a counterterrorist element. They didn't know that not only was Terminus clandestine in nature but clandestine to the State Department, Justice Department and to every other facet of the government…including the President of the United States.

But I chose not to think about it further. Of course those operatives on the team who were smarter than the average bear may also wonder about the name of this ghost in the wall who was in charge of the team. Covert aside, if you do not know who the person having oversight at the top is, somebody you could not know or see, you might be a bit dubious about what you're doing. I expected questions when we finally got together as a team.

With Bart Collins' and Ben Marshall's permission, Adriana and I took a week in the middle of August to return to Wolf Laurel, our beautiful oasis in the West Virginia countryside. Leaving the city of horns, hustle and humidity gave us that long-sought opportunity to take in the intoxicating breath of peace and fresh air. It almost made me wonder why the hell I had gotten talked into taking my new job at age 73. I think Adriana sensed what I was thinking as well.

"Feels good to be home, doesn't it," she said as we sat on our veranda looking out over the winding bougainvillea as it wrapped around the banister. "Makes me reconsider why I would go back."

I looked over at her. "Really?"

"No, I'll go back with you, but if you don't mind, I'd like to have more time here, maybe a week or two at a time."

I understood that. Her words and the reality of being back in our beautiful home caused me regret that I had uprooted her, even if it was for two years, to live in a place that she didn't like. In our waning years, we needed peace and comfort in our lives. Being so concerned about my boredom and depressed episodes earlier in the year, she had sacrificed her own solace to accommodate me. I loved her for that and I would do my best to create an environment for that solace when we did return to the busy, bustling nation's capital.

That week we spent at our WV home, Adriana visited with her friends, made a couple of pies to participate in a bake sale, and went through the house like a tornado with a mop, dust rag and vacuum. I cut our ankle-high grass, raked and blew the remaining debris into the trees and repaired the roof on our wooden shed that held all my tools. We dedicated two days to our chores and then the evening of that second day, we thanked

ourselves for our hard work by dining at one of the fine restaurants in the town voted as the Coolest Town in America.
For that matter, the town had also been touted as the Best Small Town Food in America.

I have to admit I missed our home along with my undertaker brother who lived across town in the old home place. Even though I had been away for years, we had gotten closer the last couple of decades, especially when bad guys came looking for me a few times thinking they could get to me through him since his surname was also McGowan. But, I killed them all, having no regrets for doing so. Whereas I'm usually a guy with a great deal of compassion, I can be a ruthless bastard when need be. Don't mess with my family.

Following our six days in God's country, we took our time to get back to our condo. Being refreshed and satiated from our mini-vacation in our home, neither of us felt reluctant to return. Adriana said she would try to enjoy herself and looked forward to seeing Maria again in two weeks. Having called Steed to officially offer that job, I invited him and Maria to stay with us at the condo until they were settled into theirs in Falls Church. The good thing was there were only seven miles between our residences.

First thing that Monday morning I then called each of the candidates and offered them jobs. All accepted and said they would be relocating as soon as possible between the day I made the offer and Labor Day.

The very confident and cool Mike Johnson across town was elated that the ghost in the wall and I had approved him. His residence wouldn't change and he would be ready to go on the 6th. In anticipation of that, he had already given notice of resignation to the security company.

"Well, great, McGowan," responded Angela Lovato. "See you next month. I will close my business and reassign my clients, few that there are."

"One thing, Angela. Get used to calling me *Director*. We want to keep things respectful and professional."

"Understood, Director."

"You're going to be good for this team." "Thank you, sir."

As retirement had been almost impossible for Stryker to endure, he had been ready for something like our Terminus project to drop into his lap. He was again appreciative that I had remembered him from our

Libyan mission and that he was selected above all the other choices I could have made.

"That being said, Strike, don't disappoint me. We expect great things from you." I wished I could have told him that the voice he heard on the speaker was the former CIA Director who was high on him.

"Thanks, Director. You can depend on me."

Everyone having now been notified, I sat down with Debbie to review the personnel records she had created. Team operatives, like me, would be paid out of the Office of Personnel Management. Collins and Marshall had all of us classified as independent contractors performing security duties in government facilities. Each of the operatives would be salaried at $110,000 plus per diem for their expenses. Each would have standard benefits of medical, vision and dental, which contractors do not normally receive, but nothing else. However, there would be unofficial perks for performance such as bonuses. In fact, since the unit would be unofficial in every way, the entire project continued to raise my antenna about its legality.

Debbie would go over the salary and benefits schedule with each of them on Day One. If it all was not to the operative's liking and he or she quit, they would not have learned enough about the unit to spill the beans to anyone outside of the organization. Still, they did not know the name of the organization, thinking it might be under the State Department. I knew there would be questions, especially about the benefits and who my boss really was. If, however, they went through the training and became ingrained into the organization, then quit, I would have the task of counseling them about honoring their signed confidentially agreement. I knew each of them would honor the agreement, and that if they didn't, and the story about us hit the press, I would come after them. They all knew me and knew I would do it.

Steed returned on the 5th, this time with Maria. I picked them up at Dulles at just after seven and took them directly to our condo. She and Adriana embraced and immediately began a manic-like chatter. Atticus and I smiled at each other and nodded. As we both would be away often, Steed on missions in and out of the country and me either at the HQ or tactical operations center directing the missions, they would need one another. We had a light dinner at a place called Jesudi's, named by the proprietor for his three daughters, Jessica, Susie and Diana. By ten we back at the condo for some coffee, iced cookies and conversation. Tomorrow would be a busy day…the official launch of Team Terminus.

CHAPTER 11

6th September Genesis

Each of the team operatives appeared on site before 0900. Lovato came in at 0842. Debbie placed them all in the conference room where she had set up coffee and donuts. When I entered the room, they all stood. "Please keep your seats," I said. I'm the Director, not royalty."

I shook hands with each of them and took my place at the end of the conference table. "Welcome, Terminus. Yes. That will be who we are. But that name will never be mentioned out of this room. This is the day we all get acquainted. It will also be a day of Philosophy. *My* philosophy. First, I see that some of you have note pads and have set up your cellphones to record. Put them away.

"Everything I tell you today and any other day you will record only in your brain and not be retained otherwise.

There will be no record of anything that we say to one another. There will be many things that are said and that will happen on this team that will remain confidential. Don't ever breach my orders or Terminus protocol. Your future here depends on it.

"Thank you for agreeing to come aboard with us. I know all of you have either given up jobs or your valuable retirement years to be here. You will never be on the clock and your hours will vary depending on mission conduct. You will be ready to deploy anywhere in the world 24/7 at a moment's notice. No excuses, no alibis.

"On 10 September, we will board a government bus that will take you to an FBI training camp called Hogan's Alley where we will conduct exercises that include role play, situational reaction courses, weapons training and tactics. Most of you have had some type of special ops training and therefore I would expect you to excel at all stations. You all have proven to be crack shots but that will not be good enough. You will demonstrate to me that collectively, you are the best in the world. The training will be rigorous but I know you all are in stellar shape and can accomplish the grueling tasks.

"One thing that I will demand from each of you is personal integrity. That includes behavior, mutual respect and character. As professional as you have had to be in your previous jobs, I expect it be double here. Some, maybe all of you have taken lives, and in this job you will take more. But their deaths will be necessary to safeguard and preserve the lives of the citizens of our country.

"You know that there are other counterterrorist teams within the government…the Bureau's JTTF which employs HRT and the State Department's large CT section as examples. However, Terminus will be considered this nation's primary rapid response team. My highers have instructed that when Intel is first released from the National Counterterrorism Center (NCTC), if the terrorist mission warrants Terminus involvement, we will receive it first. Within 30 minutes, we will be assembled, packed, loaded and on our way to Joint Base Andrews where a Cessna Citation jet aircraft will be waiting. It has been especially prepared for our deployment.

"There are times, however, that we may be allied with CIA SAC/SOG teams somewhere in the world. However, we will always be the lead force. When you have reached your target, I will be set up at a warehouse location near here containing the latest in communications equipment with real-time screens. As you will each have cameras and radios, I'll be able to monitor your activity on site. This will entail another day's training at the warehouse."

I spent another hour with the team going over specifics as to mission protocol and my expectations. There were questions from them as I knew there would be, but I considered none of them trivial or absurd. However, when Stryker again wanted to know the overall table of organization to include the name of the man at the top, I said, "Team, the only organizational chart you need to know is that I am the director and you are the operatives. Don't ever ask again who my boss is or who belongs to that voice in the wall."

We broke for the lunch that I asked Debbie to bring in from the deli two blocks away. It was the perfect opportunity for members of the team to get to know each other. During their exchange, I neither saw not heard any egos surfacing. There was a sharing of histories and I could see evidence of some bonding. However, I also heard some bragging from Lovato about harrowing exploits and how it was *her* actions that quickly quelled the threat. Gentleman Mike Johnson talked briefly about his tenure with CTT but I heard nothing from him as to any heroics. Steed was mostly quiet and merely content with listening. When he was asked by the others about his special ops history, he only said he was never *in* special ops. Neither did he brag that he was once considered the number one shooter in the world. It was *like* him to be humble and unpretentious.

During the afternoon, Debbie and I met with each operative in my office to go over salary and benefits. All had locked in either an apartment or condo on the outskirts of Washington. Atticus and Maria had stayed with Adriana and I the previous night. Their condo would not be ready for two more days. Adriana was ecstatic that Maria was spending the day with her. They were going to sweep through the gift shops and clothing stores in Georgetown that afternoon.

We broke up at 1600 and I informed each that we would have another day tomorrow of briefings and conversations which would then take us into the weekend. Monday, the 10th, we'd move out at 0800 for Hogan's Alley.

Steed and I left at 1630 for home. He had driven us to work, so I had left it to him to negotiate the crippling afternoon traffic. One thing about which I was only minimally concerned was how Steed's and my friendship would be perceived by the others. Although they didn't know what we had done together in the world of terrorism, they still might think I was favoring him above them. However, Atticus and I had discussed that issue the evening before over a glass of red after our ladies went to bed. He said, "Just know that I would never expect any special treatment from you. You're the Director, my boss, and I will answer to you just as the others do. If you need to dress me down or kick my ass at any time, have at it. I know I'd be deserving it."

After we had arrived at our condo, Adriana and Maria had already made us plans to dine at a four star French restaurant near the university campus. I had actually gotten to like French most all cuisine since our trip to Paris, but escargot? No. However, that was what Atticus and Maria had.

It was good to see Adriana's face lit up for the first time since we had moved to the D.C. area. I knew that Maria spending the day with her had everything to do with that, since I couldn't manage to do it myself. Atticus and I talked no shop except for one comment. He said, "I think today went very well. I sort of found a kinship with Johnson. Very urbane and grounded, never boastful all day long."

"Yes, I agree. I noticed that in you as well."

Maria then asked, "You never told me what you'll be doing, Atticus, except something about investigations."

"And that's basically what we do," I answered for him.

"We look for people who would do harm to our country and its citizens."

"Will you be traveling much?" she asked.

"I hope not much," he replied. Which I hoped as well. However, considering some of the recent reports that I had seen come through NCTC, terrorists factions were everywhere planning activities against American air bases, installations and grids, I would not be surprised that soon after our training down in Quantico, a situation would require Terminus's attention.

I then raised my glass. "Well, this is about tonight; the food is delectable and the wine warm and biting. Here's to friendships revisited and good times ahead."

We clinked glasses and turned them up.

"And thanks for putting us up for a couple of days,"

Atticus said. Adriana smiled. "It is our pleasure.

He checked his watch. As it was going on 9:00, he said, "I guess we'd better get back to your place. I need to let Bosco out of the utility room. I hope you didn't mind him staying with us. I didn't want to put him in a kennel."

"That's no problem, Atticus. He's house-trained and a friendly little cuss."

"Have you ever had a dog?"

"We have one that my brother is keeping while we're up here…a beagle. But way back when I was with the Bureau, I had a Doberman. He was a little aggressive though, and I had to get rid of him."

"Why so?"

"His favorite bone was the one in my leg."

He laughed, which seldom occurred as I remembered, the reserved personality that he was. "Well, our little terrier will never bite, but he might lick you till there's no beard left on your face."

* * * * *

Monday the 10th, Team Terminus boarded a Department of Transportation bus at 0810 and we were on our way south to Quantico. Upon arrival, we were greeted by FBI cadre who would be training our team along with their new special agents. Our's would be only two weeks whereas the agents' course was

16. Our people had already had careers in the military or law enforcement; therefore, they would only receive categorical instruction that would apply to subjects like urban offensive and defensive tactics, special weapons familiarization and situational reaction scenarios specifically tailored to our team's mission. There would be pieces of days that I alone would be training the team at either the mock village or in the field without joining the FBI trainees where I would focus on Terminus-specific protocol during missions.

Each day of training that first week I stood off to the side observing, clipboard in hand and taking notes. At the end of the day we had chow together along with the Bureau's trainees, mostly out of mermite cans. I had instructed them to stay clear their questions. The FBI kids would be curious about who our people were and why at twice their age we were going through much of the same training.

Before the team retired to their barracks for the night, I sat talking with them, giving them my rah rah speech while pointing out their collective strengths and weaknesses. Each team member clearly projected his or her own strengths, depending on the skill, which allowed me to envision what specific tasks they would be assigned when the mission flag went up. After the third day's grueling obstacle course, I saw for the first time they were getting a little tired.

At the end of the first week in Hogan's Alley, the team took Sunday afternoon off from training. Tired and worn down, they mostly used the four hours to catch up on their sleep, their cellphones and laptops, which they hadn't been allowed to have during the week. At 1900, we pulled back together in the chow hall after the FBI trainees had completed their meals. At the table, as we ate our meal of steak and fresh vegetables, Team Terminus began to let down its hair to a point where they their conversation and laughter became raucous. But I allowed it as they needed to let off a little steam. The next week that included three days in rugged terrain with our food and water would test their survival skills and ability to operate off the grid. During those three days, they would as a team be given a mission to locate and neutralize a terrorist element comprised of Bureau OPFOR personnel. That's where they would employ the individual and team tactics they had practiced during the first week.

CHAPTER 12

That same night I called Ben Marshall to advise him on my assessment of the team's first week of training.

He seemed pleased about their performance. "By the way, Bruce, looks like it won't be long after your team finishes up there, you'll be put into action.
Something's brewing that Eagle Two says could materialize into a need to scramble Terminus."

"Do you know what it is?"

"Not yet, but we're watching NCTC reports." "Well,

please keep me in the loop while I'm here." "Will do,

Bruce. Have fun down there."

During that first week, the team had raided a house in the mock village, easily flushing out a terrorist element. However, week two of the training curriculum began with the team in the field making plans to raid a terrorist hideout, a venue I had arranged with two trainers from the academy. The team would have maps, compass, and as a last resort, a GPS device to help them navigate the four miles into a triple canopy forest to locate the well-camouflaged position, one of Virginia's caves, the mouth of which was covered by fresh limbs and brush.

Both operatives and aggressors would have paintball weapons. It would not only be a take-down mission, but also involve the rescue of hostages. Could they at the same time kill the terrorists while protecting the lives of the innocent? That's what I would grade them on. It would be a two day mission which was going to be further complicated by the hard rain that began on that Monday morning. The misery index would be off the chart.

I found it was also pretty damn miserable for me as well, a former retired guy who was wondering what the hell I was thinking back in May when I signed on with the vice president and NSA. My ass could be plopped in my comfy recliner back in the West Virginia hills and me smiling and looking out the window while the rain beat against the house. There would be hoecakes in the oven and bacon sizzling on the stove. As I trudged through the forest at seven in the morning behind my four operative trainees, biting off a piece of my Bass Pro breakfast, a chaw of pork jerky, I may have caught a whiff of that bacon. Or was it just the jerky?

We had slowly and methodically covered half of that four kilometers by mid- afternoon, me watching and assessing each member of the team. We were at a point where I told Johnson to hand off the leader role and decision-making to Pierce Stryker. Stryker, who had spent most of his career with the CIA in desert and mountainous terrains such as Afghanistan, Syria and Iran, also lived and operated in the jungle villages of South America and Africa. Therefore, he was apropos most anywhere in the world. Our exercise in the Virginia woods seemed to be a cakewalk for this seasoned operative. Every movement, turn of his head and eyes, and signal was spot on. As I knew he would navigate with his rain- soaked map and compass straight to our target, I halted the team less than 500 meters from our objective and turned the leadership over to Lovato.

Although she appeared to be leading the team along the correct azimuth I had given them directly to the cave, the only criticism I had was that she was thrashing and tearing through the trees and brush like a bull in a china shop. "Psst," I signaled her. "Hold up." I then pulled the team together and asked the question, "Do you not think there are sentries and snipers somewhere around that cave who can hear and see you who will pick you all off one by one?

Suggest that you slow down, move a few, stealthy steps at a time and look deeply into the forest for the slightest movement of a branch or a piece of the wilderness that doesn't look natural."

"Yes, sir," she said. However, as soon as she turned to lead on further, she took a hit in the chest from a blue paintball. "Everybody down!" she shouted.

"Sorry, Lovato. You're dead; you can't warn them. The team can see that you took a hit and someone will step up to take over. So, who will do that?"

"I will," Mickey Johnson said. "Although Steed hasn't had a shot at leadership, he's our sniper. Mr. Steed, go set up and find the shooter."

"Good work, Johnson," I said. I then watched as Atticus ran to take up a position behind a fallen tree. Johnson then said, "Stryker, you and I will maneuver around to the left and try to envelop the shooter."

I stood in my observer position to watch what would unfold. Since I had a blue observer ball cap, I wouldn't be a target for the aggressor element. As Stryker and Johnson were hustling through the woods, two more paintballs spit through the branches in their direction. That's when I saw Steed fire. I heard the yelp twenty yards away as his paintball had obviously found its target. Then I heard the aggressors fleeing through the brush away from us. "Good shot, Mr. Steed," dead Angela said.

"That's the way we do it, team," I said. "Come on back toward me for a short After Action Report (AAR)."

Once I had given them my critique, I brought Lovato back to life and placed her back in the leader role. Much the wiser, she said in almost a whisper, "Alright, let's spread out. Slowly this time. Stryker, you flank me on my right, Johnson on my left and Steed, take point. Stop and crouch down after every ten feet and look around. The opening to the cave is supposed to be a half-klick ahead. There's a trail that looks like it leads in its direction. Stay off it. They'll be looking for us to use it. Okay, move out, point man."

Lovato had settled down and was using hand and arm signals to move the team along. As the sentries to the cave had retreated, the team found itself within a hundred meters from the contour line that had been marked on our maps.

Lovato then motioned her three teammates to low crawl through the brush to a point where she could see what she thought was some unnatural foliage covering the opening of the cave. On her radio, she then told Steed, who was twenty yards ahead of her, to verify what she was seeing through her field glasses. Through the scope on his sniper rifle, he saw the same disturbed foliage, then turned his head and nodded. On her signal, Stryker crawled to with ten meters of the objective and tossed an M80 pyrotechnic toward the base of the opening. Eight seconds later, it went off. That's when the sentries began firing from three positions surrounding the cave's opening.

Steed, seeing where the paintballs were originating, peppered the positions with round after round. Stryker then tossed a smoke grenade toward the opening, which saturated the air with an opaque haze. This allowed the four of them to run undetected toward the target. Barreling through both the smoke and the brush covering the cave's opening, they disappeared into the cave. As I did not follow them, I waited a few minutes to enter the cave to see their results. Lovato then radioed me that the action was over.

When I stuck my head inside the large, lighted cave, my team was standing around shaking hands with the aggressors. There were red and blue splotches at center mass on all three of the 'terrorists' but none on the two hostages. The three sentries then appeared at the mouth of the cave, their clothing showing red splotches on their chests. Our sniper, Steed, had neutralized them where they were perched, giving reasons why they weren't a factor when the team entered the cave.

I then pulled the team out of the cave and conducted another AAR. "You did well, individually and as a team. All terrorists are dead and hostages rescued without injury. We discussed your shortfalls getting to the objective already and I don't need to expound on them further. Lovato, you showed you are not only a leader but a good decision-maker. Steed, great shooting. I didn't expect anything less. And you two men, Johnson and Stryker, performed just as I expected you would. This was a good learning exercise for you to see how you can perform as a team. With a little tweaking here and there, you'll be ready.

Now let's get back to the compound and have a couple of beers."

CHAPTER 13

It was 1740 when we returned to the day room of the men's barracks. Lovato didn't mind seeing some of the FBI trainees in the hallway either in their underwear or towels wrapped around them following their showers. We each had a beer, a few laughs and a rehash of the two day training mission. It was good to see them bonding even more than they had the previous week. After showers and tossing their soiled clothing in the barracks washing machine, we all went off campus for a real dinner, the field rations, termite beans and protein bars well behind us. The next day, Wednesday, I would see what kind of shots they were.

We arrived at the KD range at 0800 the next morning after drawing from the armory four each M4s and Sig Sauer P226s. I also asked the armorer to load up an MP5/10, a Remington 700 sniper rifle and two Glock 17 Gen4s. Each would familiarize with the weapons, spending the better part of the day putting rounds in targets at various distances, then cleaning and reassembling their arms.

By 1500, when all the scores had been recorded, Steed, just as I expected, was the top shot with all weapons, many of his rounds being one onto the others, often looking like one large hole. Mickey Johnson was second best, followed by Stryker and Lovato whose scores were very close. According to FBI Academy qualification standards, all had fired *expert*. As they sat for nearly two hours cleaning weapons and reveling in their scores, I reminded them, "As good as I know all of you are at nailing targets, remember this…the greatest weapon you will ever have is between your ears."

I had only called Adriana twice during the week and a half I was with Team Terminus, but it wasn't like I was on a mission somewhere across the great waters or even in California. I was only less than an hour south of her. However, as Steed and I sat in the same day-room as the evening before, having a Heineken, we pulled out our cellphones. "We'll be back in a couple of days, sweetheart," I said. "Looking forward to one of your succulent pot roasts."

"That's what you want?"

"If it's not too much a bother."

"I was thinking of throwing a frozen pizza in the oven."

"Hmm. Maybe I'll just get something to eat on the way

home."

"You know I'm just kidding," she said, giggling. "But seriously, I won't be home Friday to prepare something like a pot roast. I'll be gone until about six. Maria and I are spending the day at the Smithsonian. We're taking the Metro."

"Good idea. I know how you detest driving in the D.C. traffic."

"Well anyway, I can't wait to have you in our bed."

"You got plans, do you?"

"You know it, Skippy. So bring your A game."

Thursday of that second week I placed Team Terminus in an academy classroom and spent the morning discussing the major terrorist groups currently operating in the world, especially those having the United States, its military and its citizens on their target list. I had gotten from the NCTC as well as contacts from the FBI and CIA a grouping of slides consisting of terrorist organizations and leaders, capabilities and operating locations within specific countries. I included the latest Intel the State Department, Director of National Intelligence and NCTC had transmitted through TIDE. The terrorist elements I expounded on the most were of course al-Qa'ida, both the base element and in the

Arabian Peninsula (AQAP), Hamas, Hizballah, the massive Islamic State of Iraq (ISIS) in Libya, Bangladesh, West Africa and Sinai Province, and the Palestine Islamic Jihad. My lecture was cursory in content as there were entirely too many terrorist groups, faces and operating locations for them to remember.

I then gave them a brief history lesson on terrorist activities occurring throughout the world over the past ten years. "Don't be surprised to find as soon as we return to duty at Terminus House, you will be called up for a mission. I was alerted this week by the former National Security Advisor that something's brewing which could involve us. Don't make any R&R plans."

As all we had going on Friday was to pack up and leave, I invited the team to be my guest for dinner on my dollar at a steak house just off Marine Base Quantico. There would be no discussion of the previous two weeks nor any mention of the name Terminus and tentative missions. Most of us had not brought with us anything but field or black ops clothing. However, when Lovato appeared at our rendezvous point outside the men's barracks, we were surprised to find her in a tight-fitting blue dress, hair down to her shoulders and wearing something else we had not seen to that point…makeup. Actually looking pretty. Stryker, who had stepped out of character to playfully rib Lovato a couple of times that week about women trying to prove themselves in a man's world, gave her another shot. "I like your lipstick and color, Lovato, but when you're putting it on, it's important to know where your lips end." But then she gave it right back to him. "Hey, Stryker, I've just been wondering…you being bald, what color hair is on your driver's license?"

As we all knew the ribbing was not in any way demeaning, we had a good laugh. I could tell they were beginning to like each other, but did I detect something actually budding between them? However, halfway through our dinner, my phone rang. Ben Marshall. "Bruce, the balloon has gone up. Collect your team and go immediately to Terminus House."

"Where's the mission, boss?"

"Mexico. I'll make sure you have all the Intel from the NCTC when you arrive."

"We're at dinner now and it will take us about an hour and a half to gather up, move out and get there."

"Understood. I'll see you then."

Of course, no one on the team knew or would ever know that the top boss was Eagle Two, the VP, owner of the voice in the wall. Although they had also not met Ben Marshall, former National Security Advisor, I had mentioned he was the guy with whom I coordinated on Terminus matters to include missions. They would finally get to meet him that evening.

After we hurriedly finished our meal, I paid the bill and then hustled with the team back to the cantonment area. As the team had little to shove into their duffle bags, they were ready in ten minutes. An academy bus was already waiting on us at our rendezvous point. Since we were going north on I-95 opposite the traffic still leaving Washington, we pulled into Terminus House within 50 minutes. I thanked the contract driver, gave him a fifty tip and we unloaded. I saw that Ben was already in the parking lot waiting on us. When we disembarked from the bus, I took the team to meet him. "Team Terminus, this is Mr. Ben Marshall. You might remember from the news that he served in the last two administrations as the National Security Advisor. He is who I answer to," I lied.

Lovato was the first to approach him. She stuck out her hand and said, "So, this is the mysterious voice asking all those interview questions."

Ben turned his head toward me with a puzzled look on his face. I answered for him to salvage the situation. "The only other face you'll see besides mine." The team didn't need to know there was anyone else above him pulling the shots.

Ben then asked, "Director, I know you just arrived, but

is the team ready to mobilize right away?"

I looked at each of them and they all nodded.

Ben then commented, "I'm sorry you won't have any down time, but we have an emergent development in Cuidad Victoria. Those of you having any family who are expecting you home, tell them you won't be there for a few days. I'm sure Director McGowan will consider this redundant, but never give them the name of the location where you are deployed. You will go from here to the warehouse to secure your gear and weapons. I will have a bus there to cart you to Joint Base Andrews. Director, ride with me and I will hand off your Intel and mission details. Good luck, Terminus."

As the team walked briskly to the warehouse only a block away, I walked part of the way with them. "There are protein bars and sodas in the fridge. Check your weapons, ammo and gear. Wait for me there. I don't know how long this will take."

And I didn't. As it was our first mission, I wasn't sure if it would be Ben or the VP who'd brief me. It didn't take me long to find out. It was nearly dark when Marshall pulled his Mercedes into an alley off of K Street. A vehicle back deep in the alley flashed its lights from off to on and off again. Ben then parked his car within about twenty feet from the front bumper of the Lincoln limo. Immediately, two men in dark suits exited the Lincoln and walked to where we sat. Ben rolled his window down and handed his identification off to the secret service agent who approached his door. "Follow me, gentlemen," the agent said.

Ben took the front seat as I slid onto the back alongside the VP. "Good evening, Mr. Vice President," I greeted.

He nodded. "Bruce, I hope you had a productive two weeks. Now it becomes real. Are your assets in place at the compound?"

"They are, sir, and prepared to move out. What's the mission?"

"I will make this as brief but succinct as possible, Bruce.

Our Intel sources provide that a Mexican drug cartel and sex trafficking ring has kidnapped approximately a dozen vacationing schoolgirls from the U.S. who were vacationing in Mexico City. They are high school seniors from Corpus Christi who were swept off the street after leaving a night club then carted to Cuidad Victoria a few miles to the south. Our info is that this ring has a history of taking more than three hundred young women from the streets of Mexico over the past two years, then selling them to buyers in countries such as Honduras and Venezuela. The cartel has through its resources has pushed more than four thousand pounds of Fentanyl, a boxcar load, of cocaine across its borders into Arizona, Texas and California, according to our CIA sources."

"When were the girls taken?"

"Three days ago which means we have little time to locate these pricks and respond with punishing force. I want total erasure, keeping of course the girls' safety as a priority. Locate their cache of drugs as well and destroy everything you find. You know how to accomplish that."

"Understood. We will assure their bodies will never be found."

"Our local contact who has provided much of our Intel is Father Mario deCarvalho in a parish on the outskirts of the city. A number of his parishioners witnessed the ring unloading the girls from two box vans. He will know where they are being held…that is, unless they have already been moved to a marketing location. Again, time is of the essence. Our CIA contact working the region has been collaborating with the padre. He will be at the rendezvous site."

"I know we have previously discussed the conduct of operations like these, but as I told you, I will need some IT resources to run the logistics and track our people on site."

Ben then answered my concern. "When you return to the warehouse, you will find three very capable young technicians with TS clearances who have been read into the operation. They have worked for me but do not know about the vice president or his role with Terminus. Neither do they know what Terminus is about. They just understand that your people are part of a covert Intel group made up of counterterrorist resources. They, and you, will be able to have real time audio-visual contact with the team through the latest in communications equipment to include remote drone operation."

"Seems the battery of questions I planned to ask have been answered," I said.

Collins then added, "You, Ben and I will be in continuous contact throughout the mission. There will be occasions, however, I'll be otherwise engaged with the responsibilities of my office. But, Ben will always be accessible. Your team's bird will be on the tarmac when they get to Andrews. My office has arranged with Mexico's equivalent of the FAA for the plane to enter their airspace."

"I wondered about that."

VP Collins then reached out his hand and I shook it. "You need to go now, Bruce. Time is of the essence. Rest assured, I will have your six on this. Bring those girls home."

I nodded. "Wilco, sir."

CHAPTER 14

The 'warehouse' as we simply called it, mainly because it was simply a warehouse that now abandoned had once belonged to a printing company, sat behind a row of apartment buildings. It was our TOC or tactical operations center. Strongly secured with steel doors at every entrance and which could only be unlocked by code, the building contained a large control room with desks on which sat computers, monitors with agile VIEW, ergonomic VIEW and advanced digital displays which would provide that real-time onsite visual from team GoPro body cams of what was happening on the mission. Real sophisticated shit. Back in my mission days, I merely communicated with a bulky radio-telephone if I even communicated at all. Mostly, I was on my own having no tell-tale communication that would get my ass in trouble and send me to jail. Now, a team was compelled to make the right decision and leave behind no collateral damage, especially of the human kind.

My team had already become acquainted with three young hippy-looking dudes dressed in sloppy sweatshirts and what looked like pajama bottoms. One by one, they introduced themselves. Jim Bob was the chief controller; Harold, who wore nerdy, coke-bottle glasses, was the drone operator and Diego, a heavyset kid, fortunately bilingual, was the systems operator. At first glance, I had wondered what the hell Ben and the VP were thinking, putting these scuzz buckets on my missions. But it didn't take me long to realize that not only were these kids a hell of a lot smarter than me, but aside from their idiosyncrasies, they were true professionals.

"You must be Director McGowan," Jim Bob greeted. "I reckon we'll be spending a good number of days together, eh?"

I nodded, but said under my breath "Lucky me." Then I replied for real, "Yes. Welcome, gentlemen. Jim Bob, as you will be honchoing the mission, IT wise, here's the plan." I read the brief that Ben provided. "The team leaves tonight at 0800 by bus, which should be pulling in anytime, then arrive at Hanger 15 where they will board and begin their flight to Mexico. Agencia Federal de Aviación Civil, which controls the airspace, has approved our entry into the country and landing at a small airstrip outside Ciudad Victoria." Here are the coordinates, Jim Bob. "I am placing Mickey Johnson in as team leader. Lovato, we will call on you to get the team through any language barriers that you may encounter.

You'll be met at the airstrip by one Father Manuel Garcia who will provide the location of about a dozen American girls held captive by a sex trafficking ring. At my direction you will first scout the area out and then take calculated but violent measures to safely get these girls back as the situation is assessed. Your first priority is to safely remove these girls from the hands of their captors. Then, make the bad guys disappear from the face of the earth. Leave no trace."

After hearing the bus outside, I again checked everyone's equipment and weapons. "Give 'em hell, Terminus," I said. I then shook hands with each of them and saw them out the door.

No sooner had they left, my cellphone rang. I was surprised as to who was on the other end.

"Bruce, where are you sending Atticus?" Her voice reflected her consternation.

"Hello, Maria. He and his team are on what I believe should be a short mission in Mexico."

"He has been away for two weeks and now he will be gone for who knows how long in another country. When we all talked about what his job would entail, I think you left some things out. It sounds to me he will not just be involved in investigations, but part of a group that takes on dangerous missions. When I talked on the phone with him, he was evasive about what he would be doing. Can you be straight with me about things? I am now very worried. Will he be in harm's way?"

She was putting me on the spot. I didn't want to lie to her, but needed to whitewash my answer so that the integrity of Terminus and its purpose would be protected, even if she was Steed's wife. There were things neither of our wives needed to know about what we did.

"I know you're concerned, Maria, but he will be embarking on a very important mission for the government. Considering the capability of the professionals that he is a part of, any danger involved should be minimal. They will be looking out for one another regardless of the mission. He will be fine."

"When will he return?"

"I can't answer that. I expect it will be in three or four

days if all goes well. Please don't worry, Maria. He has a body cam and I will be in touch with him and the others continuously. I will keep you informed."

"When he does return, we must talk…all three of us."

"We will. Why don't you go over to our place and have a glass of wine with Adriana. Maybe you two can stay together while I'm here in the city. I won't be back until the team returns."

When we finished our conversation, I called Adriana. She wasn't going to be happy I wasn't coming home. And I wouldn't until the team returned. I explained why.

"I don't understand. You were gone two weeks and now you're staying at least another week at your office."

"Actually at what we call our compound. The team will be in Mexico on a fact- finding mission and I will be watching them on their body cams from the time they disembark from their plane till they're on the way back."

"This sounds like the type of mission you have always left me for. And you're sure you're not going with them."

"I am not. Like I said, the team will be on a people-search…" "To find them and make them disappear," she commented.

"The people the team will be searching for are missing, sweetheart; they're U.S. citizens, lost in a remote region of Mexico."

"So nobody dies and Maria won't be doing the same kind of worrying like I've had to do over the years."

"Pretty much. But she called me and expressed her concern. I told her to go stay with you till we all return. You'll see her this evening."

She didn't say anything for a while, then sighed. "Skip, I want us to go back to that comfortable, carefree life we have at Wolf laurel. Tell your Mr. Vice President to turn all this over to someone else. I know you still want a little excitement in your life, but it appears to me you're gradually stepping back into your Zulu role."

"But I'm not, Adriana. What I am doing is merely carrying out some special projects for the VP. I'm not out on missions hunting down people and pulling triggers on them."

"Something tells me you're directing other people to do that and that's why Maria is set to worry about Atticus."

She wasn't going to let it go and as the team was soon to be in the air, I didn't have time to debate with her.

I returned back inside after my short conversation with Adriana and took on a new dialogue with Jim Bob. He said the team had now departed Andrews and would be arriving in southeastern Mexico in just over four hours. I imagined they would get some sack time as I knew they were tired from two weeks in the field. Their down-time would allow me to go back over the mission in my head as well as with my three technicians. I told Jim Bob the team was to keep me apprised of every movement and every word that came from their mouths after they touched down. He would be able to see and hear a great deal more than me considering he had on a headset and could pick up every grunt, breath and fart.

I knew nothing about Father DeCarvalho except that he had not only seen the captives but had actually been in contact with the the cartel. Apparently they trusted him, relying on him to bring them supplies, food and water. With such a relationship, I wondered if he could be fully trusted. However, he had had a dialogue with CIA assets in the area and had reported the kidnappings. Of course, he was a man of God and even if the hoods were paying I'm for his services, he wouldn't want to see the girls harmed, raped and sold off to the highest bidders. Many of them were fourteen-year-olds for God's sake. But he wouldn't be the first friend of foes like these rats, milk them for all he could, and then let his conscience take over and turn them in to the Federales. But maybe I was just being too unnecessarily mistrusting. Still, I would keep one eye open on the good padre while watching my people take out the bad guys. I prayed it could be done without harm coming to the young ladies.

We sat in the warehouse for what seemed like hours waiting, saying very little to one another, drinking coffee and anticipating when the plane would touch down. It would land in a field and be met by the priest tentatively at 2330 hours.He would direct them over another four hundred yards of terrain to the cartel's house outside the village of Ciudad Victoria. Mickey Johnson would take it from there.

At 2324 hours the body cams came on one by one and we caught the landing of the bird which jarred the team members a couple of times when the wheels bounced down. The plane then taxied to an abrupt stop. There was a flickering brightness ahead. "Radio check, Scorpion," Mickey said.

"Loud and clear, Mick."

He then asked his partners. "Lovato, Steed, Strike…you good?".

All three responded to the 'affirmative.'

Upon slapping a clip into his M4, he then barked, "Let's roll out."

I watched the herky-jerky images dance around on their cameras, as they disembarked down the steps of the plane. It was Lovato who said, "A figure bearing a flaming torch of some sort up ahead. Probably the priest. I got him. Keep me covered." She moved forward to him with caution.

The figure then spoke. "Detener, por favor!"

As Lovato came to a halt, the other three raised their weapons and took up defensive positions.

She shined her pen light in the man's face. "Do we talk in English or Spanish?"

"I will speak English with you."

"Father de Carvalho?" "Si…yes."

Mike Johnson then approached. "How many girls in

all?"

"Thirteen, señor." "How far?"

"Maybe one-half mile through that field." He pointed.

"How do we recognize the building?"

"I can take you there."

"Fine. Take us to within fifty kilometers, then I want you to drop away. How many el delivictos on site?

"Four. I believe."

"Any posted outside as guards?"

"Yes. There will be one on the roof of the house and perhaps one moving through the trees outside the house."

"What kind of weapons?"

"I believe they are the AR-15s and there is one 50 caliber Barret rifle, a very powerful gun."

"To say the least."

"Which one has it?"

"The guard sitting on the roof."

"Okay then, I'll ask you to lead on, Padre. Lovato, you stay with him. Stryker, flank right and I will flank left. Steed, you check to see if there's anyone following…anyone who may have seen the plane and the father's torch."

I watched and listened. Johnson was doing very well. Of course, it was what he was trained to do on his CTT team. They continued their approach vigilantly, taking small, calculating steps toward the edge of the village. After fifteen minutes or so, the padre pointed to a large, two story dwelling back in a grove of trees and stopped. "There," he whispered.

"What's going on, Mickey," I said. "What do you see?"

Through his night vision goggles, he saw something or someone move from behind the roofline. "A figure wearing a boonie hat…that's all I can see of him…about a football field away."

"You know what to do."

"I know what Mr. Steed needs to do," he replied.

"Take him, Atticus."

It was a mere two seconds later I heard the *spit* sound of the round exploding from Steed's suppressed .308. Five seconds later, Johnson whispered, "Bingo.
Damnation! Never seen a man's head fly apart in that many pieces. What's that round made of, Steed?"

"My own special recipe, my man."

CHAPTER 15

Steed always had the best in .308s and night vision devices those years in the Marines and as a hit man. I had seen him fire the best shots I had ever seen spit from a rifle and now he proved to all of us he could take out a target the size of a mush melon at a hundred meters during limited visibility peering through an infrared device. "Mr. Steed, you are truly amazing," I said.

"Thank you very much, Director. But as we are not done here tonight, it seems we have other fish to fry. Now where's this roving guard?"

Johnson stepped into the conversation. "Mr. Stryker, I'd like you to take care of him…swiftly and deadly-like. I do recall how you love using that K Bar."

It was then I saw from Johnson's night vision scope Stryker disappear like a ghost into woods. It didn't take him twenty seconds to locate the guard's position.

Then within half that time, he returned to where the team was squatting in the dark. His knife cast the faintest of a glint as he wiped the blade onto the handkerchief he pulled from his pocket. "Target neutralized," I heard him say.

So far, all handled quickly and quietly. "Now go get this done," I said. "You *and* these girls could be home in a matter of hours, not days." In reality, I wasn't sure what the team would find in that house. The girls could have been moved or already carted off to their predetermined destinations which could be further into Mexico, South America or even Chinese work camps. Tragically, some could even be injured or killed in the team's raid. We'd find out momentarily.

Johnson then said, "Lovato, you're on. Make it believable."

"What are you planning, Mick? Talk to me." I demanded.

"I have positioned Steed to set up outside the door preparing to spring in after Lovato goes in…"

"What…what do you mean? How is she going in?"

"She'll knock on the door and hopefully be invited in."

"Uh, Mick, did you smoke anything on the plane?"

"No, it'll go down like this. She knocks, they come to the door with guns drawn, and she tells them in Spanish her car broke down and she needs some help."

"What it they start shooting as soon as they open the door? Anybody who presents him or herself at that door is going to be a threat to both their human cargo and drugs."

"A chance we're going to have to take. We talked about it on the plane, Director. We all agreed this would work."

My heart suddenly began pounding. "Steed, meet me on 3."

When he switched frequencies and answered, I nearly shouted, "What the hell are you people thinking, Atticus?"

"I have to agree we need to give this a chance, Director. We just can't bust right in. If they buy her story and don't see her as that threat, she'll be a distraction. We will be on them before they realize what happened."

"And if they kill Angela without as much as a word?" "I
know, Bruce. She won't come out of it."

After a long pause, I let out a deep sigh. "Alright. Go
back on 1." When everyone was back on, I told Lovato,
"Be convincing, Angela. Tell them you're in dire need
and like some water. I assume you've dropped all your
gear and weapon."

"I look like a poor, tired low income type with a
broken-down 74 Ford Pinto and have walked through
desert terrain for hours. There's dirt on my ankles and
feet and my damn hair's just a mess."

"It's always a mess, Lovato," Stryker piped in. He then
laughed.

"Eat shit, Stryker."

"We're ready to make this happen, Director," Mick said.
"If you're not good with it, I'm listening."

"You're the troops' leader on the ground. You've made
your decision. Go."

As she no longer had her body camera, I couldn't tell
what was happening, but I was able to follow her from

the distance through Johnson's camera. When she got closer to the door, Steed, who was set up off in the bushes to the side picked her image up for me through his cam. However, as the lighting was poor, all I could see was her form. That's when she knocked. Following the knock and yelling something in Spanish, she was suddenly greeted at the door by two figures who shoved guns up to her head. One stepped outside to look around, swinging his AR in three directions so as to anticipate something like we were planning. However, as Steed and Johnson were well hidden in the bushes twenty feet away, they were not detected. Lovato stood on the outside of the door pleading loudly while the second man held a .45 to her head. Finally, she fell to her knees in tears and placed her hands softly around his shins.

With his left hand, the man grabbed a handful of her hair, intending to pull her to her feet. That's when she latched her hands tightly around his lags and pulled them out from under him. He then hit the floor hard on the back of his head as his gun went off. Apparently the gunshot frighted the hostages and shrill screams ensued. Steed, still perched in the bushes, fired the one shot that struck the kidnapper with the rifle through the throat. As he went down, Lovato slammed the blade of her knife into the chest of the man she had tripped onto the floor. Stryker then burst through the rear door as Johnson entered the front and both began pumping rounds into the last man in the room who had held his weapon on a huddled mass of young girls. Crying and shaking, they began wailing even louder, obviously thinking the people from our team had now come in to kill them.

With all the bad guys lying in their blood on the floor, the horror of the death scene appeared to be too much for a few of the girls and they screamed even louder. Lovato and the rest of the team, in order to quell the girls' fears, laid down the weapons and went to them with smiling faces. It was Johnson who first said, "Please, please calm down. Don't be afraid."

"We're here to take you home," Angela added. "Everything's alright now."

The team's consolation and calm dialogue seemed to quell the young ladies' fears and apprehension. Still huddled together against the wall, they began standing up and hugging one another. Several were crying tears of joy and relief. Angela used her soft side to approach each of the girls, hug them as well and hold their hands. My voice was not being heard above the noise in the house which had peaked at what seemed to be fifty decibels. I kept yelling "Johnson, Lovato, what's happening?" I could make out most of what had occurred but no everything. Finally, Mike Johnson came on the mike and said, "all bad guys are dead. No injuries apparent to the girls. But, Bruce, they're going to need a good deal of counseling after this. It's not just the emotional trauma of being kidnapped and held in this shit hole, most of them for over two weeks, but they saw all these dudes die here tonight."

"Understood, Mick. How many do you find? Count 'em."

"That's what doesn't jive, Director; the priest said there were thirteen. I count nine. The others have either been sent away earlier and the number is wrong."

"Get all their names and where they're from. We need to cart them back to their parents and account for the others who were expected to be there as well. I am sending three cushy vans to pick them up. In the meantime, you folks get them water and food ASAP. Find that priest and solicit his help. I'm having Ben Marshall contact USAID and the American Consulate in Mexico City. They will go through a medical exam there and checked for sexual molestation. A pool of psychologists will need to meet with them as well, then we'll arrange to fly the girls back their families. Furthermore, on your end, try finding out what has happened to the other girls. Maybe those you rescued will know."

"Roger, Director. I'll get the responses you want."

"Wait there with them until you hear I have the vans on the way. And Mick."

"Yes?"

"Don't think these were the only bad dudes in the area that might soon be coming for the precious cargo and drugs. Do a search and sweep, then blow the shit out of that house, bodies with it. Leave no trace of human remains, Fentanyl, coke, nothing. Neither that place nor the cartel ever existed."

"What about the police or Federales? Somebody close by should be hearing tonight's gunfire or see the smoke when we blow the place."

"That's why you need to de-ass the area as soon as everything we spoke about is accomplished. The vans will take the team and hostages to the airport at Tampico. I'll have a bird waiting there." I then paused. "Mick, you did a good job on this. Good plan after all."

"Thank you, sir.

Mick Johnson had the team consolidate the dead bodies and their weapons, locate picks and shovels, and quickly bury the remains in a desert area near the house deep enough that coyotes wouldn't dig them out. After walking the young women about a hundred meters out, Stryker and Steed spread gasoline throughout the house and set it ablaze. It was estimated that the forty large bags of cocaine and Fentanyl on which the girls were compelled to sleep could have been worth more than fifteen mil. Within ten minutes, helped along by exploding ammo, the rotted out carcass of a house went up like a tinderbox.

Nine teenage girls aging from between fourteen and sixteen sat along with our team on the desert floor a half mile away watching the ever-raging inferno burn away their two weeks of fear and misery. On a road off the horizon, a dozen red and blue flashing lights sped toward the blaze finding nothing but two melted vehicles outside the ashes of some kind of building. Apparently nobody had died in the inferno. However, somebody out there was going to be pissed.

Terminus had made quick work of the cartel and had arranged for the return of nine emotionally distraught teens to their families all within two days. Sadly, the girls had told team members that four of their fellow captives were picked up by two masked men about the same time the team was flying out from Andrews.

We were that close to getting them all. Where they were now was anyone's guess.

There was no media, fanfare or other celebration for the girls when they hit the base tarmac. Just weeping, grateful parents. After all, the mission was as covert as they come. If later the girls told their stories to the press, they had no knowledge as to who it was who stormed in to rescue them. The media would go nuts trying to find out and blame the government for concealing the story.

And even the president himself would not know how they came about to be rescued. Some kind of mercenary group maybe?

CHAPTER 16

When the team arrived back at Terminus Headquarters, we did a bit of glad-handing then sat down for a debrief. Ben Marshall was there and beaming like a Christmas star. Off to the side he told me the VP was ecstatic and that he wanted to personally meet to offer me his congratulations. "It wasn't me, Ben. Our team accomplished this on its own. I merely watched on a screen wishing desperately I was on the ground with them. Go in and offer your kudos to them."

Following about an hour-long AAR, I sent the team home, gave them the next day off, and told them to be back at Terminus Central on Thursday. Steed tossed his gear into my Suburban and I drove him back to his condo. Maria had just gotten there from having stayed at our condo for a few days. Based on what I had told her, she was surprised to see him so soon, throwing her arms around his neck and drawing herself close to him.

I smiled and turned around as soon as I landed on their porch. "I will leave you lovebirds alone and catch up to you another time. I have my own romancing to do."

"Must do this again sometime," Steed said. "Good little mission." That of course was for Maria's benefit, leading her to believe that even though where he had been was not all fun and games, easing her mind a bit as to what we were about.

But I did have a bit of fun and games to play with my Mrs., the ever-long-suffering worry wart. Of course, this time she didn't have to be concerned about me coming home with holes in me. Not much chance of that where I was camping out…except maybe until I hit the streets of our dangerous nation's capital.

Adriana, as usual, went through her 20 questions routine, this time wondering whether Atticus was in any danger in the badlands of Mexico. "What makes you think my team was in any danger?" I asked her.

She put her hands on the sides of my head and said, "Because I know you, Mr. Bond. Even if you weren't going to get *yourself* into any scrapes, you'd make it easy for those around you to do so."

"And you think you know me that well, do you?"

"Let's discuss this further over a glass of Shiraz and then enjoy a few moments of serious touching."

"Mmmm, now that, my dear, is what I've been looking forward to…especially that last part."

Only moments after my lovely wife put me to bed, a phone call from Ben pulled me back out. "You have no idea how much I *didn't* want to hear your voice tonight, Ben Marshall. I thought we said it all this afternoon."

"I hope I'm not interrupting anything, Bruce."

"If you had called five minutes from now I'd be sore as hell at you."

"Sorry, old boy. Got something new and compelling."

"Uh huh. I wager not as compelling as what I am about to get into."

Adriana righted herself on the mattress, loudly sighed and with a bit of sarcasm said, "Nice romantic evening, husband dear."

"Uh oh, I heard that," Ben said. "But this is huge, Bruce. Whereas the little Mexican mission was quick, well-executed and allowed us to see how Terminus works as a team, this will have national security implications. See me in the morning at Terminus HQ, 0700, for the answer. My line is secure but yours isn't."

"Fine. I'll be there."

"Just you and me. The VP is going to be tied up with the president on this deal as he is this very minute."

"Sounds serious." "Very."

After Ben left the line, Adriana said, "Well, I think the mood is officially broken now."

"Mine isn't."

"Yours never is. You're going to have to do a bit of work to get me back into it."

I smiled and cuddled back up to her. "Remember, my dear, I'm the guy with the magic fingers. Just close your eyes and relax."

I knew it had to not only be something big, but imperative. Ben sounded like World War III was about to happen, if it had not already begun. So, at a quarter till seven, I pulled into the Terminus parking lot. To my surprise, Ben was already waiting for me in his car. *Very* imperative for sure. He and I exited our vehicles at the same time after which we exchanged morning greetings. I unlocked the side door of the building and he followed me in, two cups of Starbuck's coffee in his hands. Once seated in my office, I immediately began badgering him. "Okay, what's going on, Ben."

"Big time threat, Bruce. Very credible Intel indicates several military bases in the middle east have been targeted by terrorist elements from two different countries: Syria's Ahrar al-Sham, which is also called Free Men of Levant, and the Yemen Houthis."

"The same Houthi bastards that I encountered in the streets of Sana'a."

"And Levant of course is also ISIS or ISIL. Both Syria and Yemen are allied together in this threat. They're planning missile attacks."

"Is this just a threat or are these attacks a reality?" "We

believe the latter."

"There have been two regimes in power since al-Assad was dethroned; who is running the country now?"

"There is a provisional government in power headed by one of the rebel force leaders named Mustafa Ashtar.

We don't know much about him, but besides having to battle other rebel elements in their civil war who are vying for control, his government has to contend with the Turks and ISIS factions. Our Intel is that Ashtar and bin Rabah are in bed with one another."

"Hmm, homosexuals, huh? I thought that lifestyle was

forbidden in Islam.”

“*You* know what I mean.”

I stroked my day old growth of chin whiskers. “Is this not too big for Terminus? It's obviously something where the president would be assuming his role as commander-in-chief, collaborating with the Defense Department to take these elements out before they send the first missile.”

“The president *is* engaged and is already meeting with the NSA, Secretaries of State and Defense, the VP and etc. He has not informed the media nor the press at this time about the threat. The Intel comes from dependable covert sources and the administration doesn't want the terrorists to know that *we* know about it. Else they would lose their planned element of surprise.”

“But if our military is poised to quell this threat, why would we be needed?'

“Because there is an indication the president wants to sit on this for a while. He doesn't want to start that World War III you mentioned. However, VP Collins and I have received through the VP's own Intel sources that attacks are imminent.

Along with that Intel we have pinpointed the locations of both the ISIL and Houthi leaders as well as their missile sites." Ben then leaned into my desk. "The ISIL head of their mission is Abboud bin Rabah, who was a seasoned brother-in-arms with none other than bin Laden. Your task is to locate him and kill him, Bruce. And as we are certain of the location of a half dozen missile launchers with warheads that can reach fifteen American bases, we want them destroyed as well."

I sat in silence for about ten seconds in thought and then posed, "A lot of logistical questions…who and where would our contacts be, how do our people get from here to there, how soon do they move out? And don't we need more than four bodies to get the job done?"

"All good questions, of course. The team leaves tomorrow. Your four can get this done but there will be other players along the way who will facilitate. I will fill in all the other blanks this afternoon. You'll need to have your people here at 1500 hrs to meet with us."

I then asked, "If the VP is meeting with the president and national security team, has he informed them of his own Intel findings? I assume the president knows that bin Rabah is the big player in all this. I'm sure he and the military would also be cooking up plans to go after the dude."

"The VP will advise me on that this afternoon before our meeting. He believes that your team covertly taking bin Rabah out and neutralizing the missile sites via Naval bombardment will thwart the probability of an all-out war, saving billions of dollars and thousands of lives."

"How many missile sites have they spotted?"

"At least twenty-five alone in Syria. Your team will place itself in a strategic proximity where they can direct missiles fired from our ships and submarines located in the Mediterranean. Vice President Collins has already been planning this Naval offensive through the Secretary of the Navy with whom he enjoys a history. As you know, Mr. Collins preceded Secretary Young in that position before he became our VP."

"And again, the president will not be privy to any of the VP's plans? How is that possible? Collins engaging Naval resources on his own sounds like he's on the brink of a political coup. I brought this up before, Ben, and at least two people on the team have expressed the same concerns. Could we all be going to prison if Terminus is found out? Collins is *not* the commander-in-chief."

"Our lily-livered president is already wanting to negotiate with these terrorists and they haven't even fired a shot. Bruce, Vice President Collins is staying within the authority of his office by covertly taking the offense to put out a brush fire before it becomes a raging inferno. There is nothing treasonous in his actions nor is there a seizing of power. Nothing is illegal about Mr. Collins' plans."

"I hope you're right about the legality issue. You should know. You were a constitutional lawyer before holding all your other offices. Most of all, you've been a good friend and we've trusted one another many times over."

"The bottom line is, I think you have become unnecessarily concerned about the vice president and his plans for Terminus, Bruce. Rest assured his intent is not a take-over of the government. As he realizes the soft approaches this administration has been taking in response to nearly every credible terrorist threat, he just wants to take the bull by the horns to assure America and its interests are protected. But, I think we have said enough about this. If you continue to have reservations, my friend, you are under no obligation to stay in the game."

"You're right, Ben. It's just that in knowing me all these years, you must realize how careful and calculating I am in everything I do. But, don't worry; I'll lower my antenna and drive on with you guys. I like this team we've put together and it's felt good to get back into the mix. So let's talk mission logistics."

Ben left Terminus HQ around ten after which I contacted my team to give them an alert order. I apologized for cutting their mini-R&R short, telling them to come in at three. Ben and I would give them a synopsis of the mission. None of the four gave me any push-back. Although I gave them no clue as to the nature of the mission, all sounded pumped, especially when I told them there would be a hefty bonus at the end.

It wasn't long after I had talked with Steed that I received an unexpected call from Maria. I immediately detected that her nose was out of joint.

"Bruce, you're sending Atticus back out and he hasn't been home 24 hours? This was not at all how you explained things would be with the job. He just returned from Mexico where he went within hours after coming home from his training in Quantico. I'm not sure why I am even here in Washington if I'm never going to be with him. I should just go on back to our home in Antigua."

I had to think a few seconds before responding so that my words would not sound indifferent. "I'm sorry, Maria. I was sure we had talked this out. I had explained that our missions could be back-to-back with little time in between, yet there could also be weeks or months till the next assignment. We respond as needs arise. I had hoped you understood that. What can I do to quell your concerns?"

"I guess nothing at this point. I either accept it or go home. And I'm sorry, too. I don't mean to sound disrespectful or unappreciative for considering Atticus as part of your team. I just want to have more time with my husband is all."

"I understand that, Maria. I have over the years had to address the same concerns with Adriana. Perhaps if you talk with her…"

"And I have but, don't worry; I'll get through beyond this and look forward to the times when he'll be home for those weeks at a time. Again, I'm sorry, Bruce. I just had to get this off my chest. Forgive me for calling you."

"Nothing to forgive, Maria. I'll always try to consider you when the balloon goes up."

"Balloon?"

"Just an old military expression, is all."

When I hung up with Maria, I started to call Adriana to tell her about the conversation but thought I'd just wait till I went home that evening. She would be the one who could better address Maria's fears and discouragement.

CHAPTER 17

All team members arrived within two to three minutes of three o'clock. Ben came in a few minutes later. We assembled to our small conference room. I had cookies and coffee on the table. Before we began our pow-wow, I pulled Atticus off to the side. "Did Maria tell you she called me?"

"Yeah. Sorry about that, Bruce."

"No worries, Atticus. Just a concerned housewife. I have one of those as well you know."

"And I had a long talk with Maria," he said. "Won't happen again."

"It's alright. I'm glad she did. I felt it kind of cleared the air."

"I think she'll be more accepting the more missions we have. She's a new wife and just not used to all this."

I nodded. "When I get home this evening, I'm going to suggest to Adriana that she and Maria spend a few days back at our place in West Virginia. I will be camped out in the warehouse and may not be home nights myself."

"I'm sure Maria would like that. Good idea…and thanks."

I smiled and placed my hand on his shoulder. "*No problem*, as those young restaurant millennials say."

When we had all settled in our chairs and the chit-chat subsided, Ben began the briefing. "Gentlemen…and lady…Director McGowan and I appreciate you being here, especially since you just returned from the Mexico mission. And thank you again for bringing those young ladies home. This time the mission will be quite a bit more complicated as well as much more strategic. It will be something that will test your skills like they've never been tested before. None of you has to my knowledge ever been involved in a mission like this. You will be taxed to your limit…each of you. It will require you to not only work together but utilize your unique individual strengths to see this thing to the end. And it will require you to take lives without reservation."

I watched their faces to see any signs of demur or vacillation, but there were none. Each appeared stoic and unflinching. I saw nothing but enthusiasm in their eyes. It was what they had signed up for.

"You're going to Syria to kill a terrorist bastard by the name of Abboud bin Rabah. With the aid of military satellite communications and up-to-date Intel it is also determined that Rabah has positioned not less than twenty five missile sites ready to strike U.S. bases throughout Europe and North Africa. Before you take down bin Rabah, you will trek into the Nusayiyah Mountains to these missile sites to verify they are real and not dummy sites. They appear real from satellite view, but we have to be sure.

Another antagonist from Yemen named Karam Fahid is allied with Rabah on this. We believe that knocking out Rabah and the Syrian targets will compel Fahid to back off as he will not want to go this alone. You will be moving out from here to Joint Base Andrews at 0700 tomorrow morning. I will ask you this now…do any of you have any misgivings or uneasiness about entering Syria to conduct this mission which has every chance of going wrong and could lead to capture, imprisonment or death?"

Each member of the team shook their heads. Actually, Lovato also responded with an 'I am ready' smile.

Marshall continued. "The lead on this mission will be Atticus Steed. He is the recommendation of your director. Are you ready to assume the leader role, Mr.

Steed?"

Steed's expression did not change. "Absolutely. I welcome the role."

"Excellent. Okay, here are some specifics. The SECNAV or Secretary of the Navy sent orders to the Chief of Naval Operations to coordinate a Special Operations Flight for Terminus from Andrews to Rota, Spain military airport. From their you'll be taken to the Spanish and U.S. Navy Combined Base to meet with the commanding officer of the U.S. Navy Nuclear submarine USS North Dakota, SSN 784., Commander Philip Livingston.

"After meeting him, you'll be taken to your barracks and then to the base conference room where you'll undergo a day and a half of classroom indoctrination on nuclear submarine operations. Yes, you'll be boarding a submarine, but you can't just set foot on this boat without having this training. None of you are claustrophobic I assume."

Again, all slowly shook their heads.

"As I understand each of you is a certified diver, you will undergo a refresher Scuba diving session. That's not to take away from your Scuba experience, but it's imperative for what we will be asking you to do. The sub commander has to be convinced you will be able to depart the boat into the water to assume your mission. From that point, you will be in position to move onto the Syrian shore and rendezvous with your contact."

"Who's our contact, sir?" Stryker asked.

"A double agent known only as Quasim. You will meet him at coordinates 35.2500 degrees North and 36.1000 East near Tartus at a time to be later designated. The rendezvous will be set up for you by Commander Livingston's people."

"What does this Quasim look like?"

"We don't know. Nobody has ever seen him. At other meetups his face was always hidden behind cloth."

"How do we know we can trust him?" Johnson asked.

"Good question," Ben answered. "We know very little about him but Naval intelligence tells us he has been utilized by the Israelis and Mossad says he's come through for them."

Steed said, "I'm not sure that does it for me. If I'm going to lead our team into hostile territory, I want to know more about somebody who hides behind a mask and is vouched for by foreign agents."

"Understood. Mr. Steed. I can appreciate your apprehension; however, everything in the counterterrorism world is at some point unreliable. We just have to trust the information and stay vigilant. Before you go after your target, bin Rabah, you will be reconnoitering several kilometers of treacherous mountainous terrain to verify the missile sites. Our Intel and satellite imagery place these sites all within twelve square miles, partly located in the Nusayriyah mountains and desert to the east. All rugged as you can imagine."

I followed up with this tidbit: "For those of you who don't know, there has been a civil war ongoing in Syria since Al-Assad came into power. There are not only various rebel groups operating throughout Syria such as the Free Syrian Army and Syrian Democratic Forces, all having political and arms support from the U.S. ISIS elements are also prevalent in the country of which bin Rabah is the kingpin. He has allegedly obtained the missiles aimed at our bases from Russia and Iran. Besides possibly contending with the Syrian Army forces and the National Police, you may encounter elements engaged in their civil war including Turkish military. The entire country is a powder keg and there could be danger in every grid square. This will likely not be an easy set of tasks. Killing bin Rabah, however, will be a huge setback for the Assad government as well as ISIS which has been in bed with the government."

Ben Marshall then continued his portion of the briefing well into the 1600 hour aided by his charts, maps, photos of Rabah and the Syrian terrain, and videos. I kept a tight lip until the end. It was Ben's dog-and-pony show. Anyway, he had all the Intel specifics. When he was done and after about fifteen minutes of questions had cropped up, I said, "If nothing further, come with me to the warehouse where we will talk weapons."

Again it was a short walk to the Tactical Operations Center or TOC where all our gee-whiz weapons and equipment were stored. We went immediately to the armory where a plethora of firearms were for the taking. Whatever I decided on, however, the weapons would be both powerful and waterproof. And they would be traveling light, given the rugged terrain.

Jim Bob and Diego, my commo and information technology assistants, were not at the warehouse since to this point we had no current mission on-going; however, I had put them on notice earlier in the day to free themselves up for at least the next two weeks. They were good at satellite communications as well as other geeky shit, and had performed well on the Mexico mission. As it was anyone's guess how long this one would be, I still anticipated the Syrian operation may take weeks.

I opened the gun room safe and took the team to the wall that contained .45 automatics of three different makes, magazines of ammo and a selection of ka- bars and Fairbairn-Sykes combat knives. "You will take one each pistol and knife. Two of you will also bear M4s. Now over on this wall you see two special pieces, the latest in military weaponry. One of you will carry this, an AA12 Atchisson Assault shotgun that fires five shells per second for close combat. Mr. Steed, since you're our long-range sniper guy, you'll carry this one…the AI-AXSR with a .300 Norma mag…"

"But, Director, I am perfectly at home with my Remington .700. Is it not acceptable?"

"The AXSR according to the Aussies is a more rugged weapon that can take the abuse and has longer range."

"In keeping up on sniper rifles I did read that, but have never tested it."

"You will have an opportunity to test it in Rota during your day and a half there. Most of your refresher training will be classroom but it has been arranged for you all to test and zero your weapons on a range. If you don't like the AXSR, Atticus, the Navy will get you a Remington. Mike Johnson, I suggest you and Lovato carry the M4s, and Stryker, you'll have the shotgun."

Stryker nodded and smiled. "Five shells per second, eh. I can get into that."

"Your ruck sacks are hanging where you left them. A Navy corpsman will set you up with your rations. Keep your rucks light with limited rations and water. There should be adequate water in the Al-Ansar streams."

"How about explosives," Mickey asked.

"You shouldn't need them. You're not going to blow the missile sites…just report whether the Topol-M or scuds are real or fake. Countries like Syria and Iran are notorious for setting up prop missiles that look like the real thing from a drone or satellite. You will again be operating with SINCGAR combat radios and one of you will have a GoPro Hero 12 camera to transmit real-time activity back here to me in the warehouse. When you're moving on the ground, I will be able to see and hear everything happening. Your radios and the camera are there," I pointed, "in that crate. So now you have all the info *I* have. I want you to be here tomorrow at 0600 when we will perform last minute combo and weapons checks before the van is here to take you to Andrews. Any questions?"

They all shook their heads.

"Okay, that's it then. Have a good dinner, get a good night's sleep and bid fond adieu to your loved ones…those of you that have them. Now get your asses home. No hangovers in the morning."

When I told my darling wife that evening that there would be many nights that I would spend in our 'warehouse' honchoing the latest mission that took my troops out of country, she said she had already talked with Maria about the two of them returning to Wolf Laurel for a few days. I then suggested that they stay there a matter of weeks or until my team came back to the U.S., whenever that would be. I could tell she was not too happy with me being away from her for that amount of time, but she *was* elated she would be going back to her beloved WV. I suspected she might find Wolf Laurel to be her refuge on many occasions away from the hustle and bustle of the nation's capital over the next couple of years…years that I had committed to Terminus. I hoped our time away from each other wouldn't be putting a strain on our marriage. If at any point I felt it was, Ben and the VP would be receiving my letter of resignation.

We had a nice, quiet evening of dinner and wine at a small local Italian restaurant a couple blocks away. Upon return to our condo I turned in early around ten after sharing a coital nightcap with the lovely Adriana. The kind of nightcap that wouldn't leave me with a hangover the next morning.

It was still dark when I arrived at the warehouse at a quarter till six that Friday morning. The Terminus team had yet to arrive as well as Ben Marshall who was always early no matter where he was going. However, the quietude gave me a few minutes to sit at my desk near all the large tracking screens, close my eyes and do some contemplation. I was envisioning every step the team would be taking from the time they made Andrews, through their short training in Rota, and then their submarine venture in the Mediterranean and onto the shores of Syria. Steed would take it from there. He would be tactful and calculating. As he had always been steady and unfailing, I knew I could depend on him. Still, my ticker was palpitating a little as I was not in total control. I was used to taking the bull by the horn myself and often working as the Lone Ranger. In this case, other people, no matter how good they were, would be making decisions in cases where they were sometimes going to be out of visible and audible range; and I was a bit nervous…for them.

I then brewed a pod of coffee in the Keurig and before I took the first sip, Ben Marshall opened the door. "Got one of those for me? Breakfast Blend if you have it."

I put in another pod and while the dark stream poured into the cup, offered him a chair. He seemed to be more apprehensive than me. "Well, old friend, this is a big one. It'll be a true test of their gonads."

I chuckled. "Remember, one of them doesn't have any."

"Well, Lovato is a real hellcat and it wouldn't surprise if she *did*." That caused me to laugh out loud.

Our laughter was then broken up by the door being opened again. All four of our warriors came through it together. I suspected they had rallied outside and had had a rah-rah moment before receiving the kickoff. They went immediately to the Keurig but as they each had to wait to insert their own pod, coffee making would take a while. It reminded me to ask Ben for a traditional 10 cup coffee pot.

"Good morning, Terminus," I greeted. "I hope you all had a good night and are ready to push off. I see everyone is dressed tactical and looking bloodthirsty. By the way, Lovato, appears black is a good color on you. Goes well with that goth lipstick." She pierced me with her eyes but said nothing. Would hate to trade punches with her in a dark alley. After each had manufactured their cup of coffee, I said, "Okay, everyone, follow me to the arms room and I'll get you set up."

After pulling their respective weapons off the wall they grabbed their rucks. Allowing them a few moments to get acquainted with their firearms and do an ammo check, I chatted a spell with Ben Marshall. When they had ratcheted their weapons and were satisfied with their operation, they snatched up their gear and walked to where I was standing to receive my final words of wisdom. Since it was six-forty and the van had rolled up early, I was brief.

"Make me proud, team. Verify the missile sites, find and kill Rabah, then get the hell back to the rendezvous site. And don't get yourself shot up. I know there're people in all your lives who will be very upset with me if you do." I then shook each one of their hands. When I stood in front of Angela Lovato, she said, "And I don't wear black lipstick, Director. It's the natural color of my lips." Learning that made me very afraid. I had to look twice to assure she didn't have fangs.

I watched as they loaded themselves into the van which would drop them at Andrews. "Godspeed," I said under my breath. They then pulled away.

I saw that red clouds had begun forming in the eastern sky. Sailors say it means storms sometime during the day and to take warning. I hoped that was not an omen for the team. It would be the early hours of tomorrow before they would be in Rota. There they'd catch some sleep unless they had sacked out on the aircraft. That being the case, they'd be wide-eyed when the sun rose over the Spanish countryside. I'd be out of touch with Steed for another eighteen hours or so. There was no need to bring in my IT guys until the team had completed their training and ready to board the North

Dakota. I would personally have a few hours to spend with Adriana…that is unless she had already taken off the Wolf Laurel.

As Ben and I watched the van's taillights disappear from view, he placed his hand on my shoulder and said, "Let me buy you some breakfast, Director.
Nothing more to do here."

CHAPTER 18

After our breakfast, around nine o'clock I closed up the warehouse and went back home. Adriana had been up for a couple of hours, and surprised to see me, gave me a squeezing hug. "Are you just home for the morning and then going back later?"

"I'm yours all day if that's okay." "Sweet!" she

exclaimed. "Except…" "Except what?"

"Maria is going to spend the day here. She just didn't want to be alone today, the first day of Atticus' Middle East 'vacation.'"

"That's okay. Tell her not to change her plans. I'll take you ladies to lunch and maybe give her a few words of comfort that will quell her fears."

"She's awfully worried about him being sent out to God knows where and facing the danger he'll likely be in."

"She thinks he'll be in danger?"

"Both you and I *know* he will. Especially if he'll be involved in the kind of missions you had."

I didn't know how to respond to that. In my conversations with Maria, I had down-played the danger aspect, giving her much the same impression about his activities as what I used to give Adriana. But both of these women were insightful and wouldn't be easily fooled. Adriana knew for sure about the danger aspect and I was sure she had shared her past experience as a worried housewife with Maria. Especially the part about me coming home with bullet wounds and pieces missing.

We *did* go to lunch at an Irish bar called O'Hara's, famous for their corn beef, sautéed cabbage and Guinness, the latter which I can never stomach. It's also a popular watering hole for jocks, golfers and Washington politicians. This day the pub's patrons would include two glamorous ladies and their trusty watchdog.

Our server took our drink orders, which were water all around. No iced tea, cokes, wine or hard stuff, although I was in the mood for a Heineken. Maybe later I thought.

As I am always checking people out, I noticed the jock-looking guy sitting with two other pretty boys at the next table which seemed to have been placed a little too close to ours. Tanned and showcasing his bulging muscles behind a ridiculously-tight short-sleeve shirt, he appeared to be thirty or thirty-five with dark curly hair. I was thinking Tony Curtis or more recently, Henry Cavil. Anyway, he couldn't take his eyes off both of my table companions. A couple minutes later, he leaned toward us and said, "Hey, grandpappy, how is it you have two dishes sittin' at your table and I've got none?"

"Dishes?" I said.

"Yeah, chicks that look like they just stepped out of Playboy."

I smiled. "Well, first, I think these ladies should be a little offended that you call them dishes and chicks, and second, one of them happens to be my wife."

"Lucky you," he replied. I took it that he picked Adriana to be my wife since she was a tad older of the two, especially since I was 'grandpappy.' So he turned his eyes solely onto Maria. "Well then it's you, sweetheart, that can join me for lunch. What say?"

"I don't think my husband would like that," she retorted.

He grinned. "I don't see no husband. Maybe you're just tellin' me that."

"Oh, believe me," I answered for her, "she has one…someone you wouldn't want to meet."

"Uh huh, why not?" He began flexing his biceps.
"Because he kills people."
He laughed loudly. "*Sure* he does."

Maria then said, "For your good health, you should listen to my friend. Like he said, you definitely wouldn't want to cross paths with him."

"And who is your friend here? Does he kill people too?" He laughed again.

"Okay, you've had your fun, Casanova," I said. "If I were you, I'd de-ass this place." That's when I intentionally moved just enough in my chair to expose the .45 in my shoulder holster.

His eyes became the size of shooter marbles. "Uh, you're probably right, sir. My Guinness is getting warm anyway." His attention then went back to his friends.

Adriana looked at me and began biting her lip to keep from laughing out loud. Maria gave me a nod of thanks. I nodded back and gave her a 'you're welcome' smile. I then said, "I think I *will* have that Heineken."

Our food came and yes, I ordered corn beef on a hoagy. I needed the big sandwich since breakfast with Ben was a bowl of oatmeal peppered with raisins and walnuts. When we were all finished with our lunch and the Greek god next to us had moved out with his friends, having not one more time even glanced at my chicks, I began talking with Maria in a low voice. I placed my hand on hers and began.

"Maria, I know you're apprehensive about where Atticus is going, how long he'll be there and what he will be experiencing. But understand he is very good about what he does and has good people there with him, all of who will be taking care of one another. Their mission is to thwart all threats being made against the United States. He will mostly be gathering on the ground intelligence that will enable our aircraft and ships to destroy specific targets. Once the Intel supports what our satellites have picked up, Atticus and the others will skedaddle. This entire team is the best our country has at this moment and they will be just fine."

"Can you guarantee he will not be killed in conducting this mission?"

I grimaced. "Tough question, Maria. There are no guarantees that any of our people won't be casualties. Atticus knew what he was signing up for and I was sure you knew as well. The best thing you can do is to not worry about where he is. He's very good at what he does and knows how to keep himself safe. He wouldn't like you to be agonizing unnecessarily. Just say your prayers and have faith in his abilities."

"I guess that's easier for you to say than what I can accept. You've done what he's doing now…"

"And I've always come home to Adriana."

Adriana formed a smirk. "But not without bullet holes and shrapnel wounds."

I narrowed my eyes and gave her my best frown. She wasn't helping my counsel with Maria. "But that was mostly when I was chasing after terrorists, some right here in this country. And my dear, unfortunately you caught a terrorist's bullet in our very yard. You're still here."

Maria then said "I know you're trying to console me and ease my fears, Bruce, and I appreciate that. But don't let me bleed all over you any further about Atticus. I know he'll be okay. I can feel that." She paused a short moment. "And saying that, let's talk about something else."

As the two women had decided to take my advice and stay for a couple of weeks at Wolf Laurel, Adriana and I followed Maria back to her condo. They would leave that very afternoon by three to beat the traffic on I-66 which would an hour later become a parking lot. After throwing her two suitcases and a handful of hanging clothes into my Suburban, Maria rode with us to our place. Adriana had already packed up as well and transferred their belongings to her van. It was the best scenario for them…and me. Maybe Adriana's companionship would be good for Maria, and my wife would not be so lonely in not seeing me over the course of the mission even though I was only blocks away. I could then devote all my waking hours following the mission.

After they left, I took a two hour nap in anticipation that beginning the next day I wouldn't be getting much sleep. It would be my first contact with the team given they were still in the air and after arriving, starting their indoctrination at the Naval base. I'd be bringing in my IT guys early the next morning who would be setting up communications. I'd have only cursory dialogue with Steed while they were going through base training but lose contact once they were aboard the sub.

Nonetheless, beginning somewhere around 0600 the next day, I'd be bunking at the warehouse to be accessible to the team at any point we needed to communicate.

After a good night's sleep, at first light I packed up a few clothes and my toiletries to take to the warehouse where I would be camping out with my IT boys for days, maybe weeks.

* * * * *

Mickey Johnson was the first of the team to exit the Gulfstream G650, stepping onto the tarmac where a stern, forty-something Navy OR-8 stood waiting. "Good morning. COB at your service, sir."

"Good morning, Mr. Cobb."

Without the slightest change of expression, the chief said, "COB stands for Chief of the Boat, sir. It's not my name."

"Oh. Sorry, sir. You can see how much I know about the Navy"

"Which is the reason for me standing here. As we have been expecting you men…and lady," he said after seeing Lovato descending behind Johnson. "It is finally good to meet you. I will be your trainer who will prepare you for your voyage out to sea."

Atticus Steed then stepped around Johnson and offered his hand to the COB. "My name is Steed, COB, team leader for this bunch. I don't know how much you've been told about us, but…"

"Been told nothing, Mr. Steed, except I'm not to ask any questions about you or why you'll be sailing with us on the North Dakota. I am to acquaint you with the boat and arrange for you to enter the waters on the Syrian coast of Tartus. We have about a day and a half of classroom, field and boat training set up for you. I hope you had a good flight and a bit of sleep because once you have settled in at your quarters, you'll have lunch at the base mess hall and begin your training in our conference room."

Steed nodded. "Acknowledged. Lead the way, sir."

As the rest of the team followed them, Steed conveyed to COB that Lovato would have more knowledge about Naval and specifically submarine operations than the rest of them considering she was a former SEAL, in fact one of the first women to be selected as a SEAL. Steed himself was a Marine and saw duty on a nuclear sub for four months out of San Diego. Therefore, as two of them, Stryker and Johnson, would require more comprehensive training aboard a submarine, he and Lovato should only need a refresher. However, all were certified scuba divers. COB was glad to hear that.

As the team had about an hour and a half to relax in their quarters, Steed sat at the desk chair in his room and sent Director McGowan a text that they had landed and would begin their training in the afternoon. Considering the time difference between Rota, Spain, and Washington, D.C. was six hours, it would be just after 0400 EDT. Steed figured McGowan would be rising in about an hour as usual. The director would not be sitting at the controls in the warehouse with his IT people until Steed advised he and the team were on Syrian soil. Via satellite communications, McGowan would then follow their actions and maneuvers.

After the team had finished their lunch, COB John Douglas took Atticus aside and said, "I want you and your team to meet our commanding officer. Everyone, military or civilian, who comes aboard the North Dakota he personally meets.
Although he will generally have little to say to them, he wants to get a look at them. He's a very perceptive person and seems to have a knack for sizing people up."

"Has he ever refused boarding to anyone based on their looks?" Atticus asked him.

"Not to my knowledge, but he has observed behaviors and mannerisms and ordered me to keep certain individuals in my sights…especially reporters and sailors of other nationalities."

"Doesn't sound like he's a very trusting guy."

"He knows who to trust; he's just careful. After all, the

North Dakota is *his* boat and he's responsible for everyone of his people and for everything happening on the sub."

Steed gave him a slight smile. "And I will assure my people will behave, sir. I am responsible for *them*."

COB nodded and returned the smile. "If you would, gather them up and follow me."

Steed did as instructed and the five of them walked to Captain Philip Livingston's base office. COB rapped sharply on the door. "Captain, sir. I have the guests."

The response from the inside was, "Bring them in, COB."

Team Terminus marched in smartly behind COB and stood at attention in a straight line. It was Lovato, separated only three years before from the Navy, who popped a salute. Livingston returned it.

"Mighty impressive, young lady. COB told me about you. Six years in the Navy *and* a SEAL. But you don't need to salute me." He then looked at the other three. "You all seem to have a degree of military bearing and I like what I see. I can see you are all going to work out fine on my lady."

Douglas added, "They are about to begin today's training. Even though they are all certified divers, we will see what they look like in the aquatics pool."

"Good, Mr. Douglas.

And they *did* look good, showing off their proficiency and skills, impressing their instructor Petty Officer First Class Bob Michael, in buoyancy, breathing, snorkel to regulator exchange, and both underwater diving and navigation. At 1545 they were out of the water and in the classroom for an indoctrination on nuclear submarine operations. Again, this was brand new to Stryker ad Johnson, but as they were naturally fast learners, they caught on quickly.

At 0730 the next day, the team was escorted by the COB and Chief Michael along with their gear to the North Dakota where they were introduced to significant members of the crew. It was with these sailors they would be learning specific functions and operations of the sub and with whom they would mostly be interacting. They were then shown their bunks. Even though none of them were particularly claustrophobic, Stryker wondered if he would have trouble experiencing the mere 8 inches of distance between his nose and the bunk above. Johnson then said, "Not to worry, Strike, I'll be sure not to have beans at evening mess." He then laughed. Steed then chided them.

"Act accordingly, gentlemen."

For most of the day, Team Terminus was acquainted with the sub's controls, navigation system, periscope operation, sonar and communications. Finally, they were taken to the dive chamber where Chief Michael climbed the ladder and opened the inner hatch. The team followed up behind him.

"There you see all of your dive gear including your weapons which my crew stowed for you. Then to your right you'll see the diver shuttle which will transit you into the water and toward the shoreline. I showed you on film how this works earlier in the classroom. I will assure that you are within 100 yards of the Syrian shore where you will exit the shuttle. From that point you will swim ashore. I'll then return to the boat's chamber, close the outer hatch and descend the ladder. Everybody good?" Collectively they answered yes.

At 1210 the team ate lunch with Bob Michael and went over last moment details. Just as the COB did not do, Michael asked no questions as to the team's mission. All he knew was that they were a special ops team who'd be going into Syria to conduct a covert operation.

At 1300 the North Dakota slipped away from the pier into the Mediterranean, turning out to sea.

CHAPTER 19

At a bottom depth of 600 feet below the keel, the sub's Commander Livingston contacted the Sonar Division to ask for an announcement whether there were any contacts in the area. Sonar responded, *Con-Sonar, the only contacts are a fishing trawler 3,000 meters at 245 degrees relative and a freighter inbound at 2100 meters, 015 degrees relative.* Steed, listening and watching intently, learned from the captain that 'relative' meant in relation to the submarine's directional heading.

"So, no suspected enemy craft lurking close by."

"Actually, Mr. Steed, the trawler is actually always a Russian spy ship taking all available readings from Navy ships and submarines, recording their propeller turn counts, noise decibels and engine readings. It's common not only on the high seas but we've picked them up hanging around outside all Naval bases worldwide."

Livingston then ordered his Navigation and Diving officers, "Navigation, chart our path to pass the freighter on its port side to blind the trawler. While it is blind, Diving officer, dive the boat!" He then paused to explain to Steed what was happening. "To do this, all vents to the ballast tanks are opened, letting out the air and filling the tanks with water; this creates the dive."

Obeying the commander's order, the diving officer bellowed, "Dive the boat! Stern Planesman, make the bubble 5 degrees down bubble!" In short order, the boat was totally submerged. With soundless stealth, the North Dakota passed by the freighter submerged .

Once fully past the freighter, Commander Livingston then ordered, "Diving officer, make our depth 350 feet."

"Aye, aye, Skipper, diving to 350 feet." When the sub reached the 350-foot level, it leveled off and continued cruising in the Mediterranean toward its objective. For the remainder of the afternoon, their voyage was relatively uneventful.

At 1800, the team joined Bob Michael and ate their dinner in the crews' mess. While at the table, the team heard Livingston on the intercom in the control room say "Prepare for Angles and Dangles." Chief Michael did not change his expression but casually placed his hands on his plate. Within seconds, the team felt the sub go into a dive, at which time their plates and glasses began sliding off to the edge.

"What the hell?" Steed exclaimed.

Michael explained that upon the captain's orders, the sub took a sudden dive with a 20 to 30-degree down bubble on the stern planes, then rose up the same degrees, bringing the boat back to its original depth.

"And the purpose of this exercise?" Lovato quizzed.

"To assure there are no potential leaks or loose items that would spill or make noise throughout the boat. Yes, it will be your plates and glasses that get spilled. Everyone knows to grab anything that will fall or spill when the command is given. The cooks hate this, especially while they are cooking, as pots and food can go everywhere. The exercise can go on for an hour. Sorry if it frightened you."

"Pretty unnerving is what it is if you're not expecting it." Stryker said. "I thought there was something wrong with the submarine."

Chief Michael smiled. "Thought you were gonna die, eh?"

"Scary enough being hundreds of feet down on this tin coffin, especially one that has nuclear power on it."

"Yeah," added Johnson. "What the hell else is on the schedule that could scare the shit outta us?"

Lovato chuckled. "You pantywaists need to get a set of gonads. You're safer on this boat than you are on the freeway. Damn, do I need to be worried about you freaking out on me every time you think we're in trouble?"

Steed then broke in. "Alright, team. Let's not get all panicky. Stop the bickering. I don't want to risk the C.O. turning around and dumping us back in Rota."

"And don't think he won't do it if he senses you're a risk to this boat," Michael echoed.

"We got it," Johnson said. "Sorry we didn't handle ourselves all that good."

Their dinner ended a bit sooner than they expected, considering all of the jockeying around. Half their food was off the plates and on the table anyway. Like Chief Michael, others in the mess area had secured their plates and glassware when they heard the commander's 'Angles and Dangles' warning on the intercom.

The team turned in at 2200. Stryker quickly got over his 18-inch claustrophobia, having fallen asleep in a matter of minutes. Lovato's bunk was in the women's quarters, two of which were aboard. Steed was assigned to bunk in the junior officers' area, primarily because he was the team leader and at officer level. Years ago, as a Marine Lance Corporal, he would have been jammed in with the lower-ranking leathernecks.

At approximately 1035 hours the next morning, Sonar reported the following: *Con-Sonar, contact at 034 degrees relative. Submarine operating at a depth of 240 feet. Computer identifies vessel as a Russian Akula Class Nuclear at a speed of 14 knots, heading of 274 degrees. Has apparently not located us, however.*

The Officer of the Deck responded," Very well, Con-Sonar, maintain monitor. I want to put as much distance between us and them as possible. Diving officer, make our depth 460 feet. Let's put a little more depth between us and the Russians by going below the next water temperature layer. That will prevent them from picking up our sounds."

The diving officer responded, "Stern planesman, 3 degrees down bubble, make our depth 460 feet."

Steed and the team sat with their soft drinks and lemonades most of the afternoon in the boat's conference room, going over maneuver plans after reaching shore. "As we learned," began Atticus, "Tartus is a port city. Our rallying point will be a klick and a half west of the city as we don't want to surface anywhere near the port waters. The area would be heavily patrolled by Syrian Naval boats. Even if we weren't spotted coming up by the boat crews, fishermen might see us and report sighting four suspicious-looking divers in the water. Anyway, we have the grid coordinates of the location where we're supposed to meet our contact."

"And again, just who is this contact and how can we trust him?" asked Stryker.

"The director says Quasim has collaborated in previous missions with one of our CIA boys with favorable results. They took down Syrian Captagon cartel leader Merhi Al-Ramthan based on Quasim's Intel. Not only did the CIA operative personally take out this kingpin but coordinated the U.S. airstrikes that destroyed cartel drug inventory valued more than six mil."

"I worked with a Company operative who was on that deal. Do you know his name?"

"No. All I've been told is that he has been reliable. Mr. Marshall says the operative's information on Quasim is that the man has come through several times in the past.

We are to meet him between 1700 and 1900 on the 5th. Once we are ashore, I will reestablish contact with McGowan. We will not advance forward until we get his go-ahead. Then from that point on, we meet Quasim and go from there. We'll be using his information to locate Rabah after we locate the missile sites."

Mickey Johnson asked, "In our briefing with the director, he told us there were 15 to 25 suspected missile sites. Is that still correct and in those mountains, how difficult do we anticipate locating them?"

"Probably *very*. Coordinates provided by satellite imagery just before we departed Washington may not be accurate. If they *are* missile sites and not dummy props, smart tactics would be moving them around every 3 to 5 days. Our deal is that we locate them based on real-time satellite Intel sent by McGowan and determine their authenticity. The missiles and crews were reported to be in the Tarik area of Nusayriyah. Tarik is a well-known military base occupied by about 300 troops. Latest Intel reveals that a small contingency of Yemeni troops are there as well."

"Lovely," said Lovato. "Getting anywhere near that Tarik area is going to be hairy. Not sure we're getting paid enough for this mission."

Steed smiled. "It's all for the ol' red, white, and blue, Angel. And not to mention saving thousands of lives on all the military bases in the European and Middle East theaters."

She smiled back. "Okay, Steed. Go ahead and shame me like that." After the evening mess, the team met with

Commander Livingston and COB Douglas in the captain's quarters. The commander told them whatever they were about to do, he wished them the best of luck. At such time, he received orders as to when and where to rendezvous them in the water; the North Dakota was sure to be lurking close by in the Mediterranean. Being the spiritual man that he was, he formed them in a circle and said a short prayer for their safety.

After being dismissed and knowing they would be embarking on the mission in a matter of hours, they turned in to their bunks early.

On Tuesday the 4th at 0040 hours, the North Dakota entered the 150-mile point west of the Tartus coastline. Commander Livingston ordered a change in depth to 180 feet. Team Terminus then met with the diving instructor again to review departure plans from the boat within the dive shuttle at 0230 hours, where it would be sent in the direction of the objective. They would then depart the shuttle at 50 feet below the surface and swim to shore. The instructor asked each team member if they understood and if there were any questions. There were none.

At 0135 the commander ordered the boat to periscope depth of 65 feet. After scanning the surface for contacts using sonar and receiving an all-clear, he performed a complete periscopic scan rotation to confirm. Livingston then ordered, "Proceed with the mission."

At 0218 Chief Michael ushered the team into the forward engine compartment and climbed the ladder into the dive chamber. The team then donned their dive gear and stowed both their land dry gear and weapons in waterproof bags, placing them in the shuttle's storage compartment. After they had climbed into the shuttle, Chief Michael dogged the inner hatch closed. When the four of them were in their seats, the chief flooded the chamber, opened the outer hatch to the sea, took the front seat, and departed the boat. Driving the shuttle to the 30-foot mark, he came to a stop. The mission team then grabbed their gear and weapons, signaled an *all clear* to the chief. As the shuttle backed away and turned back toward the boat, Team Terminus began swimming toward the Syrian shore.

Atticus Steed looked at his dive watch as they cautiously waded ashore. 0309. After entering the rocky shoreline and finding a small grove of date palms and scrubby maquis 100 yards in to conceal their movement, Steed performed a 360 scan of the terrain with his night vision scope to assure there was no movement. As it was a new moon, they should not be readily visible. Satisfied that they wouldn't be greeted by hostiles or civilian crabbers, he instructed the others to peel off their dive gear, bury it in the sand, and don the dry clothing found in their water-tight bags. Once they had done so, they pulled out their weapons and waited for Steed's signal to move out.

It would be late night, the preceding day when Bruce

McGowan received Steed's contact. "Scorpion, this is Steed. Are you accessible?"

For more than twenty seconds, Steed heard nothing on the other end. "Scorpion, Steed. Do you hear me?"

"Roger. Lima Charlie. And you?"

"Loud and clear as well. Ashore and on the move." "

Excellent. It should be 0316 on your end." "Yes."

McGowan then said, "We will activate video at first light. But until then, find some place to bury yourselves. The latest info is that the concentration of toys has moved. I will send you the coordinates when my video is up and running in the next six hours. My boys and I will be fully operational at that time. I don't want to send the coordinates over our audio devices as there are ears out there and eyes that can see the numbers on a text. Will send via free space optical, the same device we're using in tracking you. Will test it with you at 0815. You are likely to be slogging through some rugged terrain and lacerating foliage like thorny broom and arbutus, so be prepared to lose some skin when you move out toward the Nusayriyah mountains. You could get cut to ribbons moving in the dark, so don't. You will have three days to locate the toys. Keep double and triple canopy forest above you to avoid aerial detection during the daylight hours. Per our latest

Intel, it appears you are currently 5 klicks away from the general area where the toys are located. Till then, dig in and be vigilant. There are roving patrols working your area."

"Understood, Scorpion."

"Get some rest. Will re-contact you in five hours."

CHAPTER 20

No one shut an eye the remainder of the early morning hours. Every sound of nature, every bird and every creature that crawled in the bush served to unnerve them in the dark of night. Steed continued to scan the surroundings with his starlight scope, focusing especially on the slightest noise he had heard. It was how he worked. Be vigilant but strike first at anything or anybody moving upon them. Defense often required a calculated offense. Avoid capture at all costs. After all, he thought, they were on unfriendly soil, knowing that if captured, they would be treated as spies and likely tortured or killed. And as they were not supposed to be there, and only two people knew where they *were*, and who would come for them.

The sun began peeking through the trees at 0715. After each had consumed a breakfast protein bar and some gulps of water from their canteens, they waited for the director's contact. He would be able to see where they were and where they were going from their body cams. He would also have the latest coordinates of the 'toys', thanks to the latest imagery. Steed's concern was how many hostiles would be guarding the missile sights and if there would be roving patrols in the path of their approach into the Nusayriyah.

Precisely at 0800, Atticus heard on his radio "Steed?"

"We're here."

"Everyone okay?"

"We're good," Steed replied. "Ready to move."

"Fine. I have five coordinates for you. Turn on your cam and see what I've recorded."

Steed did as instructed and on his small screen first saw McGowan's face. "So this is what you look like at 2:00 in the morning. Scary."

"And you look like a jungle rat," McGowan retorted. "Are those suitcases under your eyes?"

"Funny, Director. Come trade places with me."

"Yeah, sure. Okay, enough jocularity; let's get down to it. I have my IT kids here and Jim Bob will flash the coordinates on the screen. Got a pen and paper?"

"I'm ready. Shoot."

When the coordinates appeared, Steed began scribbling. Once completed, he said, "Got 'em down."

"Good. Go to the first location which should be just over two klicks for you. Looks like you'll be climbing for a while. Lots of vegetation as well which hopefully prevent you from being seen in the open. Satellite may not pick you up much of the time, but we'll still have radio contact."

"Okay. On the move." Steed signaled to the team to follow. Using the Universal Transverse Mercator system on his directional grid finder, Steed began following the arrow. The last time he was on a mission with the Marines, which was more than twenty years before, he navigated with compass and map. This device was better than the latest in GPS technology, he thought.

McGowan was right. It was not more than 200 yards until the terrain began to rise somewhere around 20 percent. But with the aid of rocks to stabilize them by giving them natural hand and foot-holds, they were able to negotiate the rugged pathway. All the way up to the nearest crest, they were concealed by eight foot wild olive and turpentine foliage.

When they had covered 1500 feet f the rocks and biting weeds, they took a break to listen. Apparently, there was a road nearby as the guttural groan of a motor straining to climb the high ground could be heard through the forest what seemed to be a quarter of a mile away. The motor belonged to a larger truck, Steed thought.

While they drank from their canteens and listened, the truck's motor faded. Lovato then broke out into a chuckle. Everyone had small cuts on their faces and hands from broom thorns and Stryker's shirt sleeves revealed a dozen lacerations. That may have seemed funny to her, but not to the others. Ticks they had picked up and biting flies were feasting on their blood. They all took a moment and began pulling the ticks off with the points of their knives, careful not to leave the heads embedded. Johnson then pulled from his belt bag a bottle of *Skin So Soft* to repel the flies. The fragrance would also serve to counter the sweat-induced body order all of them seemed to have. "This was left over from my marriage a few years ago. My wife was an Avon lady. Thought we might need it."

"Good thinking, Mike," Steed said. "Seems to be working. The flies aren't landing anymore. Maybe it will also help with the ticks."

As the team moved on, the landscape began leveling off into a plateau. However, what came with that was a vast clearing along with a dirt road. Likely where they heard the truck. The concern was, they would be exposed…not only to the human eye but to military aircraft.

"Okay, folks, I think we can still stay on course by skirting this open area while moving along that tree line." He checked his watch. "It's just after 1330 and we still have about half a klick to our first objective. Let's break inside that grove of Aleppos."

When they had settled in on some rocks, they broke open their rations which was provided by the mess team on the sub. All were UGR-E Express rations, self heating, and actually not that bad, especially when hunger pangs are gnawing at the gut. Their rations included typical breakfast food and lunch/dinner items such as corn beef hash, beef stew, buffalo chicken and tortillas with chicken or beef. Each had three days of rations in their rucks.

Johnson finished his meal first, kicked back on a large rock and said, "Excuse the grammar. but it don't get no better than this."

"Except if I had a cold beer to down this burgundy chicken," Lovato replied.

Steed gave her a quasi smile and nodded. "A cold, cold beer."

"A Coors light," added Stryker.

Suddenly, only a hundred years away, a large truck similar to a U.S. military deuce-and-a-half sprang up over the hill toward their direction. In the rear were four Syrian troops one of which stood behind the cab holding on to what Steed recognized as a Russian KPV-14 heavy machine-gun. The team scampered to assure they were hidden deep in the grove of trees. The truck continued headed in the direction of the first coordinate. Holding his camera on the departing truck, he said, "Do you see it, Scorpion?"

"Got it. I think that's going to answer our question as to whether the missile sites are real. They wouldn't be paying any attention to a dummy site."

"Agreed, Director. We're going to trail it." "Good idea.

Try to keep it in earshot."

When the truck was out of their line of sight, Steed said, "Okay team, on your feet. Let's hustle through the clearing along the tree line and keep your ears on the sound of the motor. We're going where they're going. They should be leading us to the first missile site. My calculations is that we're less than 500 meters from it."

No sooner than they struck out, they came upon two Syrian peasants moving slowly in a wagon pulled by a mule, one male and one female, the man wearing a long kaftan and red head cover called a taqiyah. The woman wore a simple smock that covered her head and face. Seeing the team approach them from behind and carrying weapons, they registered their surprise by jumping from the wagon and scampering into the woods.

"What do we do with them?" Asked Lovato. "They could report us to the military."

"Leave them," replied Steed. "At our pace, we'll be in proximity to the target before they can find or call anyone. And as you can see, their mule has turned around and is going back down the mountain. Anyway, even though we're western-looking people, maybe they didn't get a good look at us and thought we were connected to the Syrian military just the same. It was our weapons that more so attracted their attention."

The truck they were following had been traveling slow enough up the mountain slope that it kept them in earshot of its whining motor. Nonetheless, they stayed near the road which gave them more foot speed even though they were at risk for being spotted. Of course, American operatives just being on Syrian soil was a hell of a risk, anyway.

At a point where they could no longer hear the truck's engine, Steed held up his fist, signaling the others behind him to stop. He whispered after checking their location on his finder, "They have stopped somewhere in the grid where I've calculated the first missile sight to be. Veer off into those palms and keep a low profile." Lovato closely followed Steed, then Johnson and Stryker in that order.

At 1420 the forest ended and 200 meters forward their position sat their objection. "It's real, alright," Steed whispered into his cam. "Mounted on a transport erector is a big-ass missile. Looks like one of the missiles you displayed on screen in our briefing."

"Hold your cam on the target for me to get a good look," McGowan said. Steed did so and McGowan said, "Yeah. This is an Iranian Khaibar medium range missile capable of reaching U.S. bases in Qatar, Kuwait, and Saudi Arabia among other countries. Bases such as the Army's Camp Patriot, Navy's Port of Jebel Ali, and Air Base Al Udeid are capable of being reached. Looks like the site is well-guarded as I see troops in proximity."

"Yes, we followed the sound of a transport vehicle moving toward the site, probably a reinforcing element replacing the night shift."

"I have what I need on my end. Get your ass out of there and head toward your second objective. Should be just less than 800 meters; but you have more climbing to do. The target on my map is Hill 4934 dead on the second set of coordinates I gave you. After you have moved on a few meters, take a break and swallow some water. You're going to need it."

"Roger. De-assing as we speak."

CHAPTER 21

Finding a small mountain stream that appeared to have clear, potable water, the team took that break and refilled their canteens. What loomed ahead was a nearly 5,000-foot mountain peak. By Steed's calculations, given their climbing foot speed, they should be in proximity by 1800 hours.

Steed recontacted McGowan. "Scorpion…Steed. We should reach the second target before dark. If the second objective is still at the most recent coordinates, we should then assume all sites are valid."

"Agreed. If this site bears out, we will bring you back down out of the hill country and move you earlier than planned to where you will meet your contact. I will have the Company operative set you up with day, time and location to meet him."

"Copy. I wouldn't see the need to locate all targets. That's all I have. We're now well-rested and ready to move on."

"Will await your next."

It was indeed an arduous climb. Weapons were strapped to their rucks as they needed to scale certain areas of pathway with use of their hands. If the missile was at the top of Hill 4934, there had to be a road somewhere for a truck to be capable of delivering it to the site. Steed figured it was on the reverse side of the mountain. Just their luck. Still, they'd need to stay off such a road to avoid being spotted. He was sure no uniforms would want to tackle the trail they were on.

His only concern was that aircraft could be reconning the area and they were clearly in the open.

As the team progressed, each continuously scanned their surroundings and kept their ears open not only for the sounds of approaching aircraft but distant voices which would carry through the valleys. Even though the team as a whole was in good condition, their breaths were laborious. The *Skin So Soft* had also apparently broken down and as they were profusely sweating, the insects were back. This time, biting gnats and mosquitoes. The 92 degree sun added to their misery.

Still, they trudged on, taking rest and water breaks every ten to fifteen minutes.

At 1745, they came to an oasis of olive trees where they took a longer refuge. That was when Steed told them they were close to the top. "I've got us at something near 100 yards from our target coordinates. Except we can readily see the top but nothing's there. If there is a missile site there, it has to be on the military crest side of the hill. That presents a problem. Can we get there without being seen?"

Steed then conferred with McGowan. "We're within only a few feet of target two but I'm going to wait till dark before we move in. It's an open sea all the way to the top. Target is on the reverse slope of the hilltop."

"Understand. Keep me apprised."

Well-concealed beneath the trees, they broke open their self-heating rations and waited about ten minutes for them to get hot. Keeping their conversations at a whisper, they discussed mostly how fried they were from the climb and the heat. Stryker and Lovato, sitting close together, talked the most to one another, making it obvious that they had formed even more of a bond, a romantic one at that. The words between them were warmer and gentler than would be expected of two hard-core hired guns during a potentially perilous mission.

Although the two of them had never let on to anybody associated with the team how involved they were with one another, Steed knew. McGowan knew. And maybe even Ben Marshall knew. But no one cared. They were professionals and would never let their relationship interfere. Mission first.

As darkness had almost totally shut out the evening twilight, Steed said "Time to move. Strike, you and I will low crawl to the top, and Angela, you and Mickey remain here. If we run into any trouble, you come up. I'll either contact you by radio or you'll hear the gunfire. Let's go, Strike."

It had been since the Marine days since Atticus had done any distance low crawling, except for that one occasion in South Carolina when he crawled upon some high ground to get a good position to take out a target, a child molester named Charles Hollingsworth. Yes, Steed remembered the names of every one of his kills in his hit man days. Quickly brushing those days from his mind, he now concentrated on negotiating the rocky slope to locate a different target.

Although still in good enough shape to crawl that hundred yards to the top, he wondered about Stryker. Could he keep up? Looking back, he saw that Strike was unwavering, maybe six feet behind him. A little older than Steed, Stryker was still matching him, powering his way, looking like an eighteen year old swimmer, one arm then the other, pulling his body over weeds and rocks.

Less than ten minutes later, they had covered that hundred yards, both nearly exhausted, waiting for their afterburners to kick in. But then they heard voices which brought them to a halt. Two, maybe three men only a dozen feet ahead. Suddenly, a large rock which had become dislodged from the earth thanks to Steed's left foot began rolling down the hillside past Stryker. Obviously, catching the Syrian soldiers' attention, they began hustling from the top of the hill toward Steed's direction. Immediately spotting him, the Syrian fired at him but missed. His rifle still strapped to his ruck, all Steed could do was pull his .45 from his hip and sent a bullet into the man's chest. When a second guard, yelled out for his comrades to come, Stryker already had his monster shotgun off his ruck, firing that one second blast of five cartridges that caught not just the man who yelled out but two others running from the top of the hill.

Both Steed and Stryker sprang to their feet and charged the hill. How many more were on the reverse side? If there was a squad or more, the team was in deep ca ca. But behind Steed, running at full speed came Lovato and Johnson, M4s ready to spray anything appearing. One of the adversaries then popped a flare which was to the team's advantage. Now they were able see more troops , perhaps five more, scampering like rats, running to see what the shooting was about.

Team Terminus then spread out in a line as Steed yelled "Commence firing!"

Taking the first shot, Steed nailed the closest men with his AXSR rifle. Lovato's and Johnson's M4s began spraying the rest of the men with two and three round automatic bursts, not giving them a chance to spring into action.

However, out from a truck parked at the site, came a lone uniformed troop who fired at Steed, the bullet passing through the top of his cap. Immediately, Stryker's Atchisson shotgun blasted the shooter 10 feet, taking much of his head in the process.

It wasn't much of a fire fight considering the team attacked the remnant of the Syrian element before it had an opportunity to react. Whether it was the night shift or their replacements had yet to arrive was anyone's guess.

After securing the area, Steed looked over the missile and found this one to be a Topol-M, SS-27, Russian manufactured. So it appeared Syria was purchasing or being supplied with both Russian and Iranian missiles. However, neither of these had nuclear warheads. Steed held his cam close to the missile for McGowan to see. As darkness had totally fallen and the flare was now out, Stryker located the generator and switch that turned on two makeshift area lights. Steed then brought McGowan up on his camera. "Scorpion, are you there?"

"Watched it all on your body cam as shaky as it was. Good work, Mr. Steed. And I see the missile. Not nuclear but a hell of a warhead. Your people okay?"

"Not a scratch, but death being a matter of inches, my cap has a hole in it."

"Well, that's a sure example of Mighty One's grace. Now I won't have to tell Maria you aren't coming home. Enemy casualties?"

"100 percent. We need to dispose of the carcasses as I'm not sure if these people were her for the night or others are on the way."

"No. Just destroy their communication and get the hell out of there. Get completely out of the mountain range as quickly as you can. If another security detail is on the way and find evidence of their people being taken out, they'll mobilize a shit load of troops to comb the mountains looking for you. In the meantime, I'll be arranging for fire and brimstone to be poured on all sites before your night is over. Another reason you need descend back toward Tartus ASAP."

"Do you have new instructions about where and when to meet the contact?"

"Yes, a day earlier than we had planned. He will be at the base of the Nusayriyah mountains near the Tartus city outskirts. I have arranged for you to meet him at the following coordinates on Thursday the 6th, 1900 your time.

Contact point is 34* 53'N 35*53'E which is somewhere on the outskirts of the city. Company operative set this up only an hour ago anticipating that all sites need not be verified. Get down toward the city and make yourselves scare till then."

"Wilco, Scorpion. Out." Steed then instructed Stryker to shotgun blast all radio equipment just in case other troops were on the way.

Using the dark of night to their advantage, Steed and team highjacked the two- and-a-half truck they discovered on site and took the road on the reverse slope toward Tartus. Lovato, seated shotgun opposite Steed remarked, "A hell of a lot easier going down than up."

"Yeah, we should be in the Tartus suburbs in a couple of hours."

"If we still have just less than 24 hours till we meet the contact, where do we go till then?"

"I'm sure we'll be able to find a rooming house to sleep in tonight. If not, maybe a barn or chicken coup."

"Lovely," se replied. "And this contact, Quasim, will be giving us what information?"

"He will supposedly know where Rabah is hiding out."

"But if the missiles are destroyed, why do we need to go after this dude?"

"He might then flee to Yemen and collaborate with Karam Fahid to deploy *their* missiles. This Rabah is intending on being another bin Laden or Saddam Hussein, and just like those cockroaches, he will continue to be a threat to the U.S. and Israel. He's not going away until he's killed. And we happen to be the people assigned to do it."

"Well, you're the guy in the know. That's why you were assigned lead this mission. So, boss, find us a bed. I'm tired as shit."

"Everybody is. But take a moment and reload. We spent a lot of ammo back there."

Atticus Steed, seeing the Tartus city lights looming ahead, decided not to drive the truck any further. Even though it was unlikely anyone by now had found the deserted missile site and bodies of its security, someone spotting the military truck would assume it contained members of the Syrian military. Not only would the team *not* look middle eastern, they wore black ops civilian attire. Another problem was, with all the planning that had gone into the operation, no one thought to have Steed pack a few Syrian pounds, the country's currency.

However, they shouldn't have needed it if they were only hiking into the mountains to locate missile sites and then locate and kill Rabah. Now they had just under 24 hours to find a place to lay their heads and then keep low during the next day until time to rendezvous with their contact.

Steed then saw his opportunity. As he had been skirting the water's edge of the Mediterranean, he stopped the truck on a desolate dock and said "Everybody out." Parking the vehicle with the front bumper looking out over the water, he found a heavy stone to lay onto the accelerator. Moving the gearshift from neutral to first gear while pressing the clutch, he opened the driver's door and jumped onto the pavement. The truck then lurched and tumbled off the dock into the water. At first, he thought the water was too shallow as the truck didn't immediately go under. However, as it began filling with water, it gradually began sinking. Five minutes later, it was completely gone. Canvassing the waterfront area for anyone who may have seen the incident, Steed was satisfied no one appeared to be in proximity. "Let's go before someone sees us," he said.

Quickly, they hustled to an alley that lay between two large warehouse buildings about 50 yards where the truck drowned. The alley would provide them concealment for the time being until they decided where to spend the night.

About a half mile back before reaching the waterfront, Steed had noticed a row of small houses with signs on them that read *'ijjar*. As he read and spoke Arabic he figured they were likely motels or boarding houses. The word meant *rent*.

However, without pounds, no one was going to let them in for the night. "So, looks like we stay in a chicken coup, huh? Johnson commented.

"Maybe not," Stryker said. "I might have something that will get us a room." From a velcro pocket in his ruck, he pulled out a large coin of shiny gold. "Hate to part with this; it's both valuable *and* sentimental. During my Company years when I was in Morocco, I met someone. She started out as a contact but then it budded into a…"friendship'…of sorts."

"Yeah, I can just imagine," Lovato remarked.

"Anyway, her father was wealthy and paying monies to a Moroccan cartel that sent drugs into the U.S., the kingpin of which had threatened the family with death if her dad didn't keep pouring a steady stream of moolah into the cartel. It was she who collaborated with a CIA operatives, namely me and two more, to bring down the cartel. And that we did. When we were through, no one in the cartel was left alive. Her father gave me this gold coin which is valued at around 10 K. I've kept it all these years as I feel it has brought me good luck along the way."

Mickey said, "You would part with that coin so that we would have a place to stay for one night? $10,000 for one night?"

"It wouldn't make me happy, but yes."

Steed then said, "Let's see if we can work something else out instead. If we can't, that's mighty magnanimous of you, Strike."

Steed then led them from the alley back to the main street, retracing their route to where he had spotted the row of shanty motels. When an occasional vehicle happened along the road, they either ducked in between buildings or behind shrubs to avoid detection. In less than ten minutes, the team stood looking at the units. Sizing up three of the better-looking funduqs, Steed walked to the door. His three teammates remained hidden behind a large garbage container.

After knocking for about twenty seconds at the door, an

old man with a well- weathered face and one good eye opened the door. His left eye was nothing but a socket. "Madha turid (What do you want)?

"Gurfat lilaylat wahida,"(a room for one night) Steed replied.

The man stared at him for a moment, obviously noticing he was not Middle Eastern. Maybe it was also that his Arabic was a little rusty. The man then held out his hand and said, "Thalathumiayat junayh" (three hundred pounds).

Steed shook his head. "La,miayatayn" (No, two hundred).

The innkeeper then shook *his* head. "La, aidfae alan" (no, pay now).

It appeared he *would* have to cough up Stryker's coin. Even if he went to the other inns, he would be having the same conversation. Middle Easterners were all the same, no matter what country it was. He told the man, "antazir" (wait).

A minute later, he returned with the coin. Holding it toward the porch light, it shined like a $10,000 gold piece. The man's good eye opened nearly as large as the coin. He snatched it from Steed's hand and nodded, then waved him in.

Steed had not told the man there were three others. He again said "Anyazir." Looking back toward the bushes, he signaled for them to come. When all four came through the door, the innkeeper held up his hand and shook his head *no*.

Steed said, "Ant tahsul ealaa 'ajr jayid" (you are well paid).

The man shook his head again. Steed then approached him and snatched the coin back out of his hand.

"La, la! tamaam!" (Okay). He held out his hand again and motioned for all of them to come in, obviously knowing the value of the coin. Steed wondered if the man was alone or whether anyone else was staying at the place. Anyone could turn them in.

The room had one single bed, a wash basin, a window with a soiled curtain, a rickety wooden chair and cracked plaster walls. No bath. Lovato scoffed, "A $10,000 coin bought this?"

"You get the bed," Steed replied.

"And no bathroom or toilet," she added. "This is bullshit."

"Again, you get the bed."

She looked at the yellowed sheets. "I don't think I want it. And is it being offered to me because I'm a woman?"

Steed smiled. "Well, you got me there. But, I'm sleeping on my ruck anyway. This is just a place to be off the street."

As soon as they settled in, each went outside behind the building to relieve themselves. Of course, it was what they had done in the woods all that day. Steed then gave Lovato an order to take the bed. "And don't give me any your feminist sexism arguments. Just take the damn bed." She then nodded and let out a sigh of resignation, being too tired to quibble about it.

CHAPTER 22

At 2018, while the team was heating up their dinner rations, McGowan called Steed. "Did you find someplace to crash? Harold has you on the locator and it appears you're just out of the Tartus city limits."

"Exactly. Five-star hotel."

"Sure. I'll bet. I hope it's a well-built hotel. Even though you're far from the madding crowd's ignoble strife, you're about to get shaken up. I'm sending a hell-storm courtesy of the boat that brought you in to the Syrian waters. Hunker down."

"*Allll-right.* I love fireworks displays." "Watch and

listen."

After stepping outside onto the gravel, they did just that. First there were the whistling sounds as the tomahawks whizzed through the night air. Then the sky above the mountains lit up as bright as day, followed seconds later by the earth shaking, thunderous shock waves that nearly knocked the team off their feet.

"Well that was fun," Steed said, smiling. "The Syrians gotta be burying their heads in the sand like ostriches."

Mike Johnson nodded. "Yeah, looked and sounded like what I imagined Armageddon would be."

The missile attacks continued for several minutes and Steed wondered if there would be anything left of the Nusariyahs. When the attacks stopped, the silence was almost as deafening. However, it wasn't long before sirens were heard in the city. Jumping back inside, the team watched from the window as Syrian military and National Police units screamed by on the highway leading to the mountains. After a few moments, the sirens subsided. When all was quiet, Stryker moved further back into the room, found him a spot on the concrete floor and plopped his head on his ruck. Lovato made her way to the bed.

Johnson looked as though he was about to fall over. "We're all tired," Steed said. "Let's call it a night."

"And what a night it was," Lovato added.

It was 0310 on his watch when Steed suddenly sprang to his feet after hearing the sound of a vehicle pulling onto the gravel. "Everybody up," he said. "Seems we have visitors. Lock and load."

Taking a peek through the nasty curtains on the front window, he saw two improvised trucks, maybe Toyotas, with six men piling out, cradling machine guns and loaded for bear. "Be ready. If they barrel through the door, they'll not be stopping to ask questions."

The four of them knelt close to the floor, weapons pointed at the door, ready to fire. Police or military, Steed didn't care. The team would resist capture at all costs…in this case the cost would be Syrian lives. For a moment, all the team heard was the sound of men talking outside the front door. Steed figured they were likely discussing what was waiting for them on the inside. Was the team asleep or was it ready to unload on them when they burst through the door.
There was only one way out of their predicament, but that way would bring the entire National Police Force down on them. There would be no rock big enough for them to crawl under.

The voices stopped and then suddenly the door was bowled over with a battering ram. As soon as the first man came through the door, he fired a short burst which went over the teams head. That's all it took. As others came through behind him, the team opened upon them…two M4s on full automatic, Stryker's shotgun and Steed firing his close combat .45. hen the firing was over, a faint haze of gun smoke lay over the bodies of all six uniformed cops. As the team began pulling their carcasses into the room so they would not be seen from the road, a lone figure appeared on the front door stoop. The innkeeper had a gun of his own in his hand and was pointing it at Stryker. Lovato was first to see the man and react. Given that she had spent her entire magazine and had no other weapon on her, she took three running steps and threw a drop-kick into the old man's throat. He went down hard like a sack of cement. She leaned over him for a matter of seconds, finding that she had broken his neck. "That's what you get for bringing the cops down on us," she said.

Steed then snatched up his rifle and ruck. "Come on. We gotta get out of here. Grab your shit. Somebody's bound to have heard the shooting. They'll be down on us like vultures on roadkill."

"Where are we going?" Johnson asked him. "I don't

know. Just stay up with me."

Having run approximately 150 yards toward the Mediterranean, Steed stopped where a growth of trees and towering weeds near the water's edge offered them concealment. Lights from the distant city's illumination gave them just enough visibility to see one another and for Steed to notice a shiny gloss to the left side of Stryker's face.

Blood. "Looks like you caught one, Strike. How bad?"

"The bullet grazed across the top of my head. I'll live."

Steed went to his ruck and pulled out some alcohol, tape and gauze. But then Stryker, who looked as though he was fading a bit, eased himself onto a large rock. The entire side of his head, left shoulder and arm were saturated with his blood. The bullet had dug into his skull but apparently didn't take any pieces of bone with it. "Yeah. You'll live, old boy," Steed said. "Another couple of centimeters and you wouldn't have."

Stryker didn't appear all that concerned, but Lovato did. She sat quietly by and watched with caring eyes as Steed patched him up. No sardonic quips this time such as "didn't the Marines ever teach you how to duck?" When Steed had finished applying a large patch of gauze and strips of tape, Lovato sat down beside Stryker. "Hold out your hand," she said. After giving her a confused look, he extended his hand. In it she placed his gold coin.

"How did you…?"

"When I bent over the old fart back there to see if he was alive, I lifted your coin from his pocket. You're $10,000 richer than you were a half hour ago."

He smiled, picked up her hand and kissed it. "You're amazing, Angel."

They then sat down in a small circle to continue catching their breath. "Okay, here's the thing," Steed began. "They're going to know it was us who not only killed those guys, but will suspect we also had something to do with that firestorm on the mountains. The good part of the equation is that no one alive has seen our faces. If the four of us are found together, they'll put two and two together. That doesn't mean we're going to split up, but we all can't be seen during the daylight hours in any part of these suburbs. If we have to stay in this grove of pines all day until meeting Quasim, so be it. I…"

"Lovato then interrupted. "Steed, what's that down by the water?" She was pointing to a small, run-down building a little over 100 square feet in size.

"Looks like a storage shed of sorts," Johnson replied.

"Steed nodded. "Exactly. Let's see if it's in use. Should be a good place to hide out."

Steed then left the team and with his pen light groped his way out of the tree line toward the building. The front of the shed sat on a half caved-in dock and the building itself looked as though it could fall into the water with the next puff of wind. The dock groaned and wobbled when he stepped on it. However, finding the door unlocked, he tested the shed's sturdiness. It had a good floor sitting firmly on land but a few of its side boards were missing. The shed, obviously not in use, he found nothing inside but an oar, a bucket and a flipper. Returning to the team, he said, "I think we can make it do. I doubt anyone will come looking for us in there tonight. But be assured, when they do start looking as the morning light filters in, there will be a shit load of uniforms coming for us."

"And you think they won't look in the shed?" Stryker asked.

"Not at first. They'll be all over places initially. But excuse the reference to Tommy Lee Jones' quote from The Fugitive, they'll be making *a hard-target search of every gas station, residence, warehouse, farmhouse, henhouse, outhouse and doghouse in the area.* This storage building is sitting on a rotted-out dock that would fall if more than one person stepped on it. And *we* have to be careful when stepping onto it ourselves. One at a time, and even then you might be going for a swim."

"Let me go in first since I'm a 118 pound fighting machine," Lovato quipped. "Stryker, you, the 180 pound pasta eater, need to go last." The hellcat was back, surprisingly at the expense of her wounded boyfriend.

Each member of the team negotiated the crumbling dock without bringing it down and entered the shack just before 0400. As the small building was even more dark inside, they couldn't see their hands before their eyes. However, Steed cautioned them against using pen lights or striking matches as there were three sideboards missing which would open the wall to light. It was a good time to lay back down on their rucksacks and make up for their lost sleep.

Unfortunately, there was little room for anyone to stretch out.

When the sun's early rays filtered in through the cracks in the sideboard, the team opened their eyes. Steed had kept watch most of the night with Johnson taking over at 0400. It was an important day, the day they were to make contact with Quasi to determine the whereabouts of Rabah. Would it be the day they would kill him?

All at some point stepped softly out of the shed onto the dock and took turns running into the nearby brush to void themselves. As fires were still burning in several areas of the Nusariyahs, woodsmoke was thick in the air. Sirens could still be heard up and down the Tartus main highway as they were all night. There were still 12 hours before Steed was to meet Quasim. But just who *was* this Quasim? Steed had questions. After the team heated their morning rations, he summoned McGowan. It was still yesterday just after 2300 Washington D.C. time. McGowan would still be up.

"What's your status, Mr. Steed?"

"Watched the 4th of July extravaganza and thanks for that. At three something this morning we had six guests at our door. We vacated and left them there. They didn't go home." "Fatal?" "All."

"Seems you people are trigger-happy."

"Just trying to stay alive, Scorpion. Still have several hours before meeting our contact (Steed was careful not to mention his name in case someone was eavesdropping on their conversation)."

"Are you safe?"

"Trying to be. Gotta know something about the contact."

"Shoot."

"Why couldn't we gain info before now as to whereabouts of the target through our Company man? And what does this contact know about the target the Company couldn't find out on its own?"

"The contact knows the target personally and is in his good graces. As the target moves around almost daily, the contact will know on a real-time basis where the man is at any time. He will advise the best day, time and location for you to go to work."

"Understood."

"Your questions have merit. But once you gain the information about the man's location, do not send me specifics over the airways. Just do the job and go meet your ride back home."

"Wilco, Scorpion. I have turned the cam off today to allow recharge."

"Fine. Everyone well?"

"Strikeout his scalp creased in this morning's interplay. Minor flesh wound."

"A matter of inches."

"That's what I told him. Other than that, we're looking forward to some steak and brew on the ride back."

"Those people do it up right."

"That's all I have. Long day ahead in hiding. Chao."

CHAPTER 23

By noon the temperature inside of the minute shed was sweltering. Occasionally, over the past three hours the team could hear voices, loud, boisterous voices they surmised came from police or military people. At one point, the voices seemed to come from the small wooded area which had during their escape and evasion had offered them temporary shelter near the shack; however, none of the voices were close.

The inside of the shed was almost choking-hot and as Steed himself at times was on the verge of passing out, he was concerned for the others. Twice he laid his hand on Lovato's steaming moist forehead and asked her in a whisper if she was okay. She nodded both times but didn't respond. At a point when the voices faded away, Steed opened the door, stepped lightly onto the dock and looked in the direction to where the voices had been heard. Whoever it was had gone. He then went back inside and helped Lovato to her feet, telling her to stand in the doorway. So that both of them were not on the dock at the same time, he stepped off of it onto the ground and motioned for her to come outside. When she did, he pulled her off the dock. Picked her up and placed her into the shallow edge of the Mediterranean. She nodded to him with a smile and immersed her entire body in the water. After a couple of minutes, she stood and climbed back onto the bank. "Thanks for baptizing me," she said.

One by one, with Steed keeping watch, Johnson and Stryker came out of the shed and took dips into the water. Finally, Steed laid his .45 onto the deck and slipped into the cool water himself. All now refreshed, they returned inside, this time leaving the door open. Doing so would help a little; however, they would have to be vigilant, watching out for uniforms who might decide at some point to check out the shed. If they heard someone approach, Steed would make sure the door was re-closed and Stryker's shotgun ready to blast whoever opened it.

Jammed into the shed like sardines, they not only noticed but commented to each other how gamey they had gotten. And for some reason, since their clothing was had not yet dried, they all smelled like fish. Johnson remarked, "When we get back to the sub, I will bypass the kitchen and the steak dinner to first hit the showers." Lovato nodded.

"Absolutely."

It was 1540 when the team once again heard voices headed toward the shed. Silently, Steed closed the door and set Stryker up with the shot gun. As it could fire 5 cartridges a second, it was *the* weapon to take them out. As the voices of perhaps two or three men were now within ten feet of the shed, it was obvious they'd intended to check it out. The first set of boots were heard on the deck and then the second; but when the third man stepped on the boards the entire deck crashed onto the rocks below, carrying the three of them ten feet down into the water. Fortunately, the shed only shifted downward about three feet, shaking up its occupants inside. However, careful not to utter any sounds of surprise, the team didn't let themselves be detected. But, outside they heard groans and loud conversations. It was obvious at least one of them had hurt himself.

Sounds of them climbing out of the water onto the bank, the men gave the impression they were more concerned about their own plight rather than looking into the shed. Steed surmised the police, or whoever they were, figured no one could be inside because the rotted dock would have fallen with them. However, the shotgun was ready to roar if they got nosy. But the men left, still talking and groaning, their voices waning as they went on. When he could no longer hear them, Steed opened the door just enough to peek around the corner of the shed to see two of the men in the distance hobbling and half-carrying each other. "Well, now I'm concerned our quarters might tumble into the Mediterranean along with the dock. As I don't think anyone will come back this way, we're going back to that patch of woods."

After gingerly climbing out of the shed and jumping down onto the rocks they hustled into the brush for concealment. The team still had just under four hours until they reached their rendezvous point. But what was located at their meet-up point…a house, a barn, a cave, a grove of trees? Maybe somewhere back up in the mountainous area. Steed had the coordinates and found the area on his locator, but exactly where it was, was anyone's guess. By his calculations, the contact point was to the northwest just inside the city limits, four hundred fifty meters away. That meant they would be trekking along a secondary road in broad daylight. The four of them together would certainly attract attention. But would all four of them need to be meeting the contact? Steed did not think so; however, he didn't want to split the team up. He contacted McGowan for guidance.

"I understand your dilemma, Atticus. You definitely don't want to expose yourselves as a team, knowing that anyone out there, including civilians, would see you and report you. But I agree, you don't want to split up.

However, securing this information is important. We don't want to lose our target and if we wait too long, he will likely jump ship and wind up in that other country.

Do you still have your head covers?"

"We do. Sheikh keffiyehs for us guys and Lovato has her hijab."

"Good. With your faces covered, travel slowly but determinedly in twos. Man and man, man and woman. First two leave and a couple minutes later, the second two. Keep each other in sight. Wearing your head covers, you shouldn't attract any attention. Use your radios sparingly. "

"We'll try that. If we were meeting at night, we could more easily accomplish it."

"Keep your guns in their weapons bags slung over your rucks. Cover the bags with a shirt."

"Already ahead of you on that. Do you know what key terrain is located at the contact point?"

"No information on that. Something you have to figure out. Good luck and let me know the result."

"Roger. Out."

When Steed heard the Calls to Prayer that had occurred at dawn and noon, he knew there were three more coming, which gave him an idea. The adhan had announced the first two prayers by loud speaker clearly enough to be heard throughout the suburbs. Each of the prayer times usually lasted about fifteen minutes; therefore, the team would wait for the third call, asr, which was the first evening prayer, don their head covers and move out quickly. At each call, every muslim of faith was commanded to stop what they were doing and take up the prone position to praise Allah. The team could cover a lot of ground while most of Tartus had their noses stuck on prayer rugs. There would be few if any other people on the roads and streets to see and care about who they were.

According to Steed's calculations, if they moved out at around 1700, they should be in position to meet up with Quasim on time. But they still had about an hour to wait. Keeping watch from the parcel of woods where they had sought relief from the sun, the slow tick of the clock in Steed's head was trying his patience. But then at 1658 came the call to asr on a loud speaker.

Steed stepped slightly from the woods to watch as several people hustled to their prayer place. "Let's go," he said. "We'll hustle after them to give the impression we are also responding to salah."

Covering about half of the 450 meters during the time of asr, when a good number of people began returning to their daily routines, the team slowed their pace and split up into pairs. Steed and Lovato, and Johnson and Stryker.

Although their clothing was black western-world attire, their head covers said Arab. Steed banked on nobody on the street caring.

As the setting sun cast its long shadows across the road, the team was within ten minutes of reaching the coordinates McGowan had given him. Would Quasim recognize Steed and the team as his arranged contacts? Would he be in a location by himself or in a marketplace with other people? Steed was not sure how the meeting would be going down.

At two minutes before 1900, he clearly saw the rendezvous point. The coordinates were dead-on a large, ornate marble building, a mosque. Finding an alley just short of the mosque, Steed and Lovato ducked in to wait for Johnson and Stryker to catch up. Seeing that no one else was coming out of the mosque after asr was done, he led the team up the steps and through the entrance. At first, he saw no evidence of anyone moving about. Then lying on what is called the mihrab where an imam would stand, the team saw a bloodied body.

Without word, each member pulled from their canvas bags their weapons and scanned the inside of the mosque. Steed walked over to the body and saw the man had been bludgeoned and beaten to death. His eyes were swollen and teeth knocked from his mouth. Every part of his body and clothing was bright red with his blood. Was this his contact? Was this Quasim?

Suddenly, descending upon them from beyond the mihrab were six men cradling AK-47s and 105s, four in black clothing and wearing hooded masks and two in the uniform of the Syrian military. If there was any question as to whether the Syrian government was in cahoots with al-quads or ISIS, it was just answered. "Place your weapons on the floor," one of them ordered. Realizing they were completely surrounded and weapons ready to fire, Steed laid his rifle down. The rest of Team Terminus dropped theirs to the floor as well. If there was any question One man then stepped forward from the others and Steed recognized him immediately from the slides in Ben Marshall's briefing. Abboud bin Rabah.In nearly perfect English, he said, "And so you came here looking for Quasim, my betrayer. There he lays. There is also your fate." His eyes were fixed on Steed. "You are their leader, I believe. Do you have anything to say?"

"You know why we have come here, Rabah…to kill you. And we will do so."

Rabah laughed. "How do you propose to do that when I have six guns pointed at you?"

Steed didn't answer.

Rabah then turned to Lovato. "This woman, you bring her into our holy place to defile it. It is she who will die first, but not before my men have their pleasure with her." He motioned with his head for one of them to take her. "She will give pleasure to *all* my men, one by one. Then my men will take pleasure in killing the rest of you."

The largest of Rabat's men, Hamar, stepped forward and grabbed hold of Lovato's hair. She tried to resist; however, he was too powerful. Stryker then lunged at him, but another man struck him in his already sore head with the butt of his rifle.

After Lovato was half-dragged to somewhere behind the mihrab, Steed glared at Rabah. "You say this is a holy place that has been defiled by our presence, yet you allow your men to molest an innocent woman? Is this what your religion condones?"

"You are infidels and our law commands that we treat you like animals if we must and to kill you, which we will do."

"You are all ruthless, lawless bastards, and lower than monkey shit. How do you feel now in seeing all your missile sites destroyed and still burning on the mountain? Yeah, asshole, we did that."

"It matters not as we have other missiles and allies who will fire them."

"If you mean your Houthi friends in Yemen? Our

missiles will wipe them out as well."

"If that happens, you will not be involved. You will be dead." As Rabah had been staring at the team's communications equipment on their web gear, he surmised it was from their devices the information was likely provided to the forces that fired the missiles. He then ordered his men to rip the radios and cams off. Once they did so, they smashed them on the floor with the butts of their rifles.

Stryker kept eyeing the passageway behind the mihrab, hearing Lovato protesting. He wanted to run to her aid, but knew he would be cut down by a spray of automatic weapons fire if he did.

Inside a small room where the imams prayed before salah, the large man pinned Lovato down with his body and began pawing her, first tearing her shirt at the breasts and then fumbling with the zipper on her pants.

But as he was concentrating on ripping off her clothing, he made one huge mistake. Her .45 and M-4 having been taken earlier, no one checked her for any concealed weapon. From the side of her boot she pulled her ka-bar and shoved it into the front of his neck under the chin. As she had severed his larynx, he was not able to cry out. Making only a soft gurgling sound, the man's head dropped sharply onto her shoulder.

Lovato then rolled him off her and ran toward the door.

From that small room, the team then heard Lovato moaning as if she were enjoying coital pleasure, in climax, screaming aloud. Rabah sat looking at Steed, grinning and shaking his fist in delight. "Your bitch is getting Hamar's best. But it sounds like he is done. Asad, the lion, you are next."

Steed stood up to face Rabah, fists clinched. "You think you are men, but you're nothing but algarf (shit). If you were a real man, you would lay your AK down and fight me one-on-one."

"You will sit back down or I will kill you now. It is my purpose to see your mind in pain before I cause your body to have pain. Listen to how Asad treats your bitch. He is a big man also but it is his quadib (penis) that is the biggest among us. She will scream very much."

Stryker then said, "You bastard. If I had my hands around your neck, your tongue and eyeballs would be popping out of your head."

"You will all be quiet or you will die now." His grin widened. "I want you to listen to the music of habun (passion). But do not worry; after my men have had their delight, she will no longer be alive to remember. Now go, Asad."

The man, Asad, entered the door to the small room and closed it. Stunned to see Hamar lying on the floor, his neck and chest covered in blood, he tried to yell out but his voice was cut short. Lovato, standing behind the door sliced the blade of the ka-bar from the left side of his throat to the right, cutting deep into both carotid arteries. After his body hit the floor, she waited about two minutes, then began moaning again. A minute later she stopped.

Rabah laughed loudly. In his Arabic tongue, he said, "I think Hamar wished to stay and watch. But it seems Asad did not last long. Maybe he killed her with his powerful quadib. Mariq, it is your turn. Go entertain the woman…if she is still alive." He laughed again.

Mariq, a young man perhaps 20, had an eager but imbecilic look on his face as he marched off to the room, a look that said he had never had sex with a woman. Rabah shouted after him a few words some of which Steed was able to decipher, such as, "tell those meatheads to come out and let you have the woman without them watching." But when Mariq opened the door, the first thing he saw was blood…everywhere. He then screamed out something that Steed fully recognized, "Rabah, yajib an tati (You must come)!"

When Rabah ran toward the room, the remaining three men were distracted…distracted enough for Steed, Johnson and Stryker to jump them. Knocking them to the floor, the team bludgeoned them with the men's own weapons. Rabah, hearing his men cry out, stepped out of the room just long enough to see them lying on the floor and the Terminus three standing over them. When Steed brought up the Syrian AK to fire at him, Rabah ran back inside and locked the door behind him. Steed planted three rounds into the door. Stryker was the first to run toward the room but finding the door locked, began hammering it with the stock of the AK. But then Mike Johnson yelled, "Stand back, Strike." Like a 200 pound fullback, Johnson barreled through the door which landed both him and the door onto the inside floor. With Steed and Stryker on his heels, the three of them found only young Mariq cowering in a corner off to the right.

Rabah *and* Lovato were gone.

CHAPTER 24

I had not heard from my team for over three days. My IT commo guys had not been able to reach them by radio or camera. I know that Steed would have called in if I had not contacted him first. Now, I was getting concerned. The last communication I had from Steed was that he was moving toward the coordinates to make contact with the man called Quasim. He would have real-time information as to Rabah's whereabouts, and shortly after the meet-up, Rabah's days would be over.

Just in case Steed had taken down Rabah, then somehow lost communication with me and had on his own made arrangements with the commander of the boat on which they would be riding back to Rota, submarine Captain Philip Livingston. Jim Bob set me up with him in less than two minutes. "Commander Livingston, have you by chance heard from the team of folks you dropped at the Syrian shore?"

"I have not, Mr. McGowan. We had anticipated hearing from him by now, given his dialogue with my COB just before they pushed out to shore. Could it be possible communication was lost when we put tomahawks on your targets?."

"It's possible but I had contact with Mr. Steed after that."

We talked for only about two minutes, but at the close of our conversation, Livingston told me as soon as he heard from the team, he would personally contact me.

It was 1130 hours on Monday the 10th when Ben Marshall and I met at J. Hollinger's, a favorite D.C. lunch spot. While I sat talking with Ben, I couldn't help but think about the team, where they were and what *they* had been eating. Commander Livingston told me the team had taken enough MREs, the self-heating kind, to last about ten days. No one apparently had any Syrian pounds on them in case they had an opportunity to eat off the local economy; however, they were not planning to be anywhere in the Tartus area where they would make themselves seen.

"I'm giving it another day or so, Ben; then we have to go after them."

"I'll relay their status to the VP, but as you know, no one in the Department of State or the Pentagon knows we have a covert team in there. If we utilize our resources to go get them out, the word gets back to the president. And if that happens, we are in a mess of shit, Bruce."

"Don't we have CIA assets in Syria? And couldn't they be tasked to conduct a search beginning at the location of their last communication with me?"

"That would go to the CIA director and again, it would get back to the president."

I shook my head. "It seems amazing to me that what we have accomplished so far, dispatching the team to Rota, utilizing Naval resources to get them into Syria, sending missiles to knock out enemy sites and et cetera, all of this has been contained covertly by VP Collins."

"He has both a professional and personal association with the Secretary of The Navy and all operations are being conducted through Naval resources."

"Then send a few SEALs in. I have to know what's happening with the team. They could be dead for all I know."

"I understand, Bruce. I'm concerned about them as

well. But there's only so much with logistics and human resources we can do. Like you said, we'll wait a couple more days and get back together about this."

"If communications has not been re-established by end of business Wednesday, I'm going in after them."

"You? Alone?"

"Me alone if that's what it takes."

"And how do you propose to manage that?"

"I'll find a way, with or without your help, Ben. I'm going in to find my team. If you give me any resistance on this, then fire my ass."

Ben placed his hand on my shoulder. "Okay, my friend, be easy. This is *our* team, And I don't mean to come across negatively. Just be assured I will help you any way I can. I will be advising the VP this afternoon about the team. He's the one to decide if resources can be released to go in."

The remainder of our lunch went smoother, conversation wise. Ben praised the work of the team in verifying the missile sites to set up the tomahawk barrage. Steed had displayed outstanding leader skills thus far in the mission. We then switched gears to talk about Adriana and how she was doing back at Wolf Laurel. And how good was that calamari and crab Rangoon appetizer? A much lighter conversation to try taking my mind off the team for a while.

When I returned to the 'warehouse,' my three techies were having *their* lunch. "Nothing from the team?" I asked them.

"No sir," replied Jim Bob. "We keep trying to reach them, but dead silence."

"Thanks. Don't give up." I then went to my makeshift desk to do some pondering. The threat I had made to Ben about going into Syria myself and coming up with a way to do it was more a reflection of my frustration than anything. Ben had asked just how would I propose to get myself into Syria. I blew a little smoke by saying I would find a way. Of course, I wouldn't be able to just cross the border and walk or drive in.
But the more I thought about it, maybe there *was* a way…a less than conventional way.

Being former Special Forces and having made one hundred fifty-seven jumps, would I be able to make just one more? Although it had been more than forty years since I went out of an airplane, there was no doubt I could do it again. But how could it be arranged? Recently, a friend of mine from the old days, a retired master sergeant named Bob Mandrake, also the president of our Fayetteville, NC, SF chapter, phoned me to ask if I'd be interested in doing a couple of jumps after a short refresher. I wanted to, but the Queen of my Kingdom put the squelch on it. "It is a good way for you to break every bone in your body, you know. I'd prefer you not do it," she said. She probably had a point, considering all my bones were a little more fragile than they were forty years ago.

As I had done three High Altitude Low Opening (HALO) jumps, why not *jump* into Syria rather than go through the same training aboard a sub as the team?

Going the sub route, however, it would take several days to get me there. To get into the country and locate the team's whereabouts, I wouldn't have that much time. But then a HALO jump meant the plane would still be be vulnerable to enemy fire at lower latitude.

However, there was something called a HAHO, the High Altitude High Opening jump. I had never done one of these. If I could get the training scheduled at the HAHO/HALO SF Special Warfare Center and through it in a day, I could likely cut the time in half. But I'd have to get it arranged immediately.

After pondering the possibility, I pulled out my SF contact card and called MSG (retired) Mandrake. His voice hadn't changed. "Captain McGowan, he answered. Long time, sir."

"Good to know you're still alive, Bob."

He laughed. "Back at ya. Someone told me a jealous husband who caught you with his wife, put you in the ground with his .45. I'm glad to see both of us made it this far alive."

My turn to laugh. "I've thought about you many times over the past few years. Say, Bob, you still active in the Special Forces Association?"

"Yep. Still president."

"A while back you contacted me and asked if I'd like to participate with your chapter in doing some jumps. Are you still setting those up?"

"Yeah, you interested now?" "Yes I am."

"You're not dyin' and doin' one of those 'last wish' things, are you?"

I laughed. "No, nothing like that. I just wanted to do a couple of HAHO jumps."

"HAHO? Why?"

"It's complicated, Top."

"Sounds like it's *you* who's complicated, friend. Are you still workin' for the gov'ment in some capacity?"

"In some capacity."

"Somethin' Top Secret, I presume. You gonna parachute into some hot bed somewhere?"

"You're very insightful, Bob. You didn't need to play 20 questions."

"Man, you amaze me. I thought by now you'd be kickin' back in retirement on some farm somewhere with a good lookin' broad."

"Jeepers. How do you know…never mind. So can you set me up, like yesterday?"

"It'll take me a couple of days. You know that I am at the Yuma Training Ground conductin' the HALO and HAHO training. Not at Bragg anymore. Can you be here Wednesday morning? I have a stick of Rangers who're set up to go. Since you've already been through the course a hundred years ago, you'd be goin' through refresher training'. Will last a couple of days. Two jumps, two days. We need to also give you a physical to assure you won't pass out on us at high altitudes."

"Perfect, Bob. Where at the Proving Grounds?"

"My office at Building 217. Be here at 0900." He paused. "I still don't get you, Captain."

"I'm not easily gotten, Top. I think you've always known that."

"Yeah, Guess I have. Anyway, De Oppresso Liber," Mandrake said, quoting the Green Beret motto.

"Whatever, whenever, wherever," I replied.

And so I had made the decision to go into Syria full canopy. After re- certification, I needed to get Ben Marshall on board to set up my flight over the country and all the jump gear I'd need. To determine if it was via HALO or HAHO was a matter of how hight the bird would need to fly to avoid both detection and being shot down. That would also mean whether I was going to need a SOLR oxygen mask if the plane was to fly over an 18,000 feet altitude. I knew I couldn't score something like a Globemaster high flying aircraft which would carry several sticks of jumpers at extreme altitudes but maybe Marshall would be able to secure a much smaller civilian plane such as a Cessna 172. But it needs to be faster and take me up around 15,000 feet. But could it fly at a range where an ordinary arsenal couldn't reach it with conventional weapons?

Probably. But could it avoid ground-to-air missiles? Doubtful, unless the aviator performed some crazy, evasive maneuvers. And where would the government find a civilian or military pilot willing to risk getting blown out of the sky to drop little ol' me into a hostile environment? A lot of uncertainties as to whether I would be able to pull this deal off. But unless I came up with another plan to put my ass on Syrian soil, I had to try it. I had to find out if my team was dead or alive.

And then there was that other concern. A domestic one. I couldn't tell Adriana I was going in. I was supposed to be a desk-jockey commander, no longer a terrorist hunting warfighter. As we had talked several times while the Terminus element was on sea and ground with the mission of finding a malevolent terrorist bent on killing American military, she was content with me living in my warehouse HQ directing the mission. However, even though I wasn't going to tell her my plan to go after the team by myself, she would wonder where I was when she couldn't reach me for who knows how many days.

CHAPTER 25

Wednesday, the day I took a zero dark thirty flight to the HALO/HAHO school at the Yuma Proving Ground in Arizona, I had still heard nothing from the team. It was now going on a week since I had my last communication with Atticus Steed.

It was good to see my old friend Master Sergeant Mandrake. I had attended several SF Association gatherings through the years at Ft. Bragg, but the last one was more than 10 years ago. Bob was now 78 and although balding with deep, furrowed wrinkles, still the picture of health.

"Don't be intimidated by these young Rangers, Captain Bruce. Even though I know you were one yourself, you"re gonna have a time keeping' up with 'em."

But I didn't. Whether it was the fact I was still an avid runner or the fact I had to make this happen to find out what happened to my team, I pushed myself to the max during the physical part of the training. We spent the better part of the morning in the classroom going over equipment, masks, and procedures and determining whether I wanted the chute to open soon after exiting the plane (HAHO) or whether I was cool with free-falling at 220 mph and then pulling the cord at a low altitude.

That afternoon and the next day, I experienced both. The adrenaline rush of the HALO I remembered quite well and even though I wasn't fond of plunging toward the earth like a speeding bullet, I knew that over a hostile land I didn't need to be hanging up in the troposphere for twenty minutes. Of course timing was everything and it it was a night jump and the LZ unlit, the ground could come up to meet me prematurely. An analogue altimeter with a phosphorescent face was a must. I'd have to know wind and other weather conditions so that I wasn't blown 20 miles from my intended landing in a field.
Jumping during the daytime makes for different concerns; the plane is more easily spotted and so is that colorful parachute. But regardless of the hazards, I had to do it…day or night.

That third day at Yuma, I received my certification then immediately got Ben Marshall on my phone to see if he could not only get me the authorization to go but a plane to make it happen. "You really have to do this, Bruce?"

"I really do. I can't wait a week or more to go the Department of the Navy route where I'd fly to Rota, go through the same training as our team, then get spit out into the Mediterranean Then the Syrian Navy knowing the North Dakota likely dumped a covert team on their shore and subsequently took out their missiles, will be lurking in the Med waters anticipating more hoo-ha from the U.S."

I heard him sigh. "Alright, Bruce. I have you a plane on standby, a Cirrus SR-22. It can get you up around 25,000 feet and fly at a speed of 220 knots. Are you still in Arizona?"

"Getting ready to board a plane as we speak. I'll be in D.C. this afternoon. I can leave tomorrow if you can set it up. Will also need HALO gear and a SOLR oxygen mask. The pilot needs something as well…a set of gonads. Any ex-CIA Air America sky jockeys available?"

"I know a former Marine aviator that we used on drug missions in Central and South America.
He's always looking for the next adventure courtesy of the government. His name is Spud Olson. And yeah, I put him on notice." But then having told me about my pilot, Ben was seemingly reflective for a few moments. Finally he said, "I still don't know why I'm going along with you on this; but the vice president says to trust you. He has complete confidence in you.
And he wants this team back as much as we do."

"Not to worry, Ben. I *will* find them."

"Just don't end up like your team and disappear on us."

My plane from Arizona arrived around 1730 at Dulles. I picked up my Suburban in economy parking and hustled home at a speed of 30 mph in the Washington rush hour traffic. Why it's called rush hour is laughable. I was tired from the quick trip out and back. Plus, I think my two high-altitude jumps played with my head. I had a delectable dinner and a good night's sleep, however, so by 0700 the next morning, I was ready to meet Olson at Terminus House.

Spud was a serious chap who said very little, which made me wonder if my six-hour flight from Washington to Al-Asad Airbase in Iraq was going to feel even twice as long. Gruff and terse, wearing a Marine-style buzz cut, he spit out some colorful, raw language, intermixing the F word into nearly every sentence. "What the hell you know about jumpin', anyway?"

"Army Special Forces with 157 jumps, and as of yesterday a total of 5 high-altitude jumps."

"I flew a bunch of you (bleepin') Green Berets in 'Nam and found you to be a bunch of (bleepin') prima donna choir boys who thought your shit don't stink. You…"

"Look, Olson, if you don't want this job, I'll get a *real professional* to fly me over Syria. I'm not going to sit here and listen to you put me down, not to mention defame a noble organization like the Special Forces. And if this is the type of conversation we'll be having during our flight to Al-Asad, I'll kick your sorry ass out of the plane and take my chances flying your bird the rest of the way in. I've had some time in the cockpit of planes like your SR-22."

In his eyes I think I saw something that hadn't been there in years…fear. I wasn't sure if he was actually afraid of *me* or of losing the job, which I'm sure was going to pay him well. But I *was* sure he was a good aviator and fearless in the air or Ben wouldn't have chosen him. It was after I stared him down that Olson began coming around. "Okay, Mr. McGowan, I'm sorry if I insulted you. It's just my nature to be a son-of-a- bitch. I'm sure you're good at whatever you do. And I'm impressed that you're gonna jump into what could be a bad situation to find your friends. I will be more…obligin.' Let's start our conversation over again."

From then on, it was like talking with a different person. Even his language cleaned up a little. He said his orders were that we'd depart at 1100 hours from Potomac Airfield. Considering I had weapons, there would be less chance that TSA would be checking me since we would be driving directly up to his plane. Ben Marshall's people had already secured for me a helmet containing

an audible altimeter and an oxygen mask. They had left them with my assistant, Debbie.

Ben himself stopped by to personally ask if I was "sure about doing this"; if I wasn't going to change my mind, which I wasn't, he wished me a safe and successful mission. Moments after he left, Spud Olson and I departed for the airfield. As I had made it a hurried mission, I hoped my ruck contained everything I needed for the bush. I didn't want to be trekking through the mountains and forest areas with a 50 pound ruck on my back, so I only packed essentials…three plus days of self-heating rations, a first aid kit, soap, canteen, sleeping bag, a change of clothing, a lensatic compass and a 1:25000 map of the Tartus Governorate. I knew Syria was allowing western tourists in with visas and passports, but I would *not* be an invited guest. If I were approached by anyone in uniform, I would have no ID whatsoever, hostile as I was.

Spud and I were now on a first name basis since we had earlier cleared the air. We'd never be friends, but at least our trip across the waters would not be antagonistic. We did share some past-life experiences to break up the monotony but having heard his, I think I'd have preferred to catch up on some needed sick time. After the Marines, he led a messy, sometimes turbulent life, bordering on criminal misdeeds; yet, he was one of the government's covert pilots. Much of my work life I didn't share with him, but what I did tell him made me seem, in comparison, like an altar boy. I could tell I was boring him as he yawned a lot. I was hoping it was because he was bored and not ready to fall asleep on me.

As it was nearly 13 hours from Washington, D.C. to Al-Asad, we arrived at 0230 the next morning, Bagdad time. Spud refueled and the both of us sought on- post housing for the remainder of the morning. My Remington 700 and .45 remained in the the plane so that the APs and hired security wouldn't get excited…and I wouldn't end up in the stockade.

At 0800, I met the potato head at the base canteen for some sorely-missed S.O.S. (creamed chipped beef on toast or shit on a shingle) which tasted just as good as I remembered back when I used to have breakfast in mess halls an eon ago. He reminded me that at the 20,000 feet altitude where we would be crossing from the Mediterranean into Syrian airspace, I needed to have oxygenated at least an hour before exiting the aircraft.

What I *didn't* need was a case of hypoxia to occur on my speedy way down to the ground. Spud had gone in one day from an "I don't give a shit" attitude about my well-being to an "I gotta be sure you have a successful HALO experience, pal." Well, I guess since he was the one who would plant me into a hostile environment where there were mountains and a prickly forest near a rocky seashore, I'd be okay with being his 'pal.'

It took us an hour and twenty minutes after leaving Al-Asad to reach the point where my team had swum to shore at Tartus. As Spud Olson's plane was entering Syrian airspace, we both knew I had to exit quickly so that we wouldn't get knocked out of the sky by a missile before I went out. He would then bank the plane back out of the airspace and over the Mediterranean.

At the point where we were above the coordinates I had spotted on my map what appeared to be a lush field of some kind, he slapped me on the shoulder and yelled "Go!"

I went.

The adrenaline had already begun surging through my arteries several air miles back when I sat at the open door of the aircraft watching the shoreline come into view. As the temperature at that altitude was a balmy -15 degrees, having donned my cold weather gear, I was not going to freeze to death within plunging toward earth at something like 150 mph terminal velocity. It would only take about a minute to reach the point where I'd pop my canopy. I was pushing the envelope popping it at 2,500 feet. But during that minute, I kept my brain busy thinking about everything that could go wrong. I'm not a negative person, but when you're

alone at 20,000 feet and there is nothing to hear, you might think you've gone deaf. And then with the pressure you feel on your body, you might remember what you were told about decompression sickness, where there could be venomous gas embolisms occurring in the blood traveling to the heart. It's where the pressure of gases dissolved in the body tissues exceed the atmospheric pressure. Gas bubbles can form which could be fatal.

But then so that these defeats thoughts wouldn't interfere with my task at hand, I yelled, "Snap out of it, McGowan! The altimeter warning alarm inside my helmet screamed at me to deploy my chute. So I did. It wasn't the softest of landings, but I did touch down onto the lush green spot on my map which turned out to be a cattle farm.
And who was rushing over to greet me but a big-horned bull. It was then I decided after surviving what could have been a dangerous HALO jump not hitting rocks, trees and prickly plants, I didn't want to die from my liver being impaled by an angry bull. Gathering up my chute, I found myself in a dead run toward a grove of trees with Ferdinand closing in fast. But what the bull knew
and I did not, those nearby woods contained sabra fruit, which I had previously read was a prickly cactus.

As the bull stopped well short of the cactus, I did not. Although my cold weather gear absorbed most of the lacerations, I still had scores of cuts on my face and neck.

It actually took me a couple of minutes to tear myself away from the cactus, compelling me to leave my heavy coat and pants hanging in the spiny plant. I wasn't concerned about them because there was nothing in my pockets for anyone find. However, once separated from the thistles and then assuring that the horny bovine had given up on me, I pulled my entrenching tool from my ruck and buried both the chute and helmet.

Now that I was safely on the ground, even with all the hurried planning that went into getting me there, I had no idea where to begin in my search. According to my GPS and map, I was more than a kilometer from my team's point of entry on the Syrian shore which was over a week ago. They could be in the mountains, in the city proper, still on the move anywhere in the governorate, escaping and evading, captured or dead.

Having my own SATCOM communications system with me on my Syrian vacation, I tried again to reach Steed and team to no avail. As I couldn't be more than a couple of clicks away from where they were in their last transmission, I was now fearing the worst. I didn't think it was a failure in *all* of their radios and on-the-move video equipment, and there should have at least been no triple canopy impediment as to the audio. Our commo equipment was battlefield- proven and not only dependable but resilient. I still had contact with Jim Bob and performed both a video and audio check

with him. "Hear you loud and clear, Scorpion," he said. "And I see what you're seeing there in those trees."

"Good, Jim Bob. Stay with me."

CHAPTER 26
Four Days Ago

Where was Angela Lovato? Atticus Steed stood with Stryker and Johnson looking down at the corpses of Rabah's two men. Blood which had spewed from their carotids was now seeping into the floorboards of the imam room. It was obvious that Lovato had killed them when they tried to rape her; then when Rabah came out of the room and saw that his other men had been taken down, he ducked back in and locked the door. After the team had broken down the door, the only live person in the room was the young man Rabah had called Mariq.

Steed walked to where Mariq was still cowering in a corner of the room. "Do you speak English?"

Mariq, eyes as large as shooter marbles, didn't respond. Steed asked again. Mariq shook his head, indicating he *didn't* understand.

Stryker said, "If this ain't a fine bucket of shit. One of our team is missing and the only person who knows what happened to her doesn't speak English."

Steed placed his hand on Stryker's shoulder. "We'll find her, Strike."

"Gotta be that that when Rabah escaped, he took her with him."

"Not so sure," Steed replied. "She would have yelled out when Rabah grabbed her. I'm thinking when he came out of the room, she went out the window. Then he went out himself after he locked the door. She's has to be out there somewhere hiding. Let's go."

"What do we do with the bozos we left in the other room?"

"Leave them. They won't wake up for hours and this Mariq kid won't be a threat."

But just at that moment, they heard the sound of sirens and tires skidding on the gravel at the front of the mosque. "Come on," Steed said. "We have to go out that same window."

After grabbing their own weapons from the sanctuary, called the haram, the three of them ran back into the room to the window and began snaking through the opening. When they had all dropped to the ground, they began running toward the woods behind the mosque. Smart uniforms exiting their vehicles would have immediately enveloped the mosque; however, their total focus was on the front door. Not even slowing down as they zig-zagged past prickly bushes, they ran around 200 yards to where a chunk of the mountain's foothills began. They were hoping Lovato was hiding someplace in those woods and spring out on them at some point. As she went out the window, those nearby woods would be the first place she went for concealment.

When they had reached an agglomeration of huge rocks on a bit of high ground, they stopped to catch their breath and to catch a glimpse of the mosque which was partly obscured because of the forest below. Men in uniform had now engulfed all of the grounds surrounding the mosque. Even though Steed saw a dozen or more, he knew there had to be twice as many combing the property that he could not see. Men were dead and severely beaten inside the mosque and both the military and Sabah's terrorists were not going to rest until they hunted down the assailants. Through the scope of his sniper rifle, Steed thought he recognized Rabah. Had he already joined in on the hunt? Steed could take the shot, but two things stopped him. First, he wasn't absolutely sure the head in his scope was that of Rabah. Secondly, even with a suppressor on his rifle, opening up the head and spraying blood and brain tissue over the people standing by could pinpoint the team's location. But then, as a few of them may have suspected, the team entered the woods after escaping the mosque. Through his scope, he saw men pointing toward the hillside where the team rested. Moments later, a squad-sized element began heading in their direction in a formation resembling an assault line.

"Okay, guys, we've got to go farther up. They'll be coming this way."

As it appeared there would soon be an all-out manhunt for them, Steed knew they would have to find a spot somewhere in those mountains to nest. A squad of searchers couldn't adequately cover such a vast area; therefore, the three of them would need to dig in somewhere they had good visibility of approaching bodies yet be entrenched so they would not be readily seen. Moving through what few trees they still had to conceal them, they came upon a cave positioned high up on the mountain where they had panoramic visibility. They could see anyone coming on three sides of the pinnacle.

Steed cautiously crawled into the cave, hoping a bear or mountain lion had not claimed it as its home. However, in finding something even more dangerous, a human arm suddenly swept around his neck, pulling him to the ground. Two seconds later, he felt the razor-edged blade of a knife against his neck. A woman's voice then shouted, "Don't resist, asshole! I'll slice you up like a ripe peach!"

Steed smiled. "Angel, it's me…Atticus."

She dropped her ka-bar and threw both arms around him. "Oh, God," she sputtered, fighting back her tears." You made it out of there. Can't tell you how happy that makes me."

Stryker and Johnson then entered the cave. Lovato transferred her hugs from Steed to them. "I thought we'd lost you," said Stryker. "Those men, did they…?"

"They didn't. I killed them before they had a chance to unbutton their pants. How did you all get away from there?"

Steed replied, "We overtook Rabah's men and when Rabah stuck his head out and saw us thrashing them, he ran back to the room and went out the window.

Apparently, you had jumped out the window before he did. The kid who was supposed to have his time with you we found crumpled up in a corner scared shitless."

"He was never a threat to me. As soon as he saw the two men on the floor with their blood spurting every which way, he started yelling for Rabah. I think he threw up all over himself."

"Anyway, I don't know how I would have avoided being captured if you hadn't come along. Now what do we do?"

"We stay inside here and watch for them," Steed replied. "The first head that pops out of those trees down there gets a bullet in it."

Johnson said, "The director must be going nuts wondering why we've disappeared from his radar."

Steed replied, "It's only been an hour or so since our commo equipment got smashed. But give it a day or so and he'll be *very* concerned. I guess this is as good a position as anywhere to sit. Maybe in a couple of days, the heat will be off us and we can go back down to civilization. We still have a venomous snake to kill."

As a few of Rabah's men were now making their cautious way up the slope toward the cave, Steed readied his rifle to take the first man out who crossed his established line of demarcation, which was about 150 meters from their position. If more than two or three made it past that line, the entire team would pick them off. Lovato had gotten her M4 back, thanks to Stryker who picked it up along with his weapon back at the mosque. Everyone had attached a suppressor to the business end of their weapons, except, of course,

Stryker, who carried the shotgun a close-encounter weapon. It would take out up to three men with one blast. Hopefully, the aggressors would never get that close. The suppressors not only muffled the sound of the rounds but made for better accuracy.

When three heads appeared out of the rocks below them, Steed figured the others went off on another tangent. He waited only seconds to be sure. As the approaching men continued on a determined climb in the direction of the bunker, it appeared they knew about the cave. Steed set up, chambered the first round of his 5 round magazine and fired three quick shots within 4 seconds that took off the tops of all three heads. Lovato, watching through field glasses, gasped as blood and brain matter splattered in the air. "Holy shit! You *are* good. McGowan said you were the best in the world; now I believe it."

"Just another day at the office," Steed replied, a slight smile forming on his lips. "The problem is, others will now be looking for *them*; when they find their bodies, they'll call for reinforcements and ultimately find *us*. We'll have to vacate."

"Well, every mountain has two sides," remarked Johnson. "I suggest we keep going to the top of this one and find a position on the reverse slope."

"You're right, Mickey. As soon as we see there's no one

coming after them, we go."

Steed again checked the mosque premises through his scope and saw there were no uniforms or terrorist types in proximity. Likely, everyone was on the search for them all over the trees below, the foothills of the mountain and even within the Tartus city limits.

Not seeing any more heads appearing below, he said, "Everybody grab your shit and go." Quickly, they exited the cave and began climbing what was left of the mountain behind them. As now they were completely out in the open and vulnerable to weapons fire, they jackrabbited up the slope to the apex. Steed stopped momentarily and scanned the 360 degrees with the field glasses, then continued down the reverse slope with the others on his heels. What was the south side of the mountain offered them more concealment thanks to a dense smattering of oaks and other trees. Unfortunately, what came with them were more spiny acacia and something Steed had seen in Africa…jacaratia, a thorny tree that can cut one to ribbons. But there was an upside to cutting their way through the razor-like shrubs and trees; the Syrians weren't going into the forest to find us. Until things cooled down, Steed said the team would make camp in some nice little nook.

Working their way cautiously through the devilish forest, Steed spotted such a place that lay by an inviting stream. Although they would have all the water they wanted to drink, they each only had one MRE left. Four

Americans trapped in a hostile environment, no communication, out of food, their contact dead, and the Syrian police, military and terrorist thugs hot on their trail, their situation couldn't be much worse. The good thing was, they were all in great shape and only Stryker had been slightly wounded.

Steed was at the point where they had to be thinking about abandoning the second part of their mission. Even if they successfully avoided their pursuers, they had no one to lead them to Rabah. They actually were in the same room with their target and it angered Steed that they were not in a position to kill him. Would he ever get another chance? He thought that if they could make it to the Syrian shore, they could somehow get their hands on a boat and get as deep into the Mediterranean as they could. But then as he knew Russia had made the deep water port of Tartus its strategic naval base, they would be picked up immediately as spies. Could they travel south and cross over into Lebanon, Steed wondered? It would be a rugged hike through mountainous terrain and the distance was over 100 miles. He was slap out of ideas.

The team camped for the night where they had stopped, eating their last MRE. Tomorrow, they would trek along the stream and let it carry them as far as it ran. They'd be off the roads and trails and hopefully not encounter anyone along the way. Along their path perhaps they would find fish life, berries, wild plants like eryngo and akkub, and bird eggs. There were also villages along streams just about anywhere in the world and Syria should be no different. The people would be poor but they'd have food. The team just had to make their day as they went along.

villages along streams just about anywhere in the world and Syria should be no different. The people would be poor but they'd have food. The team just had to make their day as they went along.

CHAPTER 27

The four of them had little sleep that first night, even though the music of the bubbling stream put them out early. Sounds of the night kept their eyes open, mainly owls calling one another and deer or other animals moving through the forest crunching twigs and branches, making them think they were of the human kind. However, twice the team came off their bedrolls, first when a swarm of biting ants invaded their site, and then around 0200 when they heard voices. But whoever was out there probably still looking for them, carried their search in another direction. And then there was that four A.M. shower that fortunately didn't last but a half hour.

When rays of the morning sun began filtering through the trees around 0730, the team gathered up gear and weapons to continue their trek along the stream.
Adding to their misery were the ant bite welts on every exposed part of their bodies. Unfortunately, nobody thought to pack hydrocortisone or calamine lotion in their rucks.

About mid-day, they encountered two peasant fishermen at a widened point in the stream. As the team had been carrying their weapons in a ready position, they lowered them to their sides as they passed by. Steed put up his hand to greet them and said, "Sabah alkhayr" which was "Good Morning." The fishermen said nothing but nodded in return. Their eyes, however, said, "Who the hell are you and what's with the guns?"

As it seemed they had been wandering aimlessly for several days along the stream. Steed was concerned that the others would get a case of the red-ass about his leadership, that he had no sense of vision as to how they could extricate themselves from their predicament. Along the way, he offered reassurances that something positive was going to happen; they just had to be patient. But the others knew full well that they were victims of circumstance and no one was at fault. They had survived several days of bad luck, and they had nowhere but *up* to go.

The second and third days of their trek by the waters, out of food for two of the days, they found berries and bananas along the way that farmers had begun cultivating in the governorate, caught a variety of fish which included red mullet and sardinella, and Steed brought down a deer they caught taking a drink ahead on the trail. Stryker suggested that Lovato gut the deer since she had become so good with a knife. Basically, their footslog those days had been nothing but a combination of a foraging for food to keep up their strength while trying to find their way to civilization. Steed knew they were going east away from the mountains,, and according to his map, out of the Tartus governorate.

It was at sunset on Day 5 when they approached a clearing and when two men in skull caps sprung out of a tree line with AK-47s. Steed and his team brought up their weapons ready to fire. However, everyone just stood glaring at one another without anyone making a move. One of the men with a full, graying beard finally stepped forward cautiously.

"You look English," he said.

"And you *speak* English," Steed replied.

"Who are you and why are you in our camp?" the man asked.

"Camp? What kind of camp? You don't look like government troops or ISIS."

"That is correct. We are neither. They are our enemy. We are the Syrian Democrat Force."

"We heard about you," Steed said. "Do we consider you friend or enemy?"

"As I don't know who you are, I cannot say. We are against the government and the Assad regime. And we despise ISIS."

"That means we're friends. And your name?" "I am

Hazzir."

"My name is Steed and these folks behind me are Johnson, Stryker and Lovato. Are you the commander of this group?"

"No. I am only a small unit leader. We have thirty men in this camp. There are other camps beginning maybe three hundred meters from here and fifteen total in this governorate. Our families live with us in these woods."

"Can you introduce us to your leader?"

"Yes. Put your weapons down by your side and follow me."

As the team made its way farther into the camp, it opened up to a rustic village with small shacks for houses and a community building. On the perimeter of the camp were posted about a dozen guards which would make up about thirty percent of the camp's male population. A few children who were running and playing in the center of the camp stopped to gaze at the strangers walking through their playground. Hazzir then stopped at the door to one of the buildings and called inside, "Najib, min fanlike akhruj! (Please come out)."

A few seconds later, a fifty-ish man with a salt-and-pepper beard and cold, black eyes appeared in the doorway. Hazzir then spoke to him in English. "Najib, we have visitors…Americans."

Najib looked the team over and said, "Why would Americans be in our village with guns?"
"Mr. Najib," Steed began, "We are on a mission."

"Again, why would people with weapons in their hands be on a mission in our village unless they intend to harm us?"

Steed replied, "We are not here to harm anyone in your camp. Our government sent us here to set up the destruction of the missile emplacements on the mountains."

"That was you?" He then smiled. "Then I must welcome you." He reached out his hand and Atticus took it.

"We verified the missiles were authentic and called back to our Navy to destroy them."

"That means you are very much on our side." But then he frowned. "The word about you has come to us. You were the people in Tartus who came to kill the bastard bin Rabah, but you were captured at the mosque. I know that you were not successful because he is still alive. His people and the Syrian police have been looking for you. You killed many of bin Sabah's men and they swear to end your lives. You must stay here because they are searching all around us. You will be safe here; they do not dare come into this camp or many of their men will be killed."

"We appreciate your hospitality but we have to find a way to get back to our Navy."

"Without first killing bin Rabah?"

"If we had the opportunity and knew how to find him, we would continue our mission, yes."

"We will help you do that. But first, where are my manners? You must be hungry. Come into my house and eat with us. My wife is a good cook."

"Thank you, Mr. Najib," responded Lovato. "I don't

mind telling you we're starved."

But then as soon as they began walking toward Najib, a sinewy figured stepped out from the doorway, sending a shockwave through the team. "And so here we all are. Hello team," greeted Bruce McGowan.

Lovato ran to him and threw her arms around him. "Bruce…I mean Director. How did you…?"

"You never know what will fall out of the sky these days. I didn't know whether you were captured, eaten by a grizzly or defected. So, I decided to come find you. What the hell happened to you?"

Steed shook his hand then jerked his head toward the door. "Come inside to watch us eat and we'll tell you a story."

Najib's wife put out a traditional Syrian spread: flatbread and meze for an appetizer, rabbit stew, kibbeh, mujaddara and baklava. Najib himself then broke out the wine. He said, holding up a glass, "This comes from the only vineyard in Syria, the Domaine de Bargylus.

Our wine heritage dates back 8,000 years. This is the best you will ever have.

As McGowan ate and listened intently, Steed filled him

in on every step of their experiences over the past week and a half. "You expended a lot of ammunition. Do you have any left?"

"Not much," Steed replied. "As we know, funeral arrangements in the Muslim world must take place immediately after the bodies are found, we kept them busy burying their dead to be sure no one was left to be on our trail."

"You were sent here to kill one man but ended up killing how many?"

"Lost count after the first dozen, Director." He then looked over at Angela. "Found out how sweet Ms. Lovato is with a ka-bar."

She smiled. "I worked in a butcher shop the summer between my junior and senior year in high school. I had blood on my hands early on in life. Maybe that was why I couldn't get a date with a guy and ended up joining the Army."

Stryker broke everyone up by clutching his throat. "If we ever go out, Lovato, I'll be sure to check your purse for a knife."

When Steed had completed telling the story of their plight, Najib changed the subject. "As it is your mission to kill bin Rabah, I must say it will not be easy. He is well-protected and moves around a lot. He is a powerful man and I believe even the president is afraid of him. There is a saying here, 'if you fear someone, make him your friend and ally so that you will live.' Bin Rabah will kill for the pleasure of it. If he likes you, you will be safe; but say something or do something not in his favor and either he or his men will end your life while he laughs. He thinks nothing but to kill someone, as you westerners say, without batting an eye. He is truly the most ruthless man in Syria."

"Why hasn't an adversary killed him?" Johnson asked.

"As I said, he is well-protected with men all around him at all times, even in the bedroom with his wife. Even if you do find where he is at some time, you will not get close to him."

"I have a rifle that can hit a target at over 1000 meters,"Steed said. "Give me the opportunity and his protection detail will be useless to him."

"Then perhaps I can help make it happen for you."

CHAPTER 28

When we had finished our dinner, the team gathered around me outside Najib's house and conveyed to me their gratitude for risking my life to come find them. My doing so turned what appeared to be a hopeless situation for getting out of Syria into sanguine optimism. I replied, "My friends, there are two focuses where it comes to leadership that I learned from the Army: mission and the welfare of those carrying it out. I suspected you were in trouble when I couldn't reach you.

I am elated to learn that it was because your radios were smashed. It was also a matter of self-preservation. I wasn't going to sleep until I found you. But actually, it was you who found me.

"We all owe these people who have taken us in. Normally, rebels against a government are nothing more than radical anarchists and killers whose agenda is to terrorize the innocent. In just two days, I have found the Democratic Forces to be good people who have because of their differences in political ideology been ravaged and terrorized by its own government. They have lost men, women and children by this Russian-backed administration. However, they have proven themselves against the Assad government and have been supported logistically by the U.S. government. They are not only going to help us locate a dangerous enemy but get us back to the shore where we can marry up with the Navy's Sixth Fleet.

"But all that being said, I am elated to finally see your faces again. Too bad about Quasim. Obviously, bin Rabah found him out."

That evening, Najib gathered the team around a fire pit and gave us a history of the Syrian Democratic Forces and a brother rebel group called the Free Syrian Army. They had been fighting a civil war with the Syrian government for over fifteen years. As Russia and Iran had been providing arms to the government, America's CIA had been arranging the procurement of arms from the U.S. Several battles had been fought through the years and rebel forces throughout had captured regional capitals to include Raqqa and Idlib. Unfortunately, the government had launched a number of Russian supported offenses against rebel strongholds that saw the death many and the annihilation of their villages.

However, as Najib's men were fierce fighters and he had obtained two cannons and a tank from Israel, government attacks had been repelled. "They don't even try to take us anymore," Najib said. "As you Americans sometimes say, 'they are chickenshit.'" We laughed at his expression.

"Not only have we fought the Syrian government, but the Islamic State has tried to infiltrate our camp many times. The ISIS are the dung of humanity. But it was good that when they attacked Raqqa in 2017, ISIS was destroyed with the help of our Kurdish-led Syrian Democratic Forces. Your Air Force assisted in defeating the ISIS force by bombing many of their positions.

"We insurgents are mostly controlled by the political opposition group called the Syrian Interim Government. There are many groups under the big umbrella such as the Syrian National Army and the Free Syrian militia. Now you see how…what is the word…complicated our country is. Many different armies and insurgent groups, ISIS and al-Qaeda terrorist groups, Kurdish YDP and the army of the Syrian government, all over the country. One does not know when he ventures out of the camp just who he will run into. But only one or two leave the camp at any time to bring back supplies. They will not have money to buy the supplies; unfortunately, they have to steal or raid stores in Tartus. If they are caught, they are immediately executed. But, through your agencies we also receive the supplies we need besides weapons and ammunition."

"You have a hard life as a people, Najib," I said, "and we are sorry that you do. But, we're glad our country continues to support your battle against this government anyway it can."

"But enough of this talk, Mr. McGowan. We will now drink more wine." He then gestured to his wife. "Music, Fatima. Bring Habab with the oud and Bratta with the drum. We will live the good life with music and wine." These were the kind of Muslims I liked…the drinking kind.

The following morning, Najib and I sat at his makeshift desk strategizing along with the team, sitting on the floor around us, as to how we could complete our mission to eliminate bin Rabah. Najib's young cousin, Yusuf Amir, was his pipeline to Tartus and the rest of the civilized governorate. Besides being his logistics and supply resource, he was in the know about happenings within the government's political and military systems. He actually had friends in the Syrian Army who sat at a hookah bar with him once a week to smoke flavored shisha. Yusuf liked the molasses brown sugar mix and often smoked it in the camp sending sweet, aromatic smoke throughout their tiny village. Najib sent for Yusuf to join them.

It was surprising as to how many of the men with whom we spoke had learned English. But there was a reason. Education was a huge part of daily life in the camp. As the population was ethnically-mixed and their village law was not sharia, schooling was open to everyone including girls. The teacher had studied at an American school in Lebanon and taught English to everyone who wanted to learn. Knowing that their guests were Americans, whenever we were in proximity of anyone, he or she spoke English as a courtesy. And I was thinking…I couldn't have fallen out of the sky near any more inviting place than this Democratic Forces village. Under usual circumstances, McGowan's Law, just like Murphy's Law, would have found me in some jihadist detention camp.

Yusuf was a twenty-something kid with a peach fuzz beard who apparently had his Syrian Army friends hoodwinked. Although they didn't know where he lived, he pretended to be a resident of a neighboring town to Tartus called Kinsabba which was large enough where people wouldn't necessarily know everyone in the small city. He told his friends he was a farmer, which was not exactly a lie. He worked the fields daily near his camp. Yusuf was Najib's spy who gathered information as to what was occurring not only in Tartus but on the political and military scenes. His friends were quite liberal and free-spoken in their table conversation.

"Yusuf," Najib began. "This is our guest Bruce McGowan and these are his friends, Johnson, Steed and Lady Lovato."

Yusuf bowed and said, "I am pleased to know you."

"They are interested in locating Abboud bin Rabah."

"Do you have business with him?" Yusuf asked.

I answered, "The business we have with him is of the lethal kind, Yusuf."

"I do not understand the word 'lethal.' I am sorry to ask."

"And I'm sorry I didn't instead use the word deadly. We are here to kill bin Rabah."

His eyes widened. "You want to kill him?"

"We want very much. He has been planning to attack American military bases with missiles. We destroyed the missiles but to keep him from planning to involve Yemen to fire their missiles, we must find him and kill him. Do you know how to find him?"

"I believe so. He is in the building with the Syrian Army commander in Tartus."

"So, you're telling me the head of the Islamic State Levant in Syria is headquartered with the Syrian army commander?"

"Yes, I believe so." He smiled. "You Americans use the term 'strange bedfellows.' That is what our teacher has told us about them in our class on politics."

"I think I like your teacher," I said.

"When will you be meeting again with the Syrian soldiers?"

"Tomorrow."

"Can you confirm where bin Rabah will be this week? Or would they know?"

"I think they will know. They do not like him because he is ISIS. Many in the army hate the ISIS, but they have been told to work with them and to share information. The ISIS together with the military are against our people and all who want freedom to choose. There have been many fights between them. Both bin Rabah and Commander Aamara of the military have ordered their people to not fight each other; if they do, they will be executed as examples."

"So then you believe your smoking friends will freely give you real-time information on Rabah."

"I will, as you say, pump them for information. Maybe I can find out where he lives and where he goes. I do not like him and his being dead will not make me sad."

I turned to Najib. "I have an idea. I noticed you have four or five Toyota trucks in your camp, and I have seen on the news where nearly every other truck in Syrian cities have hooded and armed passengers in them. Could our team use one of them? We would dress like al-Qaeda and ISIS with hoods and similar clothing and place ourselves in Tartus on the truck at some position to set up to kill Rabah either where he works or lives. No one should be able to tell whether we are ISIS or insurgents."

"I like the idea, Mr. McGowan. Our men have done the very same thing on occasion and have not been resisted by the authorities. We can provide a truck for you. We also have several hooded masks for you to wear."

"Good. When Yusuf has the information we are looking for, we'll go into Tartus."

That afternoon we all took showers where the camp had set up several 55 gallon drums full of spring water that were rigged above a wooden frame. We agreed it was the most refreshing experience we had had in days, especially the four of them who had been in the wild for well over a week. A lovely young woman from the village washed our clothes while we waited in burlap sacks for her to finish and then dry them on a clothes line. Food, showers and a place to sleep, we were being spoiled. I knew, however, in a couple of days we would leave for Tartus and things could get rough. It all depended on young Yusuf who would return with the information we needed.

CHAPTER 29

I had made two calls via my communications boys back at Terminus warehouse to mother hen Ben Marshall beginning with the very hour my boots had touched down on Syrian soil, the second after my team and I found each other in the rebel village. He of course was elated that I had made my jump into a hostile land without breaking anything or being captured, beaten or killed. Then when I made that second call that I had found Steed and team and that we were all being treated royally, his lungs expelled a sigh of relief.

But there was a third call that my boys set up that went to Greenbrier County, West Virginia. I had to handle that one delicately. My dialogue with Adriana had to give her no hint that I had physically joined the team's mission in Syria.

"I tried calling you," she said, "but I kept getting a crazy signal and message that the party I was trying to reach was not available." I would have to go into my 'white lie' routine to continue our conversation.

"I was probably somewhere out of cell range or maybe my service was down." And that of course was the whitewashed truth.

"Maria is awfully worried about her man. Have you been in contact with him?"

"Yes. The team has been taken in by a bunch of friendlies in a small village while they complete their Intel mission. Everyone is safe and sound."

"Explain to me again what your people are doing over there?"

"Uh, you know how this business works. We are talking on a non-secure line and I can't discuss anything."

"Oh, you guys and your sneaky Pete stuff. But are you living okay as a bachelor?"

"My dear, it's never okay without you."

"Well, maybe Maria and I will just drive up there this weekend. I need to see *my* man."

"Nah, as much as I'm missing you, I'm still following my team 24/7 and there wouldn't be any time for us to spend together."

"At least I can whisper sweet nothings to you over the phone."

"And I love those sweet nothings. They'll have to do until I'm able to ravage your sweet body."

"That won't be any too soon for me."

"Let me call *you* from here on. You might call when I'm dealing with what's going on with the team, which is almost always."

"Okay, but call me as often as you have a moment."

"I promise. Well, I guess I need to go. You be safe and enjoy your days at the homestead."

"I will. Bye, Skippy. Kiss, kiss."

"Bang, bang."

There. That wasn't too dishonest of me. I never said I wasn't in D.C. and I was constantly in communication with the team. I thought it went well without telling an out-n-out lie.

Mid-afternoon the next day, Najib's cousin returned from Tartus with some fairly concrete information. According to his friends, Bin Rabah spent the days he was not with his fellow terrorist pricks in their training camp at the army headquarters. Yusuf not only had the address of the headquarters building in the west end of Tartus but the location of his camp in the foothills to the north. Both, of course, were well-fortified.

Yusuf sat with me at Najib's desk and wrote directions on two pieces of paper along with sketches of streets and buildings. The second paper reflected the training camp which he said was about 25 kilometers from Tartus into the desert. The only problem with attempting the takedown of bin Rabah there was that any vehicle approaching the compound would be spotted two miles away and fired upon before it reached the gate. Steed and I sat pondering how and where we could get into position to kill bin Rabah. Wherever it was, it was not going to be an easy task. "Tomorrow," I said, "we go to Tartus on a recon."

We had decided to don ISIS and al-Qaeda-looking attire complete with masks rather than looking and acting like tourists which Syria was still allowing in.
Tourists had visas and passports. As I understood it, the Syrian police and military were randomly stopping people who did not look and dress like them to check identifications. Had we pretended to be tourists, especially when the authorities and ISIS thugs were on

the hunt for the Americans who killed their men, no doubt we would be stopped. I doubted people in positions of authority would dare accost a truck-load of ISIS thugs for fear of their lives.

The village of rebels reminded me of my experience nearly a half century ago when I lived with Montagnard tribes in Vietnam. Najib's people didn't look like the 'yards, as we called them, nor were they as primitive as them, but they worked all day sustaining their village then partied hearty in the dark. Nearly every night it was song, dance and wine around the fire pit. Children gleefully joined in on the song and dance, taking their minds off school, poverty and the constant threat of war. It was living proof that people who had little in life can be as happy as the wealthy…maybe even more.

At daybreak, we rose, put on our black ops clothing, black face masks and skull caps, piled in the small Toyota truck Najib had readied, checked the fuel gauge, and pulled through the village to the west perimeter. Najib had mounted an ISIS Levant flag on the truck's bed for effect. A couple of the perimeter guards waved at us as we passed them. There were also outer perimeter guards two hundred feet in the bush who raised a hand at us as we went by. They were the early warning force. The narrow dirt road continued for about a mile until it intersected with the M5 motorway that connected Damascus and Tartus. Tartus was four miles further to our west.

As we traveled along the M5, we passed civilians who turned their heads away, obviously wanting nothing to do with the ISIS rat patrol. However, we showed them we were a gaggle of good rats, not firing our guns in the air or spitting on them. We did see a couple other trucks containing people who looked like us; of course they were the real McCoys. But they threw their hands up to greet us anyway since we were their cousins…American cousins that is.

As none of us had actually been deep into the city of Tartus, we found it to be an attractive, Middle Eastern town of about a half-million residence with markets, resorts, cultural centers, and stately, ornate orthodox churches, many of which were now museums or businesses, considering Syria had greatly discouraged the worship of the Christian faith. We did see people who looked like tourists with cameras, maps and ice cream cones. The Port of Tartus looked as though it could be in the Boston Harbor or Annapolis, with a few prestigious yachts and other skiffs alongside the more common-looking 18 footers.

However, we also saw signs of terrorism in the city. What used to be a bus station was now a pile of rubble. It was likely the same building that suffered a suicide bombing that I remember reading about in 2016; somewhere around 50 people were killed in the attack the responsibility of which was claimed by ISIL. I imagined the Syrians didn't rebuild it to remind the people that even though the government had been allied with the ISIS and Levant assholes as of late, they should fear them and refrain from pissing them off. After all, they were now an integral part of their community.

When Steed turned down Jabalna Street, looming ahead was the building Yusuf described as the government headquarters shared with bin Rabah. Obviously, this was not going to be the place to knock him off. We not only spotted a half dozen government-type goons standing guard at the entrance to the complex but Mickey Johnson pointed out men with sniper rifles on the rooftops of adjacent buildings. We didn't even slow down as we passed by, but we did wave at the security team at the entrance.

Steed continued on through the city, which that day became nothing more than a sight-seeing excursion, until we reached the road that led to bin Sabah's training camp. Yusuf had sketched out the route in minute detail making the camp easy to locate. The road took us about ten miles into the desert where the temperature began to soar. Although we couldn't see bin Sabah's camp from the road, according to the map, it should have been another two to three miles ahead of us. I then told Steed to pull off onto a dirt road that looked as though it culminated onto some high ground. Parking the truck on higher elevation should give us a panoramic view of the camp or of vehicles entering and exiting. Luck would go either way for us. It might not be a day when

Rabah would be in his camp at all; and then if there were several vehicles coming and going, how would we know if he was inside any of them?

When we reached the highest point of the terrain just off the road, we exited the truck and took positions on a series of boulders that did indeed give us a good vantage point for what looked like five to seven miles. And there we saw it, an estimated two-and-a half miles to our west, a sprawling encampment with a half dozen buildings and several acres of desert land contained within high fencing. Several trucks and full-size cars were parked near the larger of the buildings. With our powerful field glasses and through Steed's and my sniper scopes, we secured close-up views of three men standing and talking. Although we couldn't make out their facial features all that clearly, we see that they had beards and were wearing both plain and houndstooth-patterned keffiyehs.

From the late morning until after 1600 hours, we sat boiling in the 110-degree desert sun, waiting and watching what could be a fruitless surveillance. We did find a tarp in the truck's bed that we draped over stakes constructed of tree branches, then took turns sitting under the makeshift tent while one of us kept the field glasses glued on the camp. It was 1620 hours when Lovato spied movement within the compound, specifically three black sedans leaving the front gate. "Rise and shine, boys. They're on the move."

I took over the binoculars and took a look. "Okay, folks, this has to be bin Rabah's entourage. Common soldiers of Allah wouldn't be driving these high-end vehicles. He's in one of them."

While watching them moving along the road, I contacted one of my kids back at the warehouse. "Jim Bob, patch me through to the 6th Fleet operations. I need a UAV."

"Roger, Scorpion. Give me a couple." "Make it quicker,

kid."

After 70 seconds, I heard from the Navy. "This is Interceptor 64, how can I help?"

"Interceptor, need an Unmanned Aerial Vehicle. Three targets, black sedans, Highway M5, moving east toward Tartus currently in grid 874359."

"Roger, identify yourself."

"This is Scorpion 6"

"Do you have SOI/SSI?"

"Yes."
"Authenticate Bravo Tango Sierra Juliet."

"One moment." I pulled from my shirt pocket my

Security Office Identifier (SOI). "I authenticate Alpha Romeo Hotel Charlie."

"Do you want all targets neutralized?" "All targets," I replied.

"Bird in the air."

As the three vehicles approached the intersection where we turned off the road, one after the other suddenly exploded, a second apart, flipping end over end and side over side. "Beautiful!" Lovato exclaimed. The Reaper had sent three perfectly fired AGM-114 Hellfire missiles into the trunks of bin Rahab's Cadillacs.

"Bingo, Interceptor. Nice job."

"Glad to help, Scorpion. Have a nice day."

"Plan to. However, you just ruined the *target's* day."

"It's what we do. Out." Steed then remarked, "Rabah's got to be in one of them."

"My money's on the middle sedan," Stryker said. "We'll see," I added. "Let's go take a look."

From our observation point, we drove back down the slope and stopped behind the last vehicle which was upside down. "Be ready to finish the job if there are any survivors," I said, bringing my rifle up to ready.

But in checking the sedans, there were none. There were two occupants in each car, bodies horribly mangled and bleeding, "Okay, team. You were up close and personal with bin Rabah. Which one is he?"

The four of them checked the faces of the dead and then Steed shook his head. "As I would recognize him alive *or* dead, he's not one of them."

"I agree," said Lovato. "He's not in any of these cars."

But then behind us coming at a high rate of speed was a black SUV. "Of course," I said. "These were decoys.

Into the ditch, everyone!"

No sooner had I spit the words from my mouth, the SUV was upon us. From the front and back left side passenger windows came a spray of AK-47 rounds, pinging and ricocheting off rocks at the edge of the ditch. Without my giving the command, as the SUV passed by us, we began peppering the front and side of the vehicle with both automatic and rifle fire. Realizing they were out-gunned, they continued on past, the driver kicking in his afterburner. One of our rounds must have hit the radiator as their car began spewing white smoke.

Fortunately, as our Toyota had not been hit by their rounds, we jumped in the truck and gave pursuit.

Although the vehicle was well ahead of us, we were still able to see the smoke. Their engine obviously kept churning in spite of the radiator damage, but I could tell it was slowing; we were getting closer to the smoke. "Stay back, Atticus," I said. "I want them to think they lost us." However, another car pulled out from a side road in front of us which created a visible buffer between us and the SUV. I was hoping whoever was in the wounded SUV would see the car behind them and not our truck. Still, even though we were completely shielded from view, we could see that their SUV was now chugging smoke like a steam engine. The oppressive air temperature wasn't helping them. It would not be long and their engine would quit on them.

But as luck would have it, just before reaching the city limits of Tartus, the SUV turned off the road into a a compound of sorts where the gate automatically opened. "Has to be bin Rabah's place. He's inside the vehicle." As the vehicle was now well within the compound, the vehicle's occupants could not see us go by on the road. However, as we passed by, we saw three armed guards on the gate. I was 99 percent sure it was bin Rabah's home.

CHAPTER 30

We parked our truck in an area behind a large building about two blocks down from the house where we saw the smoking Cadillac pull into the gated gated driveway. As I enjoyed watching the three vehicles snap, crackle and pop on the road courtesy of the Navy drone, I thought "why not." Why not order another Hellfire missile, this time down on the house. Even though the walled complex may not have belonged to bin Rabah, somebody living there, who had come out of the ISIS training camp, was a bad dude. However, our mission was to take down bin Rabah and I wasn't going to pass up the opportunity to nail him where he slept. Still, I didn't want our government to waste over a hundred grand on a small potatoes subordinate who might have been the person in the vehicle we shot up. I had to know.

But, we would wait until dark to do *anything*. However, Steed and I took a stroll back in the direction of the heavily-guarded house and saw that there were now four men on the gate, two on the outside and two inside. We agreed that from the security, the surrounding walls and the lighted grounds where the house sat toward the back of the compound, it had to belong to either bin Rabah or some muckety-muck high up on the food chain.

Across the street from the compound was a three-story building that appeared to contain offices. Although I couldn't determine from the sign on the front of the building the type of business it was, it looked like it belonged to the Syrian government. The Hawk of Quraish, which is on the Syrian flag, was embossed on the side of the building. Since the time was now after 1900 hours, there were no lights glowing on the inside.

As I wanted to secure a higher view of the inside of the compound, I needed to find a way to the roof of the building. To avoid detection, however, we slipped along the side of the building until we reached the rear. Immediately, we saw our way up…a pull-down fire escape which went to an upper window. After pulling it down and ascending to the window, one at a time, we shinnied up a close-by downspout that led to the roof. Once on the roof we walked toward the front of the building immediately acquiring the view we were looking for. It was the perfect perch for a sniper.

Through his scope, Steed zoomed in on several figures standing at the doorway of the house. "Got three subjects," he said. "One is a bearded man who's bent down to two small children, a boy and a girl. The girl is clinging to his leg and crying. But wait, the man's standing up. Yeah, it's him. Even at this distance, I recognize his face. Bin Rabah."

I nodded. "This leaves out the option of calling in Reaper. I don't kill children. That's all we need to see tonight. We'll come back at first light and set up."

"I've got a clean shot, Bruce."

I let out a sigh. "Not in front of his kids. Tomorrow."

Since it had been hours since we had fed our faces with the stuffed grape leaves and falafels that Najib's wife packed for us, we were considerably hungry. We also needed to use a johnny house somewhere and get a good night's sleep. It took about forty minutes to return to the camp. Per our pre-arranged signal and to avoid getting shot up by our rebel friends, Steed stopped near the outer perimeter and flashed our headlights three times. We would strategize the remainder of the evening, turn in, and then leave around 0500 to put our plan into action.

At 0430, I rousted the team. After a breakfast of labneh, which was a kind of yogurt, boiled eggs, and pita with fig jam, washed down with the camp's bitter coffee, we threw on our ISIS-looking attire and departed for Tartus. Parking behind the same building as the evening before, we checked our weapons and walked the two blocks to the rear of the office building. From there, we split up. Unfortunately, I had the only radio, given that bin Rabah's men had smashed each of theirs, so we had to rely on our pre-conceived plan and our watches to carry them out.

My only concern with the plan we discussed was with the children. If there was a way we could catch bin Rabah apart from his family, it's the way I wanted it to go down. Unfortunately, in past missions, collateral damage could not be avoided; innocents had often been killed along with the target. However, if I had adequate forethought in a mission, I had every chance to avoid killing the innocent. I've been considered by others as being ruthless, but I'm not heartless. If our plan worked this day, everything would go down clean.

I positioned Steed on the roof of the building where we set up the previous night's recon. Stryker, Johnson, Lovato and I planted ourselves in the bushes and shrubs to either side of the gate. There were three guards at the gate, all inside now, with the fourth roving the compound. Although there was still no signs of daylight, the courtyard outside the house was still lit up. And so we waited. There should soon be a vehicle leaving or entering. If bin Rabah appeared outside his front door, Steed would nail him. We wouldn't wait for him to step into his car. If a vehicle came *into* the the compound through the automatic gate, we would go through behind it, kill the guards and rush the house.

At 0817 hours, the latter occurred. A rather common-looking car, maybe a Buick, approached the gate. As it did not automatically open, one of the guards did so, stepped up to the driver's door and took a piece of paper. Seconds later, he waved the car in. That's when I yelled "Go!"

Johnson cut down the same guard with his AA12 shotgun before he could turn back toward the inside. The powerful blast blew his body ten feet further in. The two guards inside brought up their AKs to fire, but we being too quick and aggressive, dropped them with a hail of gunfire. The roving guard, which we did not readily see, fired an automatic burst from his position that struck the windshield of the approaching Buick which had been shielding us to this point. The vehicle then trailed off to the right, striking a pole which bore the Syrian flag. Before the guard was able to fire again, I saw the side of his head explode.
Steed.

As we rushed the house, three more men with guns came out from a side door. Lovato cut one down as Steed planted bullets in the other two from his position. Finding the front door locked, big-shouldered Mike Johnson barreled through it, knocking it off its hinges. The rest of us followed in. Checking each room at the front of the house, we yelled "clear" when no one was discovered.

From the upstairs we heard a man's voice shouting and children screaming. As we carefully ascended the staircase, guns at the ready, A door on the right at the top of the stairs suddenly opened and a spray of automatic fire danced across the wall. I fired three rounds through the open doorway with my .45 and heard a thump on the floor. Looking inside the room, I found the freshly retired body of yet another of the family's house guards.

As I no longer heard the man's or children's voices and we still had a half dozen rooms to check, the four of us crept silently along the hallway, two on each side, looking into all the rooms until we found a back stairway that led to the outside. I figured bin Rabah had taken the children out of the house with him. After we had hustled down the steps and flung open the door, we saw three figures huddled together at the base of a large oak…a woman and the two children. The small back yard was well-contained within the walls of the compound. There was no way he could have gotten over 12 foot walls. "Bin Rabah couldn't have gone far," I said "Spread out. Strike, you and Mike go around front. First, look for a spider hole or trap door that might lead to a tunnel. Angela, you and I are going back up to make another sweep of the inside."

It was possible we missed something…a false wall leading to a hidden room, a fake bookcase that can hold the body of a person, or on the first level, a door under a floor rug. We had already determined there was no basement or attic. At least we could find no door to them. Obviously, bin Rabah had sent his family down the staircase to the back yard, counting on us not killing them, and gone into hiding elsewhere. We had to find that 'elsewhere.'

Something I found that we did miss was a balcony off what was likely his master bedroom, the glass of which was covered by a floor to ceiling drape. When I threw back the drape and opened the French doors, Lovato stepped out first. All we found was two chairs and a large storage box. It was when Lovato opened the lid, we immediately discovered her mistake in not first pointing her rifle into the inside. Staring at her was the muzzle of an AK-47 pointed at her head.

Bin Rabah stood up, keeping his gun within inches of her nose. He had us. All he needed to do was pull the trigger. "And so, American bitch, you have come here again to kill me. And you have brought someone different. You will drop your weapons." Because his rifle could go off at any time putting a bullet in Lovato's head, I dropped my Remington and told Angela to do the same.

I then glared at him and said, "As I am not an uncaring man, bin Rabah, I will assure that your family does not see your body when we put a bullet in your brain."

He then laughed. "You are either very stupid or do not understand this moment. I will be pulling this trigger and sending this whore to hell. Then I will do the same with you."

"Before you do that, dick head, I want you to turn your face toward the building across the street as it will be the last thing you will ever see."

He turned toward the building, then laughed again. "Yes, I am sure you are stupid."

"And I am sure you are dead." I then brought my hand up.

A second later, the left side of Abboud bin Rabah's head came apart, his blood, pieces of skull and brain matter splattering Lovato's face and shirt.

"Thank you, Mr. Steed," I said.

"Shit!" Lovato exclaimed. "And yuck."

Looking down, I saw that Stryker and Johnson were still searching the yard below us. I called to them. "You can give it up now, boys. Target is dead. Come on up to the second floor."

The two of them grinned, gave each other high fives and started walking through where the front door used to be. Obviously, there were no more goons on the premises or we would have been accosted.

Lovato went to the upstairs lavatory and washed bin Rabah's head off of her face and hair. It was because she kept vomiting, she took more than ten minutes to do so. Coming out with a bloodied towel on her head, she said, "Steed owes me big time for this."

"No, Angel. It's *you* that owes *him*. We all do."

CHAPTER 31

Steed joined us in the master bedroom where Mike Johnson and I had pulled bin Rabah's body. Checking out his handiwork, he said, "Damn, the bullet only took of the side of his skull. I must be losing my touch; I was aiming between his eyes."

"Yeah, it's not like you, Atticus," I replied sardonically. "But, in fairness, he could have moved his head a little after you pulled the trigger."

"Don't try to cheer me up, Bruce. I think I need a little more time at the range."

"While you're brooding about your kill, help me wrap his body up in that rug.

We'll cart him out of here and bury him back at the camp. Angela, go down and sit with his wife and kids to keep them occupied while we carry him out. Tell her anything…such as we're still looking for him but he got away."

After we had rolled bin Rabah up inside the large rug and Lovato went down the back stairs, the four of us carried the body to our truck. Minutes later she joined us. "I don't know if the woman believed me but it doesn't matter. It's good she and the children didn't see him wearing half a head. You did right with them, Director. Under all that fierce brutality, I see a caring heart."

"You'd do the same, Lovato. You all would."

Obviously, the Syrian police and military had been informed about the gunshots at the bin Rabah compound as they came storming through the still open gate to move in on the house. Even though we were a block away still behind the large building, police and military vehicles had cordoned off the street, impeding our escape. Although we were trapped, they hadn't see our vehicle. Just in case they got smart and began searching the area block by block, Steed pulled the Toyota out of the back lot of the business and into the woods behind it. We were going to be there a while.

It was just before 1500 hours when we were finally on the road again back to the rebel camp. The authorities had started pulling out only minutes before. Now, every swinging Richard in the Syrian military, police, and ISIS organization would be on our trail. I was sure nobody was buying our cover now, so it didn't matter whether we were impersonating ISIS with our head covers and full facial masks or not. We just floored our truck's accelerator and beat it as fast as we could to the camp.

We still had about five miles to go to our turnoff when we saw coming from the opposite direction an ancient Russian GAZ-66 troop carrier loaded with Syrian military. Were they looking for us? It didn't take us long to realize that they *were*. Once they passed us, they began turning around. Through my field glasses, I saw that the GAZ was equipped with a DshK large caliber machine gun similar to the American Army 50 cal. It had been years since I had seen one of them.

I figured our Toyota truck could outrun the bulky GAZ, but we sure as hell couldn't outrun its big caliber weapon. And as soon as I thought that, the gunner fired a single round over our heads as a warning to stop. Maybe the vintage troop carrier which dated back to the Korean War didn't have a horn. But it got *my* attention.

I figured the next round may be a multi round burst and not a warning shot. "Duck into the trees any place

you can. Atticus. We're not that far from the camp and anyway, we can squeeze through a lot of trees that the truck can't. Anyway, for national interest reasons, I didn't want to get into a firefight with the Syrian regular army. Steed found a firebreak and swiftly turned into it. At the same time, we heard the slow rat-tat-tat of the

DshK, it's rounds ricocheting through the trees, coming dangerously close to the truck. At a point when both front fenders of the Toyota scraped trees on either side, I knew the GAZ couldn't continue following us.

However, its gun began spraying bullets at a cyclic rate of fire that reverberated throughout the forest, lasting more than 30 seconds. I think we pissed them off.

Steed continued zig-zagging around trees, both vertical and fallen, until we came to a creek. I thought it might be the same stream that continued west into the rebel camp. As the water was only a couple of feet deep, I told Steed to throw the shifter into 4 wheel drive and press on. If it was not the same stream, at least we were traveling in the same direction as the camp; and since it was a hot, steamy day, the water would be refreshing.

After a few minutes, it appeared we had lost the GAZ. Unless its occupants disembarked and began tearing through the woods to try finding us, we were done with them.

I was right about the stream. It led to the road where the team had encountered Hazzir, the outer perimeter guard. I was wrong, however, that we were done with the Syrian army troops. No sooner had we traveled through the intersection of the main road and the trail to the rebel camp, the GAZ pulled across the road in front of us. Out of one side of the vehicle were six troops with automatic weapons trained on us. When Steed brought the Toyota to a stop and tried to back out, three more soldiers came out of the woods behind us.

One man stood among the others in the large bed of the GAZ and addressed us. "You will drop your weapons, get out of your truck and be on your knees. Now!"

Well they had us. Yet another hiccup in our final mission which was to get the hell out of their damn country. We did as ordered. The five of us dropped to our knees beside our truck. The man in charge then stepped down off the GAZ and approached us. Standing over us, he lit a cigarette and formed a devilish grin. "So, you are not ISIS, you are not al-Qaeda, you are not Syrian. You are the Americans we have been looking for…the killers of our men and our friends. And I suspect under that rug where a pair of feet are hanging out is the body of Abboud bin Rabah, who you have also killed."

"And you are who?" I asked.

"I am Commander Aamara of this governorate. The man in the bed of your truck was my friend. He may have been ISIS but we had the same purpose; we both hate the United States."

"So you were in with him in the plan to fire missiles at our American bases," I said.

He smiled and took a drag of his cigarette. "To kill many of the American military."

"I must say we enjoyed spoiling your plan, Commander."

"I want you to watch something, American. It will also be your destiny before this day is over. Look to where I am pointing and you will see two men also on their knees. Behind them are two more men who belong to me. When I drop my cigarette into the sand, my men will put bullets in the two men's heads. They are enemies of the Syrian government just as you are. They are what you call rebels and they are from the camp just over a kilometer from here."

We looked to where he was pointing and saw that one

of the men was Hazzir. The other I recognized but didn't know his name.

"Don't do this, Aamara. I ask you to show them mercy."

"I do not have mercy on enemies of the state. Now you must watch." He then tossed his cigarette on the ground and crushed it with his boot.

None of us looked when the pistols fired. But seconds later I turned my head and saw Najib's men face down on the ground. "You're a filthy, murderous bastard, Aamara. You will rot in hell."

He laughed. "If that is the case, I will see you there. But it will be a long time because this is *your* day to go."

"Then I'll ask you one thing before I die. The others with me, let them go. I am their leader and planned everything. They were only following my instructions."

He shook his head. "They all have blood on their hands. Like you, they are infidels, and under our law, we can kill you just because you are breathing…which will not be for long. Is there anything you wish to say before you die?"

"Yes…to my people,"

"Then do it. Your time is up."

"Get down!" I yelled. The five of us fell forward onto the ground and practically buried ourselves in the prone position. We all saw them. Coming out of the trees, like a straight-line wind, Najib and twenty or so of his men opened up on our captors. Commander Aamara was the first to go down. His men who had their backs to the attackers didn't have a chance to react. In less than ten

seconds, ten Syrian soldiers lay dead.

I stood and walked toward Najib. "How did you…?"

"My people heard the big truck and another of our outer guards saw them. The soldiers had never gotten this close before to our camp as they were much afraid of us. We believed they had come for us and made ready to defend our home. Then we heard the shooting."

"I'm sorry, Najib. They killed Hazzir and one other."

Najib looked to where his men lay, their blood spilling into the sand. He then fell to his knees and began wailing what could have been a prayer. His cry was that of a wild animal. A moment later he erected himself, wiped his eyes and said, "We must bury the dead now. All of them. They may be our enemy but it is our religion that they must be buried on the same day before the sun sets. I will ask that you place their bodies in the truck bed and we will bury them in our village."

I nodded. "Mickey, you and Strike do as he asks."

Najib's men took just over an hour to bury the Syrian troops but said nothing over their graves. As it was getting late, Hazzir and Tanook, Najib's other sentry, were to be buried before dark as well. Words *would* be said over them.

There was no music and dance in the village that night. The mood was somber and tearful. Just as people do in America, sev eral women put together meals and took them to Hazzir's widow. Tanook was not married and lived alone. We sat with Nabob and his family talking for a few minutes and then went down to the creek to do nothing but listen to it babble over the rocks. Somewhere out in the woods the sad song of what sounded like a lyrebird added to our mood.
Thirteen men laid in their graves that evening. At least one of them deserved it. He was our mission. But I'm sure most of Aamara's men were not evil, abhorrent people…they were just following orders. And I hated they had families to whom they would not be returning that day. It was not us who killed them, but they had to die or we *would* have.

However, it was not all doom and gloom with us as we were pleased our mission and been accomplished. The missiles had been destroyed and the man who planned to deploy them to kill American service men and women had lost his head over the deal. It reminded me that I needed to Ben Marshall; he and the vice president needed to know.

And they needed to get us back home.

CHAPTER 32

Najib's cousin, Yusuf, who had been working part-time as a night security guard for a chemical factory in Tartus returned from the city the next morning with the news that not only one of their prominent residents was thought to have been killed in his home but the governorate commander and members of his elite special operations unit were missing. There was talk that either the rebel opposition force or the group of suspected terrorists who had somehow landed on their shore and earlier destroyed their missile defense locations was responsible. Everyone was asked to be on the lookout for four or five people dressed as members of the Islamic State who had been seen on a number of occasions in and around the city of Tartus.

"Hmm," I said to the team. "Do you think they're talking about us?"

Steed replied, "Until we're out of this place, maybe we should not go anywhere out of the village as a team and certainly not wearing full-face masks."

"I fully agree, Atticus."

Lovato piped in. "Yes, get us home, Director."

A few minutes later, I tried getting my boys back at the warehouse on my Sat (satellite) phone but found I had no coverage. Strange that I didn't since shortly after I parachuted down a few days ago, and then found the camp, I had *no* commo issues. Maybe the satellite was being blocked. We were deep in the forest and had mountains as a backdrop. I'd have to take the truck on the road toward Tartus to see if I could get service.

We had a tasty lunch of Shawarma and Fattoush prepared by Najib's wife and then I donned a gray ghutra to cover my head which is what many of the Arabs wear. I then borrowed a pair of loose-fitting sirwah pants and a plain white shirt from Yusuf, who was about my size and slid onto the driver's seat of the Toyota. I carried with me a borrowed AK-47 I took off one of the dead soldiers. He was no longer using it.

I checked my Sat phone once again, finding still no coverage. I then cranked the Toyota and began moving out of the camp.

Passing by one of the perimeter guards who had taken Hazzir's place, I was still seeing Hazzir's face in my brain. In short order I was on the main road to Tartus. I was not going to go too far outside the village, but it needed to be a location where there was no triple canopy jungle. However, when I was approximately two miles from the city's limits, the Sat phone lit up.

Finding a pull-off area just ahead, I parked the truck out of sight of the road behind an abandoned, dilapidated building that looked like it was once a church. It was. Propped up against a tree in the yard was a well-weathered wooden sign that read Tartus Greek Orthodox House of the Virgin Mary. One of the Christian churches had gone by the wayside under pressure of the Syrian government since Assad came into power.

I first tried my boys back at the warehouse but there was no answer. But as it was 0500 their time, were they up and on the move? I let it ring eight, ten, twelve times. No one picked up. Finally, after twenty minutes of trying, Jim Bob picked up.

"Boss," he answered. "We wondered when we would hear from you again."

"Did I wake you?" I asked him.

"Uh, not really. I…uh. Okay, you did. It's five o'clock in the morning."

"And one of you three are always supposed to be monitoring. I found that we no longer have cam commo, but we still have real-time audio. And then there's the device I'm talking to you on."

"My bad, boss." It was the answer every millennial that screwed up had that I ever knew. Like it made a difference.

"So stay awake and get me Mr. Marshall on the horn."

"Right away, sir." He paused. "But, he might also be asleep."

"Then wake him the hell up, Jim Bob," I said curtly.

"Yes, sir."

Two minutes later, I heard Ben's voice. "Bruce, been waiting to hear from you. What's the news."

"The target is dead. Mr. Steed busted his head with a 7.62 round." "Fantastic! Mission is complete."

"Not quite. You need to get us back."

"I've been thinking about how we can do that."

"Through the water boys?"

"Maybe, but I'm trying to get a flight arranged from our ally's location directly to Andrews. Are you still with the opposition group?"

"We are. But the whole country is looking for us. Got a solution?"

"I believe so. We're going to airlift you out."

"And how the hell will you accomplish that?" I asked him.

"Our trusted ally is sending a bird. You just need to establish an LZ (landing zone) for pickup."

"Is it from the base on the Med we have discussed in the past?" I was trying to keep our call as covert as possible without mentioning names, countries, and et cetera.

"It is. The bird can be ready to fly tomorrow. It will have one of our people at the controls. Gotta be during the hours of no visibility"

"Can be tricky in this terrain," I said.

"Just find a field and send the coordinates. Suggest 2100

hours."

"Where will it take us?"

 "To the ally's location. From their port, you will fly across the pond. One thing…don't make the LZ too far off the coast. Birds aren't good with bullets."

"Okay, will send the coordinates at dawn's early light." "My early light or yours?"

"Let's make it yours. I don't want to be getting you out of bed."

"And I appreciate that," he said, laughing. "I need my beauty sleep."

"Hmm. Obviously, you haven't been getting enough of it."

"Goodbye, Scorpion."

A really bright dude listening in on our conversation would have little trouble deciphering what our conversation was about, but we didn't mention anything specific in the clear. An eavesdropper wouldn't be able to determine the when's and the where's anyway.

The chopper would probably be an American Blackhawk and it would come from the Israeli base at

Haifa on the Mediterranean. It's crew would likely be an IDF team from the Israeli Navy's elite Shayetet 13 Special Forces unit. I had to get back to Najib's camp to talk with him about an open field where the Blackhawk could land. And yes, the LZ would need to be somewhere the bird could get in and out quickly. It would fly up the Med across the coastline near where the team came in and disappear quickly over the sea.

I was just about to leave the church parking lot and pull onto the road, when a Jeep type vehicle containing two uniforms blocked me. The passenger then pointed his AK at me and yelled, "Tawaqif warfae yadayk!" I recognized a couple of the words which translated was something like "Stop, put up your hands." But whatever he said, I knew that's what he wanted me to do. He then motioned with his rifle for me to get out of the truck. So as not to catch a bullet with my body, that's what I did.

I didn't look traditional Middle Eastern but I *had* seen a few Syrian men who also didn't look Middle Eastern. "Yaqtarib!" I think that meant 'approach.' At least his AK said that. With hands raised, I walked slowly toward the Jeep. The driver then grabbed me and took me to the ground. Patting me down, he found my ka- bar. Of course my only other weapon, the AK, I left in the truck.

Wearing patches with the the Syrian flag on one shoulder and another flag patch with the name 'Syria' at the top, I intellectually deduced the men were of the Syrian military. As they kept yelling at me in Arabic words I didn't understand, I just shook my head. The driver then slapped me across the face when I didn't respond. I wish he hadn't done that. Now I had to kill him. I just needed the opportunity.

I remember when my friends and I were kids, we'd stand on a street corner, lift our heads and just stare up in the air. People would then stop and begin looking up as well. Of course they'd see nothing at all. Maybe clouds. We'd laugh like idiots, reveling about how we had fooled mature adults, making *them* look like idiots.

So, standing there, I raised my head and began staring into the sky. And yes, the two of them *were* idiots for falling for my old trick. That's when I snatched the soldier's AK from his hands and butt-stroked him on the chin. The second soldier, who had been mesmerized by what was up in the sky, looked back down to find the muzzle of my newly-acquired AK staring him in the face. He immediately dropped his rifle on the ground before I had a chance to say "drop your rifle on the ground."

I then motioned with the AK for him to get down on the ground with his buddy. As the two of them laid in the dirt, one conscious and the other not, I took off my shirt and pointed to his friend, meaning that I wanted them to do the same. He got the message and began taking the man's shirt off. Then I pointed to his trousers, to take them off. Then his boots. A few seconds later, the unconscious man was entirely naked.

Turning my attention to the conscious man, I motioned for him to take his clothes off as well. With eyes as large as golf balls, he shook his head. I then put the muzzle of my rifle to his head. Within a matter of seconds, he was likewise naked, holding his hands in front of his privates. I put my shirt back on and pointed toward a wooded area behind the church. "Go!" I yelled. He did understand that, and began trotting off gingerly as though he were on hot coals, considering he was barefoot on gravel.

As the man on the ground was stirring, I leaned down and slapped him across the mouth, having reversed myself about shooting him. When he suddenly discovered he was naked, he had a bewildered look on his face. He immediately covered himself as well. I'm sure he wondered what I planned to do to him. "It's not what you think, Jughead." I then pointed toward the woods where I sent his friend. "Go!" Even though I'm sure his feet were being tortured by the gravel, he wasted no time getting out of sight.

One might wonder why I had them shed their clothes. If I had just taken their weapons and left, they'd jump in their Jeep, call in their cohorts and give chase. This way, being humiliated, they weren't going contact anyone, hoping they'd find a sheet somewhere hanging on someone's clothesline. Before I left, I switched vehicles, taking the Jeep and leaving the truck. The Jeep was a later model and had a radio. I didn't think the Toyota could be traced back to the camp. But even if it was, nobody was going into the camp to mess with Najib's guerrillas.

I shared a good laugh with myself then bundled up their clothes and shoes along with their weapons and tossed them into the Jeep. I'd throw their clothing into the woods on the way back to the camp and hand off the AKs to Najib to add to his collection.

I continued chuckling as I retraced my route to the village, wondering how people would react when the men were found. Or would the two of them just drive the broken down Toyota naked back to their unit where they would never live it down? According to their religion they would be shamed and maybe punished. I actually was feeling sorry for the morons.

CHAPTER 33

Back in the camp, I pulled the team together with Najib, and told them what was planned. Najib said there was a patch of land just east of the village that they farmed which would serve well as a landing zone for the chopper. To help the aviator, they could light fires at the four corners of the field which would assure a safe, nocturnal landing. "Allow me to take you there," he said. "You will see that the helicopter will not have to travel far from the coastline to get there. It is maybe one kilometer."

After affirming that the field would serve as a good LZ, around 1750 we returned to the village. I sat at Najib's desk once again with my map and wrote down both the map and GPS longitude and latitude coordinates of the Landing Zone. In checking my phone within the camp for the first time since the morning, I saw that I still had no service under the forest canopy. Unfortunately, I'd have to leave the village again to get it.

Just before dark, I stepped out of the village and walked to a lesser wooded area to try the Sat phone again. Voila! I saw that I had service.

"Okay, Ben, I have those coordinates. "Send them." After doing so, I asked him to regurgitate both the GPS and map coordinates back to me. He got them right. "Thanks, Ben. See you in a couple of days if all goes well."

That night the mood in the village was a little less morose. The people were even given to celebration…celebrating the lives of their departed souls, and as they had enjoyed our company the past few days, celebrating not only the accomplishment of our mission in killing the evil bin Rabah, but our safe return to the U.S. There wasn't as much music and dance this night as usual, but there was plenty of wine and homemade hooch.

For the first real time since we had been in the camp, we sat with Najib and a few of his English-speaking elders about their mission. Most of the people there, fed up with the new Syrian government, chose to break from the city of Tartus and the Tartus governorate to begin a campaign of propaganda targeting the Syrian citizens, slipping into their communities to talk with them, give them leaflets and set up lectures in the community houses, preaching about the evils of the government. On two occasions, the commander of troops out of the Tartus governorate ascended upon their meetings, beating the leaders and killing five of who the government referred to as 'agitators and criminals.' It further infuriated the provisional Ashtar government that the United States had been supplying the rebel villages with weapons and other logistical items to carry out their campaign.

Because the government itself had turned to terrorist acts against the rebel opposition, leaders like Najib resorted to hostile actions against the military garrison in Tartus and political icons. Najib promised his people were peace- loving Muslims and never raised a hand or fired a bullet at anyone unless it was in retaliation…or deserved. None of his people had joined the ranks of al-Qaeda or ISIS since they were ruthless terrorists conducting missions against the United States, its allies and other democracies. What it amounted to…his people were fighting the Syrian government and ISIS/al-Qaeda targeting the free world. The terrorists and the Syrian government together were allied in their hostilities against Israel and the U.S. That was why bin Rabah and Commander Aamara were friends.hat Najib also said most of the government's people practiced a different form of Islam which included Sharia Law. When the village declared they were of the Alewife sect of Islam, the government's persecution of the rebels intensified. The Alawite sect of Islam not only permitted the consumption of alcohol but did not require women to cover their heads. I had wondered about both but hadn't asked. Under Sharia Law, the rebels had also committed murder on government troops and police. Everyone doing so was automatically guilty and sentenced to death without trial. So, they were Alawites. I had no idea, but what should have been an immediate clue was the alcohol.

But speaking of alcohol, it mattered little that we were all a little drunk and didn't pass out until near 0200 the next morning. We had nothing to do and nowhere to go until 2100 that next evening.

For the first real time that next afternoon, we were able to kick back and enjoy the people of the village. Children and women naturally gravitated to Lovato, thinking it pretty cool that a woman who looked like her could also be a tough, calloused warfighter. Most of the Syrian wives merely cooked the meals and kept the home, primitive as it was, and helped the husband work the fields. But they seemed to be a happy lot, generally smiling, good-humored, and devoted to one another. And because we were Americans and supporting their quest to take their country back, they had been pleased to help us in our mission.

The village came out in force at 1800 hours to set up for our going away party. Just as in celebrations in our country, each family brought a dish to set on the long community table. There was more food than any of us had ever seen at any American party. The desserts were, as Adriana would say, "to die for;" although, I sure as hell wasn't giving up my life for a slice of baklava. Besides the baklava, somebody made their most popular dessert, karabeej halab, which is a cookie- like biscuit filled with pistachios coupled with a meringue dip called nataf. I wouldn't die for it but it was so good, I might take a punch in the stomach for it.

After the enjoying the spread, we were back to sitting by the stream, our feet in the water. No drink this night as we had a Blackhawk to bring in which would carry us to a safer land.

At 2030, we grabbed our gear and weapons and began walking to the LZ. Najib's men had already lit the four fires something like a hundred yards apart from each other and all the aviator had to do was sit the chopper down somewhere in the middle. 2040 and 2050 came and went and then precisely at 2101, we heard the the Blackhawk's blades beating in the distance. I love how plans come to fruition. And then on my radio I heard, "Scorpion, this is Blackwing. Approaching your position. I see four fires forming a square. Is that you?"

"We are dead center. I have lit something else. Identify."

"A flare."

"Yes. Are you good to drop in?"

"Roger, Scorpion. So that we will not be exposed to hostiles, be prepared to board without hesitation. Keep low."

"Wilco, Blackwing. I see you now. We are ready."

As soon as the Blackhawk's skids touched the ground, we boarded through the open door, all five of us within less than five seconds. The crew chief helped us find our seats in the dark as the aircraft lifted off. He then hooked me up to the pilot's commo by placing a head set on me. I immediately opened up a chat. "Thanks, Blackwing. Assume we're flying down the Med to Haifa."

"Roger, Scorpion. I'm Dave; are you Bruce?" "That's

me."

"We'll be flying Nap of Earth, so for a while till we get over water, it may feel like you're on a rollercoaster." Nap of Earth was when an aircraft flies over trees and hilltops, staying as low as it can. That way, if there are any hostiles, they won't hear the bird coming until it is right up on them at a speed of 160 knots.

"We're approaching the Mediterranean now and should be past the Tartus port in zero two. When we flew over the port, we picked up some verbal traffic from the Ruskies who man the port. They…"

At that moment, we saw tracers whizzing past the aircraft, Dave taking immediate evasion action. Banking the Blackhawk sharply to the right, the tracers ceased. "Apparently, the commies saw you crossing the port and notified the Syrians to expect you to return," I said.

"Yeah, I wouldn't think the Russians fired on us. They'd rather the Syrians start a war."

In another minute, we were safely over Mediterranean waters and about 50 minutes from our destination, the Israeli port of Haifa. I think everyone on my team had the same feeling I had when I left Tan Son Nhut Airbase, Vietnam, and was out over the Pacific and on the way home. I had never had such a feeling of complete peace and release. There was also that gratitude to the Almighty that He allowed me the privilege of going home when others didn't…except in a flag-draped coffin. I admit I was also feeling a little of it myself on this mission as I had once again faced death at the end of an AK. It's not that I was used to it, considering my last twenty years of experiences as a covert agent; one never is.

But time and time again, I was able to pull myself out of some immensely difficult situations, giving credit, of course, to Providence. And every time I did, I'd tell myself it was time to hang up my spurs. Nobody could continue being as lucky as I had been.

I looked at all my team members, one by one, who had been quiet and reflective to this point. Stryker and Lovato were trying to be coy around the rest of us, holding hands once in a while. Mickey Johnson, who as part of my old counterterrorist team had been in similar scrapes as me, had his eyes closed, not asleep, but just thinking…maybe *thanking*. And then there was Atticus who I had never seen unnerved, looking out the chopper's door glass, seeing nothing in the dark, probably just meditating as he did a lot. He then turned toward me, smiled and nodded. We had done it. Mostly it was *he* who had done it.

Considering all the adverse circumstances, he had done a good job in leading and protecting the team. Within the same hour, we saw the lights of Haifa Harbor below us. We'd get a well-deserved night's sleep, courtesy of the Israelis, and then off Tel Aviv to board a government aircraft that Ben had arranged for us.

CHAPTER 34

No sooner had we all turned in for the night at the IDF Naval Base visiting officers' quarters, I heard the undeniable *whump* sound of artillery rounds going off. Whoever it was began shelling the compound by 'walking' their rounds in maybe a kilometer away. It was a tactic most every arm used…fire a round, see where it lands, then add 50 or 100 meters when firing the next. Eventually, they would get rounds on target. When satisfied they had hit something such as the airfield or ammo point.

A naval officer then appeared at the door of my barracks, flipped on the light, and rousted about twenty of us males. He first shouted something in Hebrew and for benefit of our team, yelled, "Come! We will go to the bunker!"

I tried to tell him I'd be willing to sleep through the barrage, but he wouldn't allow it. "You must come."

It was a large bunker, one of several outside the barracks, that looked to hold a platoon or more. When we were all bunched up and accounted for, the officer said, "It is the Palestinians. They will do what is called harassing fire for perhaps fifteen minutes and then it will cease."

"Wonderful," Mike Johnson said. "I thought we were done with people trying to kill us. "We…" His protest was cut short by an exploding round just outside the bunker.

"You were about to say something else, Mickey?" I asked.

"Just get me the hell on that big silver bird back home."

As the officer predicted, the shelling stopped for the night a few minutes later. We waited another ten, then was given the 'all clear.'

However, when we left the bunker, what a surprise to find that we no longer had a place to sleep. Our barracks had been hit by the exploding round we heard. The IDF officer stood looking at the crumbled, burning mass of wood and said, "Is very amazing. They usually don't hit anything as it is mostly guesswork for them."

I was damn glad I didn't argue further with the officer or I'd be hamburger. Just another brush with another enemy. Thank you seren (lieutenant)," I said extending my hand.

"No problem," he replied. I was expecting a 'you're welcome' response. He must have been an exchange student working as a server in an American McDonalds.

We were all placed in another barracks after that. I assumed Lovato had been safe in one of the female bunkers.

"Goodnight, boys," I bid the team.

"Good freaking night, Director," Stryker responded.

At 1000hrs the next morning, the Israeli Navy bussed us, our weapons, and our gear to Ben Gurion International in Tel Aviv. Then, at 1330, we boarded a swanky, government-operated Gulfstream G700 that would take us home. Now *that* was first class. It seemed the vice president was appreciative of our work. Pays to know someone at the top.

It was a long enough flight, but our time in the air came with a few frills…the latest movies, a couple of gourmet meals and however much we wanted to drink. I cautioned the team not to get too loaded as we were being dumped onto the tarmac at Joint Base Andrews. A group of staggering, raggedy-looking people half-falling down the steps of an airplane and carrying firearms might cause a little alarm on the base.

It was still dark early the next morning when we arrived at Andrews. Everyone had slept on the plane; therefore, we were refreshed and happy to be back to civilization. Standing at the base of the plane's ramp waiting for us was Ben Marshall who had gotten his carcass up at 0300 to greet us.

"Mr. National Security Advisor," I said, shaking his hand.

"Welcome home, Team Terminus," he replied. He shook everyone's hand as we came down the steps. "What a team. You were the right people for the job and I'm proud of you." He then eyed Strike who was still wearing a patch on his head. "Mr. Stryker, did you bump your head?"

"Yes, sir. Bumped it into a bullet. I think the bullet got the worst end of the deal, though."

"Bounced right off his hard head," Lovato added. "Let's just say I have a new part in my hair."

"Thank God for centimeters."

"Just what I told him," Steed said.

"And you, Mr. Steed…you did a fantastic job leading this team. My boss will be ecstatic when he hears about how it all turned out."

"And that would be who, Mr. Marshall?" Steed quizzed.

"The man with the plan, Mr. Steed."

Atticus was still fishing, but that bit of information only four people knew…Ben, my assistant Debbie Nelson, and me…the fourth being my dear wife who the vice president had personally met at our house. It reminded me to call her sometime later in the morning.

We didn't have far to walk across the tarmac until we saw two black SUVs. I rode with Ben, who had driven one, and the others rode with the same female Secret Service agent I had met when when Collins visited Terminus House.

We went first to the warehouse where I woke up my boys. They hadn't had much to do considering bin Rabah had destroyed the team's commo equipment and then they weren't able to follow me half the time because of the mountains and triple canopy forest. There were things we needed to fix, communications-wise before our next mission.

I told our commo guys they could go on home and back to their bread-and- butter jobs. We thanked them for the service they were able to provide and that they would be provided ample notice before the next mission began. Ben said they'd receive their check at the first of the month.

After they left, we pulled our nasty clothing from our rucks and threw them into plastic bags. I'd send them to a nearby laundry sometime during the day. We then placed our weapons and rucks in the arms room and locked up. As the rising sun was now brightening the earth, we walked the couple of blocks to Terminus House. T'was a beautiful summer morning.

Ben had previously detailed one of his aides to prep the place for us where we found bagels, pastries and coffee waiting on us. Did I mention how everything we take for granted made us appreciate life in the U.S.? We having taken our seats at the team conference table, Ben stood and began the debrief. He asked us for a play-by-play of our exploits beginning with the team's arrival in Rota, Spain. In his precise but detail-oriented manner, Atticus took about twenty minutes taking Ben through the team's mission. It would have taken most people nearly an hour; however, I was surprised how much information he provided in such a short time. I think he was anxious to get back to Maria.

To clarify some points, Ben began pounding us with questions, questions about bin Rabah and whether we encountered someone behind him who might continue his quest; the number of police and military who got in the way of our bullets; an assessment of the U.S.-

supported rebels in the village and their needs; and was there anything he could do to better provide for the protection and welfare of the team in such missions. His Q and A extended the debrief longer than I thought necessary. However, I understood he needed every morsel of information about the mission to take back to Vice President Collins.

When we broke up from the briefing around 1045 hours, I shook everyone's hand and sent them back home for a well-deserved R and R. I caught a glimpse of Lovato and Stryker getting into the same taxi. Was their budding relationship going to hinder the Terminus overall mission down the road? They were adults and knew how to segregate relationships and duty.

Ben stayed for a few minutes to tell me about his meeting two days before when the president pulled together the National Security team about the missiles being knocked out and that bin Rabah was reported dead. He asked me point blank why I hadn't informed him about specific plans for that to happen. He said "I'm the commander-in-chief of the armed forces, for God's sake, and when the Navy conducts operations like this on foreign soil, I'd better damn-well know about it. And you, Mr. Murphy, the Secretary of Defense, never apprised me of the attacks either?" I explained that our armed forces are always conducting operations to protect and defend the interests of the U.S. and its people on a continuing basis. We have special react teams like the Marine Recon elements, the SEALS and Army Rangers that strike when the threat is imminent. I said, 'You know, sir, other presidents have not been in the loop when a matter needs to be quelled immediately. They have trusted our forces to be in ready positions and act when necessary without getting them out of bed at 2 AM.' He responded by slamming his fist down on his table and yelled, 'Well by God, *this* president will not accept our forces planning attacks and sending missiles and insurgents onto foreign soil without my knowledge and expressed consent. And I *will* get out of bed at 2 AM.' I just replied, 'yes, Mr. President' and let it go at that."

"And how did the vice president respond?" I asked.

"He just looked at me and smiled."

"Then do we need to change our motis operandi to somehow just let him know the situation and there are covert elite forces at work whenever there's a threat?"

"He knew about the threat just as we all did, but as I said before, he was content with just establishing a dialogue with terror groups like ISIS and al-Qaeda to ask them politely to not kill our service men and women. He's the kind of president that will reward them by sending them money, arms and ammunition if they leave us alone. Vice President Collins said we will continue doing business like we have and keep the president out of the equation as much as possible."

"I'm with you, Ben. Just sayin' though, I don't think I would look good in an orange jumpsuit."

He laughed. "Don't worry, my friend. It will not come to that. Remember…you don't exist and neither does Terminus."

CHAPTER 35

Atticus Steed, who had been outside during my conversation with the National Security Advisor, having his own conversation with Maria, returned to my office and sat down in the chair in front of my desk. It reminded me I needed to call my wife to tell her I was coming home…to my Wolf Laurel home…that afternoon.

The fact that Atticus had already talked to Maria and I hadn't called Adriana, would not set well with her.

"Before we chat," I told him, "let me get *my* call out of the way." He then left my office until I was through talking with her.

"Good morning, sweetheart," I greeted.

I've always said I have this sixth sense about me. I can anticipate and even feel things before they happen. And even 250 miles away and over a cell phone, I could feel there was a different temperature back in Greenbrier County, West Virginia. It may have been 83 degrees in the nation's capital, but it was a frigid 32 degrees at Wolf Laurel, at least in Adriana's voice. "You have the audacity to call me 'sweetheart' after the stunt you pulled?"

"Can you explain the word 'stunt?'"

"You know what I'm talking about, Bruce." When she calls me Bruce and not her pet name for me, Skip, I know an impending storm is coming. "You weren't in D.C. all along. You went to be with your team in Syria."

Steed, damn him. He betrayed me. He had told Maria. I couldn't wait to go jerk a knot in his tail.

"Can I explain…"

"I don't want to hear it, Skip." I was 'Skip' again. Maybe the temperature was rising.

"Atticus and I will be leaving here in a few minutes for home and we should be there around three. I'd rather us sit down and talk about this and not be in a tizzy over the phone.

"Oh, I'm more than just being in a tizzy, Bruce McGowan." Maybe the temp was dropping again. She called me by both of my given names.

"Just fix yourself a nice glass of Chablis and go sit on the veranda, my dear, just like you do when we have a little tiff."

"Goodbye, Bruce." And then she ended the call. I probably said the wrong thing. She never likes it when I patronize her. My ear was now feeling the final, frigid blast of winter coming out of the phone.

When Atticus returned to my office, I just glared at him for a moment. Then, "What did you tell Maria, Atticus?"

My question obviously confused him. He replied, "That I loved and missed her and that I was coming back to get her at Wolf Laurel."

"Did you tell Maria about me going into Syria?"

"Of course not. You barely came up in our conversation."

"Well, somehow, Adriana found out about it. The atmospheric conditions are not going to be to our liking when we get there."

"Sorry, Bruce. I didn't say a word about you being

there."

"I can't figure it. She found out somehow."

We had a quick lunch at *D.C. Deli* then hit the road just after 12. I had just reached I-66 when my cellphone rang. I thought it might be Adriana telling me she was sorry to have been curt with me and she would make it up to me with a nice dinner and some marital bliss later. But it was a male voice. The vice president.

"Good afternoon, Bruce. It's Bart Collins."

"Hello, sir. How are things with you?" As Atticus was riding shotgun, I didn't put the VP's call on the Bluetooth speaker.

"Very fine, now that you and the team are back with a wonderfully successful mission under your belt. Thank you, my friend. I wish I were in a position to pin medals on your and Mr. Steed's chests…the entire team for that matter."

"I appreciate your comments, sir. It was a bit harrowing at times, but we made it back safe and sound."

"The National Security Advisor filled me in a few minutes ago on all that you and the team experienced. You were definitely the right people for the job. A group of Rangers or SEAL team guys going in there with a 'take no prisoners hooah frenzy' would have probably cut a path of chaos and pandemonium that would end up having international ramifications. Not taking anything away from those guys but sometimes it's like they're bulls in a china store. Anyway, I was most concerned when you decided to go in on your own after you hadn't heard anything from your team for days.

Took real balls to do that, Bruce."

"I've been in worse scrapes, sir; just concerned whether they were alive or dead."

"The measure of a true leader…mission and welfare of the troops."

"Sounds like you went to the same Army school that I did. I was just saying that to the team."

"Well, I didn't want that lovely wife of yours to be worried about you. I gave her a call and told her you knew what you were doing."

"You talked to Adriana?"

"Yes, I hope you don't mind. Even though she signed off on you honchoing this team when I met with you two, I could tell she had immense concerns about it."

"Uh, sir, I didn't tell her I was going into Syria. That

was our deal…I command the team from the Terminus operation center, and they do the leg work."

"Oh man. I am sorry, Bruce; I thought she knew. I think I may have caused some trouble on the home front."

"I'll work it out. It's not anything I haven't faced before."

"Well, just let me know if I can smooth things out with her."

"It'll be fine, sir."

"Are you on the way down to the WV?" "Yes. Mr. Steed

is with me."

"My congratulations to him for his good job. And say hello to your Mrs. for me."

"Will do. Good day, sir."

I leaned my head against the seat back. So, Bart Collins, the man who could be president in a couple of months, was the one who unwittingly let the cat out of the bag. I now wondered if the guy would be able to keep the nation's secrets. I had naturally but unjustly assumed it was Atticus who had sprung the leak. I looked over at him. He was looking at me as well.

"Well, Director, sounds like someone else ratted on you. Ben Marshall's boss, I presume?"

"Yeah."

"And you're never going to tell me who it is."

"Not anytime soon. It's kind of a Top-Secret secret."

He sighed. "Like I would ever have a need to tell anyone."

I didn't respond to that. For more than ten miles I just sat and watched the road. But I was also thinking. Atticus and I had bonded these last few years. The two of us had shared confidential stuff before, mainly where it involved killing the Viper. I had helped him in taking out the Viper's brother who sought revenge on him. Okay, why not? He may be taking over Terminus when I'm done in a year or two. At least that would be my recommendation. He'd certainly know then.
Collins was probably going to be elected president anyway.

"Atticus, Ben Marshall's boss, the man who created Terminus is the vice president, Bartley Collins." "You're kidding."

"Nope. This team is his baby. Not even the president knows about us." "You're saying that Terminus is covert even to the leader of the free world?"

"If you want to call him that. As you know, he's not much of a leader. We've discussed it as you'll remember."

He then laughed. "The Vice President of the United States sold you down the river with your wife."

"Not a laughing matter to me. I have to go home and face the music."

He grinned. "The fearless Bruce McGowan. You're actually *afraid* of Adriana."

"No, I'm just afraid this might be the proverbial straw breaking the camel's back."

"Well, Mr. Cliché, I don't think she'll make a scene with Maria and I in the house. And I will be singing your praises to her about your heroic rescue of our team. We would have been in dire straights if you hadn't come along."

"Would mean little to her, Atticus. It was all about truth and trust. I didn't call her and tell her what I was doing.

When I was able to get hold of her in Syria, I didn't divulge where I was. Just told her not to try reaching me because we were having communication issues."

"Which was the truth."

I shook my head. "No, Atticus; I hid the truth and that became a lie."

"I get it. Well, own up to it, tell her you're sorry, and you'll never let it happen again."

"Like I've done a dozen times."

CHAPTER 36

The ladies were sitting on the veranda with their glasses of red wine waiting for us when we arrived. I was trusting in the wine that its warm, biting magic had mellowed Adriana out since our 'uncomfortable' conversation over the phone. And since Maria had already sprung off the veranda to throw her arms around Atticus as soon as he stepped out of the car, maybe Adriana would greet me with the same fervor. However, while our two friends were chewing on each other's lips, she casually walked down the steps toward me, *her* lips formed only in a smug, semi-smirk that told me there were troubling waters ahead.

When I had returned from every other mission, she practically knocked me down with kisses and joy.

But then I thought I would de-ice the situation with my patented, beguiling smile and one of my disarming quips, both of which would make the storm clouds quickly dissipate. After unbuttoning my shirt and exposing my still chiseled chest and abs, I said, "Look, my dear, no holes." Several times I had returned home with gauze and bandages covering gouge-marks made by bullets, knives or shrapnel, much to her horror.

Today, however, she was not amused and only replied with a "bully for you." I may have made this comment before, but it's a known fact that when the Queen is not happy, there is no peace in the kingdom. And I had this foreboding feeling that I was about to get thrown in the moat with the alligators. I will give her this, however; she wasn't about to start on me in the presence of Atticus and Maria. "You guys must be worn out. Come sit on the veranda and I will get you a soothing glass of Merlot. Then you can tell us all about your adventure." What she said sounded all nice and altruistic but I thought her reference to us having an adventure like a couple of Boy Scouts returning home was a bit condescending.

Atticus, who knew Adriana was more than just peeved at me, began the conversation. "I will say that we found our mission to locate those missiles to be a bit more vexing than I anticipated. We found them and reported their location to Bruce, but in the meantime, we lost all communication with him." What he didn't say was that the team was captured and the adversaries smashed the radios. "We were soon to be returning to the coast to meet the submarine but got distracted by a group of people in a village who were actually an opposition force against the government of Syria. They helped keep us safe while we tried to restore our communications. Bruce, who was back here worrying about us, had no idea where we were and if we were in any danger.

Even if our government had sent another team in to find us, they wouldn't have a clue about where to look.

"One thing I learned a long time ago in the military, and which Bruce continues to reinforce, is that a good commanding officer looks out for his people, sometimes taking personal risks to assure their safety and welfare. Bruce has a keen nose about things. He has the uncanny ability to find people, whether they are friend or foe. He found us in that village and made arrangements to get us out." He then looked at Adriana. "I know you would have been worried sick knowing he left Terminus headquarters to go look for us, but had he not done that, who knows if we would have made it back. Syria is not America's friend and we could have been thrown into prison or even…well, you know. Bruce is a hero to us, Adriana, and we'd follow him anywhere."

I thought that last thing he said might have been a little over the top; however, I was grateful that he jumped in to help a buddy out.

Even though Adriana had listened intently to Atticus singing my praises, obviously, this was not all about my coming to the team's rescue and getting them home. "I know you're a friend, Atticus," she began, "and loyal to the bone, but my husband needs to understand that keeping me out of the equation when he goes off to a dangerous country on a dangerous mission and not letting me know is a betrayal of our marriage. I'm not so angry that he went there as I am with him trying to keep it from me. We have always trusted one another in our relationship, not keeping secrets, telling what he thinks are just white lies, and causing me to wonder where he is or whether he will ever come back to me. He promised he would be sitting in the director's chair and not risking his neck going off on some wild tangent that will get him killed, especially parachuting into hostile territory."

I then stepped into the conversation. "Adriana, you're talking in the third person like I'm not even sitting here. Tell *me* these things."

"Like you would ever listen, Skip; like always happens…mission first, me second."

I was quiet for a moment…eyes closed, taking a deep breath. We were doing what I hoped we wouldn't…airing our differences in front of our friends. Then I said, "You're right, sweetheart. You've always been right. But please don't think I never consider you. I've been doing it wrong all these years. I've been keeping things from you because I love you and haven't wanted you to be worried. I know you sanctioned me taking this job because not only was it temporary but I was supposed to be a chair-borne leader not airborne. I wasn't thinking right when I decided on the spur of the moment that I'd go find out about my people. Even though I shouldn't have done it, I *had* to do it. I am sorry and ask in front of these good people for your forgiveness."

I sat for a few moments waiting…waiting for her response, looking for just a smile or a nod. Atticus and Maria, sitting frozen and noticeably uncomfortable to have witnessed our argument, kept their eyes on her for her answer. Then her eyes softened. When that beautiful smile began forming ever so slowly, the sun came out from behind the clouds.

After setting her half-spent glass of wine onto the floor, she stood and came to where I was standing. She clasped her arms around my neck and said, "Yes. You have it, Skip. I forgive you. But please, please respect our marriage enough to never hide anything from me. Understand that you are no longer that daring man of action and trepidation. I saw that you were moping around, bored and listless, and I thought you taking this position would bring you out of your funk. So, I'm taking some of the responsibility for this little tiff myself. But I want you to know that I love you for just being Bruce McGowan, husband and lover extraordinaire. When this stint of yours is over, come back to being that person. Don't worry, I will help make your life exciting." She then kissed me as passionately as she ever had.

Both Atticus and Maria began clapping their hands as though they had been in the audience of a Broadway play. Adriana smiled sheepishly. "I'm so sorry we started a fuss in front of you. We should have taken our little war of words someplace else and not subject you to it."

Maria said, "Not to worry, Adriana. I'm glad it came out in front of us, as it is something Atticus and I have also gone through. The way you handled it and the beautiful way it ended was a great example for the two of us. It's the way squabbles *should* end."

Atticus smiled. "I have a feeling later on tonight it will end a different way… in a frenzy of fireworks."

"You really know how to embarrass a guy, don't you, Steed."

Around seven, we went out for a dinner of steak and lobster at one of the finer local restaurants. Our dinner conversation included nothing about what had happened in Syria the last couple of weeks nor in Mexico the week before. It was all about happy things and family moments…parents, childhoods, funny experiences…life. When we returned home, I handed a cigar to Atticus and invited him to sit out on the veranda while the ladies had their coffee in the kitchen. I had a reason. He had never been much of a talker, so I thought I'd probably not get much out of him. It had been a long, dry and quiet four hours from D.C. to West Virginia earlier in the day.

"Got something on your mind, Bruce?"

"Yeah. You've been with the team about six weeks now including time spent at Quantico. I just want your opinion; what's your opinion about who we are and where we're going?"

He took a drag from the cigar and then a drink of his wine before responding. "I like the concept and other members of the team. And I was not blowing smoke about you as our our leader. You're good, Bruce, but I knew that from our experiences with the Viper and his vengeful brother."

"Except my question was not meant to be about me. Do you think the Terminus concept works?" I asked.

"Isn't it the same type of team you served with a few years ago?"

"Basically, yes. Our assignments came covertly just as ours. We were a unit imbedded within the State Department, but neither the department nor the Secretary of State knew about us. Just as the vice president is fielding this unit without the knowledge of his boss."

"And that's uncanny to me. Is that not an illegal scenario? It's like he's going behind his boss's back to conduct missions like you going behind yours."

"I'm not going behind mine," I said. "What's giving you that impression?"

"You just had an argument with her this afternoon, or have you forgotten?"

"Adriana? Okay, you're funny, Mr. Steed."

He laughed. "Yeah, just messing with you, Boss. Still, it seems rather strange that something like that is occurring at

the top."

"Don't concern yourself about it, Atticus. It's something that I had been mulling over myself. But it's all about a milquetoast president either ignoring a national threat or being wary about taking aggressive action."

"In other words, he doesn't have the stones to address terrorism."

"About the size of it. But that's not what this conversation is about."

"Then what *is* it about?"

"I've known you for several years now, Atticus. I have to admit, when the government paired us up to nail the Viper, I had my reservations about teaming up with someone I considered a murderer…a hit man. But as I got to know you, I saw you had a good heart, a justice heart, trying to right wrongs, someone caught in the government's trap, although the culprits were evil men holding you hostage to your past and not acting on behalf of the government itself. However, over these years I've observed you as not only a patriot but a good leader and decision-maker, well-respected by your fellow team members. I…want you to take over the team as its director."

I thought Atticus would choke on his cigar. "You are shitting me. Why?"

"I would finish out the year as director and in the meantime will tout you as my replacement. I know Adriana is not happy in D.C. and I'm thinking she regrets making a deal with the vice president, mainly because the job as I want to do it is causing a bit of contention between Adriana and me. You were a witness to that today."

"But, you're great at this position, Bruce, and I don't know the first thing about being a team director."

"Yes, you do. I saw you lead this team when we had good commo. As to the administration duties and the rubbing of elbows with people like the National Security Advisor and even Vice President Collins. You have both the tact and savvy to do this."

He shook his head. "I'm a doer and am good in the trenches, but as I've never been in a leader position, I can't see myself there."

"I can. Someone has to replace me and just giving up the position, I know I'll be disappointing Collins and Marshall. But my marriage is important to me…more than anything in the world."

"Even so, how do you know the vice president will be good with me?"

"As I said, I will do my best to convince my higher that you are the man for the job."

"And then there's Maria," he added. "She hates Washington. I myself had been thinking about leaving Terminus and going back to Antigua."

"You have?"

"My marriage is important to me as well. I told myself that when your commitment is over and you step down,

I would do the same."

I leaned my head back against the chair and let out a sigh. "I guess it's something we both must think about. Just do me this favor…talk it over with Maria and let me know what you decide. Coming back down I-81 today, I thought I had this all figured out."

"I will give it a lot of thought, Bruce, but at this time, the answer is *no*."

We sat breathing in the fresh night air for another half hour without saying another word about my proposal. Just as I was getting ready to go inside and call it a night, my cellphone rang. Ben Marshall.

"Bruce, corral the team. We have to move on something in the next couple of days. A place long buried in the abyss of your mind."

ABOUT THE AUTHORS

Lee Martin, a native of West Virginia, lives in the Atlanta, Georgia area. Retired from the U.S. Army with the rank of Colonel, he was awarded the Bronze Star and Gallantry Cross in Vietnam. He has a Doctorate in Counselling and is an adjunct professor teaching courses in Psychology.

Terry S. Byrnes, CPPB, after completing two years of Active Duty in the US Navy Reserve, based out of Pearl Harbor, Hawaii, serving as a (Supply) Petty Officer, 3rd Class, Submarine Qualified (SS) on board the Nuclear Fast Attack Submarine, USS Swordfish, SSN 579, and operated in two Campaigns off Vietnam until mid-1972, then returned to Miami, Florida. He maintained his US Navy Reserve status into mid-1975. After graduating from Florida International University and spending decades in the Hotel, Culinary, and Travel Industries and as Municipal Government Purchasing Manager, earning Certified Professional Public Buyer, he retired and created I.E.R. Media to publish, edit, and author novels. Terry S. Byrnes is now Co-Authoring, Editing, and Publishing as C.E.O. of I.E.R. Media, as well as a Literary Agent, Website Designer, and Marketing Developer.